WHITE WATER VALLEY

Center Point
Large Print

Also by Jackson Gregory and available from Center Point Large Print:

Emerald Trails
The Maid of the Mountain
Riders Across the Border

WHITE WATER VALLEY

Jackson Gregory

Center Point Large Print
Thorndike, Maine

This Center Point Large Print edition
is published in the year 2024 by arrangement with
Golden West Inc.

Originally published in the US under the title
Valley of Adventure by Dodd, Mead & Company.
Originally published in the UK under the title
White Water Valley by Hodder & Stoughton.

The text of this Large Print edition is unabridged.
In other aspects, this book may vary
from the original edition.
Printed in the United States of America
on permanent paper sourced using
environmentally responsible foresting methods.
Set in 16-point Times New Roman type.

ISBN: 979-8-89164-279-9

The Library of Congress has cataloged this record
under Library of Congress Control Number: 2024938332

To
My Beloved Daughter
MARIANA

WHITE WATER VALLEY

CHAPTER 1

Penelope Loring was breathless with delight when the stage deposited her in the quaint little New Mexican village with its scant handful of adobe houses, its ancient red-tiled mission church in a tangly garden, its pigeons and its pepper trees—and its white road running out to the far purple mountains.

But that tingling moment with its rapture had been quite three hours ago, and now it was a dejected and wistful-eyed Penelope who sat in one of the deep embrasured windows of the big main room of the one hotel in San Carlos. For her a shadow had fallen over the sun-smitten little town which seemed to grow tremulously unreal as she regarded it through a mist which slowly thickened until, like the first drop of a summer rain something splashed to the back of her hand and she dabbed furiously at her eyes—and even the road wavered, that straight white road, empty under the August sun, inviting to the blurring mountains toward which an eager young soul had so ardently yearned.

Plans and dreams went all to smash together. She sighed and withdrew her troubled eyes from what could no longer be any concern of hers since drowsy, picturesque little San Carlos would have none of her. She began slowly unscrewing the cap of her fountain pen and gave a little twitch to a pair of shoulders which all of a sudden wanted to droop. On a gay little writing pad purchased yesterday in Albuquerque in such high hopes of soon putting down on it all sorts of delightful adventures, she began writing. That was because she must talk with someone, and who was at hand? Not a single soul whom she knew or who had ever heard of Penelope Loring.

> "DEAR PATTY LANE:
>
> "Such a joke her destiny has played on your absurd Penelope! I've just learned the horrid truth. First I cried; that was because I was tired and disgusted. Then I said 'Damn,' which was because I was *mad*. But after all that I said, 'Who cares? Life runs large and the biggest Ups come right after the sinkiest Downs—and the Lorings never gave up a ship yet!' And that was because I was trying to be brave, my dear. But *Patty*—"

A big drop splashed on her paper. "Little fool!" said Penelope with a sniff of contempt. "If you start crying—" Then she laughed, albeit a bit shakily; that drop came not from her eyes but from a moist brow and made an awful mess of her "trying to be brave." She drew a ring about the "brave" and in the margin scribbled: "Not a tear, sap; whew, it's hot, and I'm just dripping—"

A tinkly sound which managed to convey a sense of coolness in the shadowy, thick-walled room caused her to look up. It was Mr. Bradshaw, the hotel-keeper, a palm fan in one hand and a tall misted glass in the other, advancing upon her. He was a very stout man of middle age and on the white sleeves of a collarless shirt he wore a pair of garters as supporters, very pink and frilly, yet none the less a grateful Penelope drenched him with a smile that put Mr. Bradshaw, seasoned hotel-keeper that he was, into a glow.

"You're a dear," said Penelope to Mr. Bradshaw. And to Patty:

"This is the craziest little place; you'd love it. There's a deserted looking old mission church in a garden all red and yellow roses and lovely weeds and pear trees and pomegranates. Then there are some pepper trees and a lot of pigeons and under the pepper trees three or four little doll-houses—that's where the Banker lives, and maybe the garage man and the storekeeper. *And* the straight white dusty road running by and going straight on and beginning to waver over little hilly places and getting narrower and narrower until you'd have to be very small to travel it, and at last arriving at cool shadowy places in the purplest mountains you ever saw—and that's where Romance goes swaggering about in purple and capital letters my dear. Oh, you can tell! And all that's what the aforesaid Miss Penelope Loring has gazed at and sighed for—and now—"

"Chirpy young thing, when she blew in," meditated Mr. Bradshaw. He sat at his ease behind a long counter which had all the glass and bottle ring-marks of a bar; it had also a brass foot-rail which gleamed softly after the manner of a sly wink. Certainly there was a suspicious tang and zip to Penelope's lemonade not distilled from any mere lemon peel. Mr. Bradshaw manipulated his fan slowly, sipped at his own tall glass and pondered: "Wonder what's made her all sort o' droopy?"

A man came in from the dusty road; Penelope disposed of him with a flick of the eye. He was an old fellow, straight and sinewy and brown, with a small white moustache; he wore Palm Beach suiting, the trousers stuffed into high tan boots, and a wide straw hat. She knew who he was, having glimpsed him earlier through the bank window: Mr. Lew Houston.

"Stage didn't forget your ice this trip, did it, Brad?" asked the banker.

Bradshaw without rising reached under his bar and brought forth the third tall misted glass.

"Here y'are, Lew," he said. "I seen you lockin' up. Hot, ain't it?"

"Hotter'n billy-be-damned," agreed Mr. Houston.

Bradshaw jerked his head warningly toward the other end of the room. Lew Houston glanced that way, saw a pair of shapely ankles, stepped back to see what else the deep window might contain, became promptly aware that now and then a girl could be every bit as pretty as girls had a way of being some thirty-forty years ago, sighed and returned to the bar.

"You're right, Bradshaw," he said thoughtfully. "Quite warm, isn't it?"

Penelope leaning out from her half-hidden nook and smiling said: "Please! Don't mind me. It was so hot in my room—but if I am going to be in the way—"

"My dear!" exclaimed Mr. Lew Houston. He took off his hat and made her a little bow, slightly lifting his glass. She nodded brightly, withdrew her brown curly head and went on writing. Mr. Houston glanced out of the open door. "Looks nice and cool up yonder, Brad."

"They call my purple mountains 'Up Yonder,' " wrote Penelope. "For me it's the Never Never Land! It's put some sort of a spell over me."

A horseman went clattering by; through the door you could see a great volume of white dust. Above the muffled thud of his horse's hoofs you could hear the musical jingle of the long chains on his spurs and the no less musical subdued tenor of his voice. He was singing sentimentally:

"*Ai, Morena, que por tu ventana.*"

"The sun is going down; the shadows in San Carlos are almost blue. You get whiffs now from the old mission garden. Someone will have to materialize soon with a guitar; you'll have to hear a girl laughing—I don't know where she will come from—"

"Talkin' about Up Yonder," said Bradshaw.

They spoke at length of Up Yonder and their conversation developed a trick of centring about one man. They called him Bill Mountain. At times Penelope listened; anything connected with Up Yonder had its fascination for her. At other times she wrote busily. She gained impressions like those which might have been had by looking through the flickering spokes of a wheel.

"In my land of Blue Mountains," she wrote, "there lives a wild young man named Bill Mountain! You'd think at first, of course, that somehow he'd got his name from the mountains; and after a while you'd wonder whether the mountains hadn't got their names from him! Listen, Patty: I'll tell you a tale! In the Up Yonder the sheriff is an old man named Dan Westcott; he's seventy or more. And last spring he was sick and at that time a man killed another in a fight over a horse. And Bill Mountain, being the wild young devil he is, was made a deputy to go out and get the killer. Now, here's what he did:

"You see, Bill Mountain loves just one thing on earth, and that is horses. He raises fancy stock for the border race tracks and for men all over the country, East and West, who want the best in polo ponies. So he forked saddle leather, as we say Up Yonder, and rode right over to bring the killer to jail. He and the killer sort of talked things over; the killer says, 'Sure I kilt the son-a-gun, which he needed it; I caught him a-savagin' a horse o' mine an' I jest nacherally blowed him apart with a shot gun—' And then Bill Mountain speaks up and he says: 'Hell you say, Jim? Here, wait a shake.' And he writes out with paper and pencil: 'This will certify that a certain low-life, now dead by a shot gun, committed suicide. Signed, Bill Mountain, deputy sheriff.' "

"As far as I c'n make out," Bradshaw was saying, "a certain party name of Buck Andros has got a man-sized job on his hands if he thinks he can ease in that high country an' twist Bill Mountain's tail."

"Bill shot one of Andros's men th' other day," Houston remarked thoughtfully. "Tom Gadge, it was."

"You don't say?" Bradshaw lowered his fan and leaned forward, mouth open. "Kill the skunk?"

"Guess not. Word just reached me; Dan Westcott was down at the railroad and dropped me a line about some business; tacked that on as a postscript."

"He would," nodded Bradshaw. "What was the rumpus, Lew?"

"Same thing," said the banker. "Bill found Gadge monkeying with the waterworks; he said 'Scat' and Gadge the fool went for his gun. Bill drilled him forthwith. He then picked his game up, slung him over the saddle and carted him off to Buck Andros, asking if he should send a doctor along or if Andros thought he could pull him through."

Bradshaw fanned and sipped and thereafter spoke his mind:

"The lid's goin' to blow clean off hell up that way 'fore long, Lew."

The horseman who had ridden so gaily by had put his horse up somewhere and now entered on high heeled boots, a handsome young buck with snapping black eyes and milk-white teeth, who must have been about nine parts pure strain Indian to one part doubtful Mexican and was a very picturesque young rascal with his almost liquid grace, his smile and his cowboy finery. He seemed to sense a feminine presence even before his quick eyes stabbed through the gloom of the big room to where Penelope sat; he took off his big grey hat quite charmingly, Penelope thought.

"*Que hay*, *amigos*!" he greeted banker and hotel-keeper, and came slouching up to the bar like a panther. "Eet is wan lofely day for sure, *no?*"

A moment later he was pridefully showing

them a beautifully carved belt which he wore about a lithe lean middle, and telling them of it.

"Don Montana, thees belt he geeve me," said the young fellow whom the others named Tonito. "Me, I do some leetle *nada*, a kind deed maybe for Don Montana, an' he meck Tonito the fine geeft, *no?*"

This Don Montana, it would seem to Penelope Loring, was yet another denizen of Up Yonder. It was as though these men dropping in here one after another conspired with the purple mountains and the arrow-straight road, intriguing her interest afresh at every turn, luring her on to high adventure when she knew right well that since the country in and about and beyond San Carlos would have none of her, her one proper gesture was to turn her back on it all. Throughout the late afternoon and into the warm dusk with a faint taste in it of the white dust of the beckoning road and a spicy fragrance from the mission garden, she sat, at times listening since she must, at times dreaming wistfully, at times scribbling furiously.

"I suppose I'm getting terribly garbled impressions," she wrote. "But that's the only kind I'm apt to get here where instead of being a whole year, I'm playing a one night stand. You see, I began to think that Bill Mountain and a great burly ruffian known as Buck Andros were pretty much the high cards in Up Yonder—and now the most exciting of them all, Don Montana comes along! I'm sure he is a sort of high and mighty overlord over goodness knows how many miles and miles, and something of a dandy, I am guessing, who rides a beautiful horse and jingles silver spurs and wears flashy things with silver spangles.

"I can still see my mountains though it's almost dark now and somebody's lighting a lamp. Purple, purple mountains, a deeper purple now than you can imagine. That's the colour that kings wear—"

She held her pen poised, her attention snared once more by talk at the bar. The postmaster had come in and had congratulated Brad on his ice: it would be a great day for San Carlos when the stage came every afternoon instead of only twice a week. A couple of dusty young ranchers dropped in; they'd got their mail which appeared to consist in a bundle of newspapers and a couple of mail-order catalogues, and routed their homeward ways through Bradshaw's place for a drink and a bit of friendly gossip. Keen-eyed young fellows, thought Penelope. Certainly not a man of them failed to note her presence, inconspicuous as she had made it; and having noted it, not a man of them but had something to say to the hotel-keeper in an undertone.

And they were all birds-of-a-feather, congenial inhabitants of a little world of their own, herself the only stranger relegated to an outside position.

But before that thought was more than formulated she watched the entrance of yet another man and understood on the instant that here came one who was even more of a rank outsider than herself; for not only was this man not of their easy-going fellowship, but could never be.

He looked towards the bar and those who had turned at his step promptly turned their backs on him and went on with what they were doing and saying. He hesitated a moment and the tip of his tongue ran along his lips; he sniffed at the full fragrances which floated out from the tall glasses and seemed about to step to the bar when Bradshaw, having looked at him with all the cordiality of a fish, emulated his customers and turned his back. The newcomer passed on and slumped down in a chair at the rear of the room and at no great distance from Penelope.

When he saw her he allowed himself to stare. He was a hulking young man in a new grey suit and blue socks and tan shoes; he had very big reddish hands and sandy hair and a pair of sullen, pale eyes and, for so big a man, a very small mouth. He leered instead of smiling, and she disliked him immensely for it and decided promptly that the boys at the bar were to be commended on their discernment and exclusiveness. Here was a man who did not belong; that much her instinct could tell her, but it could not play prophet to the extent of informing her that, so little did the fellow belong, San Carlos was about to see the last of him for all time.

She, like the others, was turning a shoulder against a colourless yet unpleasantly cunning stare, when there was a lively racket of hoof beats in the road, the sound of spurred boots landing on the porch, and a vastly pleasant lazily deliberate voice saying: "Wait here for me a coupla shakes, Lady." Then, before this latest arrival came into sight Penelope was intrigued by two facts: the first was that the big man in the grey suit stiffened and for a moment seemed to cease breathing; the other was that there was a glad, affectionate ring in the voices of some two or three men at the bar exclaiming together:

"It's Bill! Ol' Bill Mountain, the son of a gun!"

Bill Mountain's first remark as he dragged his spurs into the hotel lobby was:

"Gents, surge up an' befrien' me! Use whatever fo'ce seems necess'ry; gang-jump me an' hawg-tie me if you gotta do it, an pry my mouth open an' pour the good red licker down me whether I want it or not. 'Cause I'm drier'n hell's gridiron."

And then he saw the man sitting alone and pulled up and grew silent. For as long as a man might have taken to count ten he stood where he was, his hat on the back of his head, his hands on his hips. Then he appeared to forget his thirst and his friends and to bethink him of some bit of business which wanted finishing. His eyes, taking stock of the room, had disposed of Penelope with just the sort of flick which had served her to catalogue and dismiss the banker. It was with the owner of the shifty, cunning eyes that he had to do. He came straight on, walking on his tip-toes to avoid catching his spur rowels in Bradshaw's Navahoe rug until he stood towering over the other man.

"Scat, you polecat!" said Bill Mountain.

The other man scrambled to his feet, his face turning red, his pale eyes emitting a gleam in which were viciousness and anger and an uncertainty which was akin to fear.

"Just because—" he began.

"Shut up! I'm talkin' this time, you're listenin'. Get this: your daddy's only child was a daughter! *Sabe*?"

It didn't seem to make sense, thought a bewildered and fascinated Penelope. Yet the other man's mouth dropped open; he appeared to understand and there was more of fear now than of uncertainty in his eyes. With a movement of almost incredible swiftness his big reddish hand went under his coat—

But he had to do with a quickness of eye and of body which was even greater than his own. As his hand emerged, dragging out what was meant to be a flat, compact argument in blue steel, Bill Mountain leaped on him and caught his wrist in a grip from which there was no breaking free.

"Once already I said 'Scat, you polecat,' " said Bill Mountain. "Ain't that aplenty? I don't aim to do any killin' this evenin', but jus' to make you so hard to find that even the devil himself's ap' to miss you when he calls the roll. San Carlos is to see you again never, never, no-more, which is a promise I'm makin'."

He gave the imprisoned wrist so savage a twist that the gun dropped to the floor. The other man, at last allowed to writhe free, strove to bespeak his courage with a jeering laugh and the words:

"With your brother already on the run for murder, and sure to hang—"

Bill Mountain lashed out with a sudden fist and knocked the man down. Rising, the fellow made a wild attempt to retrieve his fallen weapon, but when his fingers almost brushed it he was jerked back by a hand on his collar. Penelope, shrinking back into the deep window, saw in Bill Mountain less a man enraged than some grim and irresistible force. He was as impersonal and as relentless as a storm-wind scattering leaves. And what followed next was over so soon that it left her gasping, and those other onlookers at Bradshaw's bar convulsed with laughter. Bill Mountain knocked his man down twice more, got him again by the collar and shoved him battling and cursing to the door. The man went out in a grotesque sprawling fashion of one just learning to fly and as he vanished there was the sound of a boot striking and of a spur jingling merrily. Bill Mountain shouted into the gathering dark:

"Fork a horse an' ride out'n here hell-for-leather, or so help me I'm gunna shoot you! Scat!"

He swung about and went to the bar. Bradshaw, apprehensive of that sort of a vocabulary which might be unleashed at such a moment, said something to him hastily in one of his harsh stage whispers, and indicated the girl's presence. Bill Mountain said:

"Who gives a damn? Gents, gather roun'. Here's puttin' the fires out. Ha-appy da-ays!"

CHAPTER 2

"And now what do you think?" Penelope wrote to Patty. "Already I have seen the famous Bill Mountain! And you said that I'd go and fall in love with the first cowboy that came along! If you could only *see him!* He is absolutely the last man on earth any girl would ever fall in love with. I'll try to tell you about him, but really my dear you just have to see some things to really appreciate them—like the Coliseum by moonlight, you know! As he came in at the door—Well, nothing could actually be as gangling and awkward as he seems to be. He is big and long and shaggy, and you know it isn't just his ragged old chaps and dusty boots and dilapidated old hat that make him so. His mouth is too big and so is his nose. He's absolutely fascinatingly ugly. Remember that eagle we saw one time on the ground and how funny it looked trying to get started into the air? The way Bill Mountain walks you'd think that from babyhood he'd used his feet only to wear boots on so that he could use the boots only to hang his spurs to so that anywhere he wanted to go he could fork saddle leather and ride, even if it were just across the road. The lamplight is shining full on his face now, his hat is pushed way back and to the side and he's laughing because he just met up with a man he doesn't like, said, 'Scat, polecat' to him, took his gun away and threw him out! To do him justice he isn't nearly so hard to look at when he's laughing. Mr. Bradshaw nudged him and reminded him that he'd best modify his language to my innocent ears. 'There's a lady present, Bill,' whispers Mr. Bradshaw. 'Who gives a damn?' says Bill Mountain!"

Bill Mountain pulled his hat forward with a business-like jerk and then laid his hand on the banker's shoulder.

"I rode in for a talk, Lew," he said. "I don't like to pry you loose from any good licker, but when you've got an idle hour on your hands I c'n use it."

"Just getting ready to go, Bill," said Houston. "Come along over to the house."

"Right. I'll step out an' fix Lady up for the night, then I'll be with you. Ride pretty, boys, an' addyose."

Ten minutes later Lew Houston threw open the door of one of the little houses among the pepper trees, saying, "Here we are, Bill. Walk in and call it yours."

The two men with a lamp lighted sat in Houston's front room, a liveable place with big leather chairs, Indian rugs, solid old oak table and smoking accessories. On one wall was a single oil painting, a seascape reminiscent of Waugh. Lew Houston liked on a slippered evening to sit and look at it; here in the dry country it was ever a source of delight to him.

"Cigar, Bill?"

"Thanks, Lew."

They eased themselves into big chairs facing each other. Bill Mountain lighted his cigar carefully, appearing thoughtful. With the first puff of smoke he leaned back, stretched out his long legs and was about to speak when Houston forestalled him, asking swiftly:

"Any news of your brother, Bill?"

"Yes, Lew," answered Bill Mountain after the slightest hesitation. It was not that he did not trust the banker all the way but merely that there was upon him night and day the realisation that an unguarded word might spell his brother's undoing. Though it was not to be supposed that anyone was listening to their talk, none the less he lowered his voice to add: "I'm in touch with him again; I've got him hid out where he's safe enough for the present."

"I'm damned glad to hear it, Bill," said Houston heartily. "He's a good kid and I hope to God you can manage to get him out of the country somehow. I don't doubt that Pasmore needed killing, but just the same it's curtains for Juan if they get him."

Bill Mountain nodded moodily and his eyes were sombre as he answered.

"Yes, Lew, it's curtains for the kid if they grab

him now, and the funny part of it is that he didn't kill anybody."

Houston's brows shot up and he regarded the other man more narrowly than ever.

"Juan didn't kill Pasmore?" he demanded incredulously. "If any man but you said that to me, Bill, I'd name him a liar. Sure of it?"

"Dead sure, Lew. Juan told me."

"Hm," said Houston. He shifted in his chair, bent a penetrating regard upon his cigar at which he frowned as though displeased with it, then popped it back into his mouth and began chewing it. "Damn it, Bill," he exploded, "everybody knows—"

"Oh, I know, Lew. And everybody, I along with the rest, jumped to the logical conclusion, and it's just one of those cases where logic's no good. Forget it for the moment; I'm here to talk about something else."

"*Bueno*," said Houston crisply. "In passing just remember that I'm for the kid anyhow if there's anything I can do. But before you get on with this something else, let me ask you what got into you to-night? What was the sense of man-handling young Lane just now, Bill? Aren't things bad enough already? It strikes me that he is one man—"

"And you can forget him for all time. You'll never see hide nor hair of him again. He's only the polecat you heard me name him."

Lew Houston did not in the least understand, for he had come to regard the man of whom Bill Mountain spoke so off-handedly as the rock against which his young friend's fortunes were about to split.

"He may be all that," he retorted, "but also he's in a position to pull all the props out from under you. Oh, I hate compromising with a crook as much as you do and I suppose he has already done all the damage he can, selling you out to Buck Andros, but you're doing yourself no good by treating him to a ride on the toe of your boot."

Bill Mountain further surprised him by thrusting forward a tanned and capable looking right hand, slowly closing it until a hard-clenched fist resulted and remarking coolly:

"That for Buck Andros, too, Lew."

"Damn it all, Bill," said the banker testily, "What's got into you? If it wasn't for your worrying over Juan I'd say you didn't have a trouble on your mind. I've known all too many young fellows in my time overly given to optimism when they should have been cleaning their guns; you're not turning out to be that kind of a guy, are you, Bill? Good Lord, man, it's not ten days since I saw you looking like a man that was licked clean down to the ground, and here you come at me with a 'Pooh' for young Lane and a couple of 'Poohs' for Andros as though you had 'em both in the bag."

"Don't get me wrong, Lew," said Bill soberly. "Hell's due to bust wide open all right, but I'm going to ride straight through with bells on!"

"That's better than slow organ music," conceded Houston. "Now suppose you tell me the answer? I give up."

"Here's the story," said Bill Mountain.

Those matters to which he referred had their beginnings in a day which Lew Houston could recall well enough but of which Bill Mountain himself could only know by hearsay, not at the time having been born. It was now forty years since a certain Johnny Lane, a wild, foot-loose, harum-scarum ne'er-do-well came from no one knew where into the mountainous country of the Up Yonder. But this same Johnny Lane, though no place could hold him long and though his fellows adjudged him as hair-brained as he was likeable, had what is known as Vision. And he loved running water as the Montanas loved fine horses. Money came and money went through Johnny Lane's nimble fingers and for the greater part he might just as well have expended it for the unstable gas in a flock of toy balloons. But when he gained possession of White Water Valley he was acquiring a potential fortune for a song.

Johnny Lane one day on his inconsequential way from one place to another, stopped for a visit with his old friend, Jim Montana. This Jim Montana was none other than Bill's father. He was one quarter Spanish by blood and ninety-nine per cent. Spanish in everything else. He owned some forty thousand acres of exceptionally good land, he raised cattle casually, he lived spaciously and was a happy and successful man. But as his holdings spread out from year to year as did the lands of men of his type who, when they had money to spend bought land, there came the time when he wanted more water than he could lay his hands on.

"I want to buy your White Water Valley, Johnny," he said to his visitor. "It lies adjacent to my property, it's at a higher elevation and I can use the water."

"Not for sale," said Lane promptly. "That water of mine is going to be worth real money some day. You can use it, though."

At that moment Lane was in funds and had a small account in the bank down in San Carlos. He was "on his way" and didn't know when he'd be back, so it was arranged that Jim Montana was to make an annual payment of a couple of hundred dollars, handing the money over to Lew Houston and using both the land and water of his valley in any way that pleased him. The transaction was altogether too minor a matter for either man to dream of putting anything in writing. They knew each other, they were friends; it was as simple as that.

For several years Jim Montana used Lane's

valley as though it were his own. He grazed stock on it, he deflected the water where it poured out of the higher of the two little lakes, he irrigated his own alfalfa fields. Little by little that flowing stream began to be the life blood of his entire acreage. He spent thousands of dollars making dams and flumes and ditches and even buying other adjacent dry lands on which he poured the life-giving flood. The time came when he said to himself soberly, "I've got to acquire ownership of the White Water." For it had become obvious even to a gentleman of Spanish proclivities that, were White Water to fall into some hard-headed and unfriendly owner's hands, that individual would be in a rare position to pull all the props out from under one Jim Montana and let him down into something which smacked of financial disaster.

What had all the ear, hide and hoof marks of a kind and helpful Fate ordered it that at just about this time Johnny Lane's erratic orbit brought him streaking back across the Up Yonder. Jim Montana, brooding over these matters, had ridden up to White Water and sat in his saddle on a little hill, looking things over when Johnny Lane happened to make a flying visit to his highland estate. Jim Montana told his friend exactly what he had done and where the shoe began to pinch.

"I'll give you twenty thousand cash for the whole works, Johnny," said Montana.

Johnny Lane was open-minded.

"How about forty thousand?" he asked.

"It's worth it," said Montana. "It's worth more than that to me. Forty thousand goes. Suppose we spread the payments over a few years?"

"Take your time, Jim. No hurry. I'm heeled right now, anyway. Pay in at the bank at San Carlos, same as usual, whatever comes handy. Six per cent.? *Bueno.* I'm on my way right now and in a hurry, but soon's as I can get around to it I'll send the deed up to Lew Houston, and you and Lew can fix things up. *Adios*, *amigo*."

They shook hands and Johnny Lane went on his way. Jim Montana never saw him or heard from him again. No deed ever reached the bank. A perfectly sound deal had been entered into, but no one on earth knew anything about it save Jim Montana and Johnny Lane.

Montana when he saw the banker told him of the arrangement; thereafter both he and Houston held that there was a debt owing the Lane account of forty thousand dollars, interest at six per cent. Year after year Montana made his payments, and all this while no deed came and no word reached them of Lane's whereabouts. And some ten years before this evening, on which Penelope Loring found herself wondering whether a certain Don Montana would offer any more to the appraising feminine eye than did Bill Mountain, the father of the young man who she thought was two young men was gathered to the heaven of all good easy-going old cattlemen, and Donald William Montana, alias Bill Mountain, found himself the owner of an enormous outfit and of a sizeable problem.

He had had many talks with Lew Houston. There remained ten thousand dollars payable to the Lane account and in the end Bill Mountain, having inherited enough of his father's disposition to say let the tail go with the hide, paid it in full. Then he sat back and waited.

Johnny Lane's death had been assumed long ago, otherwise how explain so prolonged a silence and the further fact that the money awaiting his call still lay rolling up interest at three per cent in Lew Houston's bank? That he had died without issue seemed a likely thing, Johnny not impressing any who knew him as a marrying man. Even should an heir turn up at some late date it was at least an even break that he'd turn out to be a man who would play in good faith, take the Lane estate as represented by the accumulated funds in the bank, acknowledge the fact of the sale and consummate the deal. Lew Houston for his part had always shaken his head over the thing.

"It was all in the cards that some day some Buck Andros would show up and start trouble," he had felt from the beginning.

Yet when Buck Andros did take a hand and

began gathering in the dry lands to the west of White Water Valley, acquiring them and a lot of moth-eaten mortgages at his own price, Bill Mountain was not impressed. When Andros said bluntly that White Water Valley did not belong to the Montana property, Bill laughed at him. When Andros accused him of unlawfully deflecting the water, Bill Mountain told him in a few selected words to run jump off a high place. And when Andros took the first step towards turning that same water out across his own newly acquired lands, Bill Mountain took to wearing an old walnut handled forty five and watching over his interests personally.

But at the next development Bill Mountain began to fear that he was beaten. Buck Andros hired a sly pettifogger down in Albuquerque and went gunning after an heir. And, being a determined man and not in the least scrupulous, he found one. Further, he secured from that heir a deed to his interests in White Water Valley.

All this was known by Lew Houston as well as by Bill Mountain. He knew also how Bill had gone to see the heir whom Andros had dug up and had argued the case with him. He found himself up against an individual hard to stomach, that same young, case-hardened, foxy-eyed fellow whom he had evicted from Bradshaw's hotel this evening.

"Tough luck maybe for you, Montana," this

one had told him. “Misunderstanding, you know. Sure your old man and mine had a deal: your old man was to pay forty thousand dollars to my old man, and for that amount was to have a lease on White Water for a span of years. The span’s up now and I want what’s mine.”

“You’ll have to go to court, you know,” said Bill Mountain, holding himself in. “My father has been dead some years, but you’ll find that even so his word is worth more than most living men’s.”

But from the outset it was clear that Andros had his man in his pocket.

“That’s why I said you were licked, Bill,” said Houston.

“I thought I was,” laughed Bill Mountain. “Then last week old Dan Westcott dropped in to see me. We sat and chinned and clinked glasses for an hour, the old devil just meandering all over the map before he got around to what brought him. ‘Kind of a bad mix-up ain’t it, Bill?’ he says after a while. ‘You know, Bill, I always had a hunch some day the heir would pop up! Quite a spell back I was over in Arizony pirootin’ aroun’, havin’ been over yonder account takin’ a couple bad hombres home that had flew the coop and got over our way by mistake. That was ’bout ten years afore your dad slipped out on us, Bill. An’ it chanced that I saw Johnny Lane then. He had been married recent, too. An’ had a kid! Yep, your dad knowed. I told him. But when he went to look Johnny up, he'd vamoosed. Never can tell, can you, Bill? I'd of swore Johnny wasn't that kind.' "

"So old Dan knew?" said Houston. "He's a funny old goat that does a lot of talking and yet doesn't ever tell you much he doesn't have to." He looked thoughtfully at his glowing cigar-end, then jerked his head up to see a sparkle in Bill Mountain's eyes. "Damn it, Bill," he said, "that's no good news to me. All this while I've hoped against hope that Andros was pulling a fake heir on us and that we'd nail him in the courts. I didn't really believe Johnny Lane ever had a young one."

"He did, though, according to Dan Westcott," said Bill Mountain. "Here's the way he told me the tale: 'Bill, m' son,' he said, staring down into an almost empty glass, 'I rec'lec' fine how all swelled up Johnny was; took and drug me into where the cradle was to look at what he said was the fines' kid that ever was. Funny thing, Bill; that kid when foaled was a filly! How come, you suppose, that it's turned out to be a man now?' "

Lew Houston sat up straight in his chair.

"I'll be damned," was what he said.

"It skins 'em and stretches their hides all in a row to sun," said Bill Mountain. "This heir of Andros' claims to be the one and only child and has sworn that Johnny died when he was seven years old. He's a liar and so is Andros, and they're asking for what they're going to get. Here a week ago I was sitting with my hands in my lap. Andros had some men up at the White Water, ready to blow out a mountainside and turn the water down on his land."

"And Dan told you in time! And you went up and found Tom Gadge on the job and fixed his clock!"

"I sure did, Lew. What's more I celebrated with a big fireworks at Andros' expense, only I took the liberty of moving his dynamite about a mile from where he thought it would do the most good. Now, still doing neighbourly turns, I'm down here to warn you to hold tight to any Lane money you've still got. As Dan says, when we do find the right heir he's going to be an heiress."

"Filly," corrected Lew Houston. "Yes, I'll hold tight. It will take a whole string of court orders to pry me loose."

"If you two rattlesnakes got any private talk to indulge in," said Bradshaw, barging in on them, "you gotta go somewheres else to do it."

"Squat, Brad," said Houston hospitably. "We're about through. What's on your mind?"

"That girl," said Bradshaw. "Name of Pennylope. The pore kid's in trouble. Sweet kid, too. Don't you think so?"

"Yes," said Houston.

"You, Bill?" asked Bradshaw eagerly.

"Didn't notice," said Bill.

"You wouldn't," snorted Bradshaw contemptuously. "If that lady that's told of in song an' story, that went through town on a white horse without much of anything on—"

"Godiva," suggested Houston.

"Her," said Bradshaw. "If Godiva rode by an' Bill Mountain was aroun', mos' likely he'd perk up an' say, 'That horse ain't much, its ears is too big an' its tail don't set in right.' "

"What about the girl, Brad?" asked Houston.

"Chirp an' chipper when she blew in here, Lew," said the hotel-keeper, "them two big eyes o' hers dancin', dimples all over the shop, feet kinda skippity even when she stood still. Jus' all full o' pep an' go, like a spring breeze or a frisky yearlin' colt. An' now look at her! I knowed somethin' was wrong; I been an hour gettin' it, but I got it!"

"You would," grinned Bill Mountain and evened the score.

"It's all ol' Sniffy Pringle's fault," growled Bradshaw.

"He's dead now, so let him be, Brad," suggested the banker.

"That's what I'm talkin' about," retorted Bradshaw. "He had no business dyin'. He was head school trustee, wasn't he? An' he wrote Pennylope down to Albuquerque and give her the job teachin' the school, an' wrote her she could board his place an' wouldn't have to pungle up until the end o' the month when she drawed her pay. Then the ol' weasel died, for he always was a weasel livin' or dead; an' Reef Johnson got to be head trustee an' hired another school marm, and shoved school ahead, an' now Penny-lope gets here an' her job's gone—An' she ain't hungry, thank you!"

"Broke?" said Bill succinctly.

"Broke. She an' her girl frien' down to Albuquerque had a fine farewell party, an' Penny-lope spends free, figgerin' all she needs to hold out is enough to get her landed here. An' now the pore little kid, brave as the dickens, too, is out on a limb. 'I'm so shamed, Mr. Bradshaw! I—I can't pay you any more'n I've got, can I? An' I only got sixty cents lef'! But I'll do something; I'll work in the kitchen a while, if you'll have me, or wait on table an' make beds an' things until I can pay what I owe you—' "

"Why doesn't she tackle her girl friend for a few dollars?" asked the banker.

"She won't," said Bradshaw. "She says she came out here with all the flags flyin', an' her frien's a nurse an' broke too an' out o' work, an' she'll be eternally damned before she lets out a cheep."

Even Bill Mountain grew mildly interested. The three men sat into a conference to discuss ways and means.

CHAPTER 3

"Bill Mountain," wrote Penelope's flying pen, "is the biggest liar in New Mexico, as I have on the excellent authority of Mr. Bradshaw who has turned out to be an angel with pink garters on his sleeves. Bill Mountain further, on the same angelic authority, is a man whose word is as good as gold! Oh, don't ask me, my dear! Besides, I'm so excited I could fly! I guess it means that he is one of those creatures that all his friends greet jovially by saying, 'Here's that unmitigated dam' liar, Bill Mountain,' and yet if a man said in the wrong tone of voice to him, 'You lie!' it would all be something different again and messy. But here's the main thing, Patty Lane: I'm off to bed now in a hurry because I'm to be up at daybreak, and in the saddle to ride Up Yonder! Yes, with Bill Mountain!"

Bill Mountain had found her sitting very still on the front porch at the hotel, looking at the stars. He said, "Howdy, sister" and seated himself on the steps below her. Penelope said a strained, "Good evening," and looked at him curiously. He, too, was looking at the stars; his back was towards her and at first she thought that he was just going to sit there and let the evening drift by while he thought up something to say.

"Brad tells me you're lookin' for a job," he said after a while.

Penelope gasped. Brad had no earthly business going around telling all that had passed between him and her. She stiffened a little, then since he still did not turn she relaxed slowly. She did not answer him.

"Teacher, huh?" said Bill Mountain. "Well, there's a teachin' job open Up Yonder. Me, I'm the head school trustee. You're hired. Be ready for an early start. We better get goin' at sun-up."

Penelope's first gasp was a very feeble sort of thing compared to the second.

"You're a school trustee! You—you're actually looking for a teacher? Up Yonder?"

"Yes ma'am," said Bill. He had been making himself a cigarette; now he lighted it and she saw his face in the red flame. He looked to be in dead earnest.

"Wh—what school?" asked Penelope in a small voice.

"Oh, the name o' the school?" He waved his match like a small torch, finally extinguished it, broke it neatly in two and rolled the bits between his fingers. His face which had had the effect of leaping out of the dark vanished again. "The name o' the school," he told her, "is White Water Valley school."

"I never heard of it," said Penelope mystified. "And when I made my application for a lot of places I had a list of schools as long as my arm."

"You wouldn't hear of it, mos' likely," he admitted.

"When does it open?"

"Soon's you get there, I reckon, an' c'n get things ready."

"How does it happen that you haven't a teacher already? Do—do you just ride around the country hunting for one?"

"Yes, ma'am," he told her. "That's the way I do. You see, I never was a school trustee before an' this is all new to me. The school's new, too; that explains everything, don't it? Jus' gettin' started for the firs' time this year. Want the place?"

Penelope had to remember that this was the biggest liar in New Mexico! Just the same, her heart beat quickened. She tried to see his face but in the starlight could see nothing but a black shadow under his old hat.

She strove to be very businesslike.

"Thank you for the offer, Mr. Mountain," she said. "But it is all rather queer, isn't it? You don't know a thing about my qualifications, you don't know who I am or what my name is—and I don't know where your school is or what the salary or—or anything!"

"I know you'll do fine," said Bill Mountain offhandedly. "I know you come from Albuquerque an' your name's Penny-lope—"

"Penelope," she corrected him, and added pointedly, "Miss Penelope Loring."

"As for wages," said Bill, "you an' me can fix that between us. Whatever you say, goes, I guess. How much was Sniffy Pringle offerin'?"

"Mr. Pringle was to pay me ninety dollars. I was to pay him twenty-five for board and room."

"Say we pay you a hundred-fifty?" he suggested. "An' you board yourself? We throw the livin' quarters in. We oughta be able to do whatever Sniffy Pringle could, an' go him one better, you know. He was a man to play awful close to the table, sort of a skinflint, to draw it mild."

"He is dead now," said Penelope softly.

"Jus' because a groun' hawg stops breathin'," he told her lightly, "ain't any reason for folks in these parts callin' it a bird o' paradise." He rose with a sigh like a man who hated to bestir himself yet felt he must. "It's boun' to be hooten'n hell to-morrow, so let's hit saddle leather early—You c'n ride, can't you?"

"Yes," said Penelope eagerly. She would run in and have another long talk with Mr. Bradshaw—but her hopes were leaping. "Yes, I can ride." Not only had that, but a certain part of her squandered funds in Albuquerque gone for a most delectable riding outfit.

He mounted the steps and went into the hotel and she thought that he was yawning. On his way in at the deep doorway he called back. " 'Night,

Penny-lope. I'll whoop you at daylight." She heard him a moment later talking with Mr. Bradshaw. Every word of their conversation came out to her clearly. Bill Mountain was telling of a new colt; it had been born on the first of May, was out of Larkspur by Daybreak, and already gave every sign of being a duplicate of its granddam, Starlight who, Brad was to remember, had been sired by Long Tom.

Penelope's attention wandered and she turned her eyes again to the stars. She would wait until that absurd Bill Mountain went off to bed, when she would have a talk with Mr. Bradshaw. The hotel-keeper she instinctively trusted; no one could see him and fail to do so. He could tell her whether it were a mad thing to go off towards the mountains, into a strange country, with Bill Mountain. Her imagination had quickened, her thoughts raced helter-skelter among facts and conjectures. This solution which had just offered itself to her problem, how unexpected it was and somehow unreal! Yet, under analysis, what could be more commonplace? New school districts were for ever being formed in the back country as families multiplied and children came along. Why shouldn't one be opening now for the first time, just at the moment of her need? Why shouldn't she happen along instead of any other girl to secure the newly created post? . . . Perhaps the hardest thing of all to reconcile to her sense of realities was Bill Mountain in the role of school trustee!

The sky constituting the dome of the heavens was a glorious deep blue illuminated and deepened by its myriad scintillating lights. But down over the ragged horizon there was a mellower glow; the moon would be rising soon and the mountains, now a solid dark mass, would reveal themselves in a new phase, their crests catching the moonbeams, their gorges filling themselves with mystery. The night was intensely still.

She drifted away in profound reverie. All heat was gone now, the air was sweet and fresh, the world as she saw it intensely lovely. A line from restless-souled Byron whispered itself in her ears: "Where all save the spirit of man is divine." She thought of what had occurred in the Up Yonder only a day or so ago, two men trying to kill each other, Bill Mountain shooting Tom Gadge; of the scene of violence which she had witnessed a little while before, the denouement of which she had found oddly satisfactory—and of those final words of the evicted man denouncing Bill Mountain's brother as an outlaw fleeing the charge of murder.

She tried to peer into the future and realized that the future which for the most part is something far off was now as close to her as to-morrow morning. It was a queer sort of realization; it was like having come right up to the door and to be standing there saying, "Shall I open it and go in? Or shall I turn back, leaving it closed?"

The moon had not yet risen, though the sky was swiftly brightening above the mountains when she became aware of the fact that she no longer had the outside night all to herself. Out of the corner of her eye she caught sight of something moving among the shadows under the pepper trees. She watched somewhat absently, still preoccupied with her own musings. Whatever it was that she had seen had grown still again and thus blended with the darkness was invisible to her. Faintly curious, she kept her eyes on the spot where it had vanished and presently saw it stir again and made out that it was a man. Immediately she became alert and really interested. One who dodged into shadows invited attention.

In the hotel the two men were still talking. Bradshaw suggested another drink and she heard Bill Mountain say, "Thanks, Brad; save it for nex' time." Bradshaw said, "Fair enough, Bill; here's mud in your eye, an' now if you'll lis'en to me a minute I'll give you a tip that mebbe some day'll save you from havin' a right bad hemorrhage—"

The man by the store moved again. Queerly, thought a thoroughly interested Penelope. He darted across the road, coming towards the hotel, and Penelope straightened up with a gasp. The starlight revealed him sufficiently clearly now and, more than that, it glinted along the steel barrel of a gun. He passed within a dozen steps of her, ducking about the corner of the hotel, speeding along towards the windows which, wide open for the evening's cool air, would give him an unobstructed view of the two men inside.

She started involuntarily to scream a warning, so sure was she of the man's intent, so eloquent of his purpose his every movement had been. Never had her mind functioned so swiftly as it did the second after realization came to her. If she screamed not only Bill Mountain and Bradshaw would hear; so would the other. The two would come running, and in the lighted room—

No, that would not do. She sprang up instead and ran as softly as she could to the door. Bradshaw was facing her and stared: Bill Mountain seeing the look on Bradshaw's face, whirled about to see what caused it.

"Quick!" she gasped. "There's a man with a gun—under the window—"

It seemed to her that one leap brought Bill Mountain to her side.

"Down!" he said. "Lie flat!"

As he passed her he caught her by the shoulder and thrust her down to the floor. Then he ran out at the door and she caught a glimpse of Bradshaw seeming to melt out of his chair and slide out of sight behind his bar. At the same moment through the window she saw a long orange-red streak of flame. There was a report followed swiftly by another and yet another. Bradshaw's head appeared above the bar, his eyes looking round and foolish.

"Down!" he shouted at her. "Keep down!"

She could make out a difference in the quality of the reports outside; of course one was a rifle, the other a pistol. And she had not known that Bill Mountain was armed.

She scrambled to her feet.

"Down—dammit!" yelled Bradshaw.

"Listen!" she called back to him.

There was the sound of a man running and almost instantly the louder sound of a horse's hoofs. Bradshaw hurried to her side and both went to the door just in time to see Bill Mountain coming back. He was head down and at first she thought that he had been shot. Then, as he came closer, she made out that he was merely reloading his gun; she saw him slip it out of sight under his left arm. The swiftly thudding hoofbeats were already dying away.

"Who was it?" demanded Bradshaw. "That bum you jus' booted out o' here?"

"No. It was Gadge," said Bill Mountain. "Herbie Gadge, Tom's brother. Didn't think Herbie had it in him. Well, blood's thicker than water after all, even in a Gadge."

"If it hadn't been for her we'd be packin' you in ice by this time," said Bradshaw.

Bill Mountain really looked at Penelope for the first time.

"Good girl," he said, and smiled like a friend.

"Damn right she's a good girl," exclaimed Bradshaw. "You'd of been deader'n a mackerel by now—Why'd you let him off, Bill? When he piled onto his horse was your chance!"

"That's when I was sure who he was," said Bill. "Know what horse that was, Brad? It was Baby Belle. The wucker was lying flat, right close down, too. No, I couldn't take any chances in the dark."

"Me, I'll pull down the shades and finish my drink," said Bradshaw, turning away. Over his shoulder he offered soberly, "You can't tell but what he'll take a long shot, Bill. Better watch your step."

"No, he's spoken his piece for this time, Brad. Scared now, that hombre is. I'm sorry for any animal he rides to-night. I didn't sell him Baby Belle, you know," he added frowning. "I sold her to Hemp Morgan and he let her go to Andros. And it will be one long, long day before Hemp ever gets another horse from me."

Penelope was looking at him curiously. There was some odd but intangible difference in the man, some subtle new quality in his speech. He had spoken swiftly, and it was as though he had lapsed into some old familiar habit.

He turned to look at her again; up shot his brows quizzically.

"You're not goin' to turn pale now, are you, Penny-lope," he bantered, and here was the original Bill Mountain, speaking deliberately, lazily and colloquially. "You was quite a heroine jus' now, ca'm an' cool-minded. Ain't goin' to get trembly, are you?"

Her face, though perhaps it had paled, flushed up redly now. If he, just because he had only a moment ago been under fire and now chose to make light of the episode, thought that she was going to be any more concerned than himself, well then Mr. Bill Mountain had much to learn.

"Should an idiotic fate ever again decree that I am to drop some bright and chatty little remark to you as I did just now," she told him while giving herself a thorough dusting off, "I'll thank you, Mr. Bill Mountain, not to throw me down and walk on me."

He drowned her last words with his rollicking laughter.

"That's the stuff," he said, and like an old and privileged friend of the family, caught her arm and drew her along with him in Bradshaw's direction. "Brad, ol' horse," he commanded, "set 'em up, an' make sure it's the best in the house for our new pal, Penny-lope."

"Not having any, thank you," said Penelope, and wriggled free. And to the hotel-keeper serenely, or at least as serenely as she could, ignoring her new pal, she added: "If the festivities of the evening are now over, may I have a few words with you, Mr. Bradshaw?"

Bill Mountain chuckled.

"I'm off to my room, where I'll lock my doors and hide under the bed for safe-keepin' while I'm getting my beauty sleep," he said and strolled away. "Night, ever'body."

"Night, Bill," said Bradshaw.

CHAPTER 4

Though Bill Mountain went straightway to his room he did not at once prepare for that beauty sleep of which he had spoken. With his lamp lighted he stretched out on his bed, draped his heels over the footboard, clasped his hands behind his head and regarded the ceiling. There he lay for an hour, mentally busy while his body relaxed after a long day. Once he heard voices and supposed that some of the denizens of San Carlos, who had heard an exchange of shots, were drawn out by curiosity to request details. Later, out of a long silence, he heard Bradshaw's voice saying good night to Penelope at the foot of the stairs, and then Penelope tip-toeing down the hall, and closing her door softly.

After a bit he rose, extinguished his light and went downstairs. The house was dark, but he lighted a lamp and made himself at home behind Bradshaw's little bar. Alongside the hotel register he found pencil and paper. Perhaps not so much letter writing would be done in this place during the next six months as was done here to-night.

> "Dear Ben," he wrote, "the minute you get this get going for all you're worth, will you? It's damned important. We're

going to have a school of our own in White Water. It'll be at the lower end of the valley, so as to draw for attendance on both White Water and Montana. Pass the word that every kid old enough to walk has got to go. Get a couple of the boys and two-three Indian women to give the old Cold Spring house a thorough cleaning. The front room will have to do for schoolroom until we get a house built. The teacher will live in the other rooms for the present. You and Consuela furnish it from my diggings. Consuela will stay at the Cold Spring place as housekeeper, cook and so on. If anybody asks you about all this monkey business you tell 'em we've been planning on it the last nine years. Got that, you hound dog? I'll come home and fry you in hog fat if you miss a bet anywhere along the way. So long.

"BILL."

P.S.—Yes, I'm bringing the teacher. She's an old lady who just lost all her money and both sons; she's a little deaf but otherwise all right and a dead game sport. Addyose."

This note he folded and carried out into the night. Rounding the blacksmith's, which began to think of itself as a garage, he rattled at a window. A voice in Spanish demanded explanations.

"That you, Tonito?" asked Bill.

"No, senor. I am the cousin of Tonito."

"It's Montana speaking. Is Tonito there?"

Tonito answered for himself. Bill called to him to bestir himself, jump into his clothes and get ready to ride. Tonito bestirred himself and ten minutes later had his instructions, called a cheery *hasta la vista* to his cousin and rode out of San Carlos. Bill watched him head out towards the mountains, went back to the hotel and to sleep.

Penelope awoke with a start; someone was knocking. It was dark in her room and she had no idea that morning was even on its way. But when she asked drowsily, "Who is it?" Bradshaw's voice informed her that it was almost daybreak, that breakfast was ready and Bill Mountain wanted to get going.

"Right away," answered a suddenly wide awake Penelope.

She jumped out of bed and dressed hurriedly, donning the new riding togs; she peeped at herself in a dark and blurry mirror, pulled on a hat big and broad enough to be some protection from the sun later, jammed some double handfuls of odds and ends into a small handbag, locked her two big suitcases and ran down the stairs.

"This way," called Bradshaw from the kitchen. "Come in here for breakfas', Miss Loring. You'll eat alone; me an' Bill has already done so."

On an untidy kitchen table Bradshaw had set forth bacon and eggs and hot-cakes and the blackest coffee Penelope ever dreamed of.

"I rastled it m'se'f," he said pridefully. "If I'd of tried to get Maria up this time o' day she'd have busted me one an' run out on me. Eat hearty, Miss."

When, breakfast swiftly disposed of, Penelope hurried out into the yard, the blue night was like a Maxfield Parrish painting, the sky like a deep-tinted morning glory. Dawn was in the air, sweet and cool and fresh, and there was a faint flush of light above the distant mountains, but among the pepper trees in little San Carlos the hour belonged to night. A group of shadows coming towards her from the barn resolved itself into Bill Mountain leading two horses. The clank of his spurs and the jingle of bridle chains made pleasant music.

Bill Mountain said a casual, "Mornin', Penny-lope," and swung lightly up into one of the saddles. There, looming big against the stars he looked down at her, watching her shrewdly. Bradshaw had followed her into the yard and was about to offer her a hand up, but she made haste to mount without his assistance. She saw the head under Bill Mountain's wide-brimmed hat nod approvingly; he sang out, "So long, Brad," and added, "Come ahead, Penny-lope. We're on our way."

As they rode side by side out of San Carlos she knew that all the while he was watching her to inform himself as to the extent of her horsemanship. She was grateful as never until now that she could ride; her father had taught her, had often ridden with her in the Sandias, and had instilled in her something of his own love and appreciation of fine horses. The animal she bestrode was young and full of spirit, one of Bradshaw's best, and Penelope was not in the least unaware as the light brightened that she looked well in the saddle. And a little song began to sing itself in her heart as ghostly puffs of dust rose underfoot and San Carlos fell away behind them, a song that was all about the white, white road along which she was actually riding, and the purple mountains ahead where mystery wove its spells and romance rode in purple and gorgeous adventures offered themselves; the white, white road on which one sped through the blue night and into the golden daybreak.

At first all was a grey blur on either hand, but as the darkness thinned Penelope saw that they were voyaging an undulating sea of sand and sage. Presently the sun rose above the mountains, and Bill Mountain pointed out the way they had to travel.

"Look straight ahead," he said, "an' you'll see two high peaks with a sort o' saddle between 'em? That's Injun Pass, an' after we've got the flat lan's behind us an' done some climbin' along some purty steep mountain trails we'll head up that way. Then we'll duck down in a long narrow valley, make another climb an' slip through another pass. High Gate, jus' like the firs' one. From High Gate you c'n see purty near as far 'cross country as a feller can look straight up in the air, an' I'll show you down below an' off to the right what's known as Montana Valley. At it's upper en' it goose-necks where it hooks on to White Water Valley. Got all that g'ography?"

"You make it very clear."

"I went to school once m'self," he advised her.

"I am going to love it up there," said Penelope with assurance. "And I haven't thanked you."

"O' course you're goin' to like it," said Bill Mountain.

He set the pace, a steady swinging gallop which his rangy black mare appeared to be able to maintain tirelessly for hours, and relapsed into a long silence. What a funny sort of man, Penelope thought, for a school trustee! In the couple of hours during which they drifted across the arid level lands, her busy thoughts suggested many questions which she had to dismiss unasked. What, she wondered, was to be expected between Bill Mountain and his neighbour, Buck Andros? What of the man who had tried to shoot him last night? What of that man's brother whom he had shot only a few days before? And there was that other man, the one of the pale, unpleasant eyes whom she had seen pitted out into the road—and that man's vicious words, something about "your brother, on the run for murder and sure to hang—" To be sure all these were considerations which need not more than brush the outer confines of her own life; no doubt she was as close to all this right now, riding at Bill Mountain's elbow, as she would ever be. Yet for the moment it occupied her more than did her own plans and expectations. For after all, her adventure of locating herself in a new mountain school would be a pallid affair compared to his.

Almost before she knew it they were upon the western slope of the mountains and entering the wide mouth of a shadowy canyon, where they came upon the first scattering pine trees. A spring of clear cold water invited them aside into a place of tall ferns; they drank and watered the horses, and Bill Mountain had a cigarette and Penelope sat with her back against a tree and dropped white pebbles into the pool. Then they rode on deeper into the canyon, following an old weed-grown wagon road until it ended in a little clearing, thereafter climbing steeply a winding trail.

They were above an hour in attaining the first of the two passes. The time went by like a song for Penelope. She found herself in a land of wild beauty and always penetrating deeper into its savage heart. Bold, barren peaks stood loftily above, naked save for the clear strong light in which the sun clothed them. Overshadowing deep cool ravines, which at times revealed a silvery flash of water, and always in her ears was the whisper of pines. For the treeless lands were far behind and below now whereas at these greater altitudes forests of pine and fir cloaked the slopes. And rather curiously making for perfect peace, Bill Mountain at her side was no longer a stranger met only a few hours ago, but seemed like an old friend.

How this came about she did not at first know. She noted it with something of a start and puzzled over it. They had been chatting of this, that and the other thing; they had laughed together. In his companionship she found something at first defying analysis which was at once novel and oddly refreshing. Somehow he had struck a new note, and she was at utter loss to account for it. Being with him was like being with no other man she had ever known. When that fact dawned on her she would never have been the very thorough-going Penelope Loring that she was had she not dug down for the explanation. It came to her like a flash of light.

He was the one male human being she had ever encountered who did not treat her as of another sex than his own. He talked with her exactly as he talked with a man. He said, "Hot as hell's kitchen, ain't it?" He said, "That's a damn fool thing to say an' you know it." He looked at her exactly as he looked at a man. And all the while he was himself, really himself, and that was what made his companionship so refreshing.

You never knew a man really, that is you never did if you were a girl—especially a pretty girl. In the same way no doubt, if you were a man, you never knew a girl. There must forever be that little trimming of sails to the breeze of sex. If in ever so little and ever so unconsciously you modified your vocabulary or your inflection or your smile. This did not mean that one meant to pose; it only meant that one did pose. To do so was human. A large part of human functions operate involuntarily.

Bill Mountain did not do these things. He was himself.

She looked at him curiously, again seeking explanations. Why didn't he change as others did? Being a persistent young woman, Penelope got the answer to that question, too: This absurd Bill Mountain was the one human being on earth, so far as she knew, who was not thinking of himself and being concerned with himself while he talked with you! No, not even subconsciously or unconsciously was he trying to "put himself over." Not trying to show his best side. That was it.—After a while she decided that long, long ago he must have realized what a funny looking thing he was and had lost all conceit, and so simply forgot himself.—It was different with Penelope Loring; she knew that she was pretty and attractive; she did enjoy putting herself over. And she came to suppose that it just couldn't be done with Bill Mountain; he wouldn't take any interest. Oh, he had looked at her and he had sized her up. Once at the hotel, again when she mounted her horse. Looked at her as an individual, not as a girl.

Altogether her discovery was novel, refreshing—and faintly in the nature of a challenge.

One other discovery she made before they came to High Gate. He had ridden ahead where the trail was narrow, winding around a steep shoulder of the mountain and she, speculating upon the anomaly that he was, was watching him curiously. The thing which suggested itself to her now was that that awkwardness which she had thought to mark in San Carlos had fallen from him. (Much of these musings of hers took definite form when later she put them into a letter to Patty Lane, at which time she wrote: "He's not a man at all; he's just the top half of a centaur! You should see him on horseback; he is whole and complete then! How he can ride! On horseback he's the most graceful thing—")

"Come ahead, Penny-lope," he was calling to her. "Not tired, are you? We'll hit a gallop here through the pass; that'll rest you if you are."

Here a three mile gallop offered itself through a pleasant upland valley with a tiny clear stream to splash across at times, with a sparse growth of big pines making long shadows across the grassy floor. Only a day or two before a heavy thunderstorm had drenched the mountains and the air was clear and sweet with earthy smells. A rare sense of well-being exhilarated and buoyed Penelope along; her breast swelled to a long in-take of delicious air and her pulses drummed pleasurably. The sun shone on them genially but at this altitude, well above seven thousand feet, poured down on them none of the heat which was baking the lower levels.

They left Indian Pass behind them, went down a crooked trail into a land of steep-walled ravines and made their way slowly to the top of the next ridge. Here, with breath-taking unexpectedness as far as Penelope was concerned, they came upon one of those glorious panoramas which only the high placed of earth can reveal. "The promised land," said Bill Mountain. They looked down dizzy heights into a long valley through which meandered a silver thread, Montana Creek which had its beginnings in a second, higher Valley, that of the White Water. There were emerald squares making a mosaic with brown, there were tiny houses flashing white and red, there were clumps of yellow pine and spruce. Lines of lacy white which were waterfalls poured down from the higher valley into the lower at the Goose Neck.

"It's the vale of peace and content and fruitfulness," said Penelope.

"It should be, all o' that," said Bill Mountain.

"It's like the Happy Valley in a story called *Rasselas*—And straight down there is Don Montana's place? Tell me about him."

He looked sharply at her as though he suspected her of having swung all without warning from a mood of almost ecstatic admiration to one of jest, but saw that her eyes were glowing with the beauty of the scene spread out down there below them.

"Don Montana?" said Bill Mountain. Then all of a sudden he understood, and made the most of the moment. Sure, he'd tell her about Don Montana an' he reckoned that he knew that hombre as well as the nex' feller. A half-bred pup, that's what he was, as you'd guess from his name, a man that Bill got along with good enough at times an' that made him no end of trouble at others. "We been frien's an' we've fought it out like two ol' tom-cats. A dash o' black Spanish blood in the cuss, you know, Penny-lope—only don't you go an' call him a Greaser to his face! It makes him sorer'n a saddle boil. An' me, personal, I wouldn't trus' this Montana out o' sight. Them breeds is all like that."

She eyed him with scant approval.

"There is nothing finer than a dash of Spanish

blood," she reminded him with the first hint of the school mistress he had seen in her. "It's the blood of conquerors. I suppose he is a dashingly handsome chap with many a poor country maid's scalp dangling at his belt?"

Bill Mountain's face grew longer than ever.

"That's him," he vowed. "How'd you know? Jus' from the name? Why, you'll find girls crawlin' over that breed thicker'n flies."

"And that," thought Penelope as they rode on, "is about as hideous a simile as I've ever heard. I wonder whether my new friend is jealous?"

Their most hazardous bit of trail lay just before them. They went steeply down, with spires of rock standing above them, and their pathway narrowed so that again they rode single file, at times their stirrups brushing the sheer mountain on one side while on the other they looked straight down for hundreds of feet. Bill Mountain looked back to see how she was taking it and she managed a smile, the sort which comes to the lips only. She wanted to get down and lead her horse, but seeing how indifferent he was, stuck bravely to her saddle.

He waited for her at a spot where the trail broadened rather more comfortably just before narrowing again to worm its way about a sharply out-thrust place of crags.

"Makin' out all right?" he asked.

Penelope was just beginning to breathe properly

and before she could voice the assurance that she did beautifully, thank you, both were startled by a sudden crash of sound shattering the brooding silence. At no great distance rifle shots started up echoes that clanged and crashed among the iron cliffs all about them. And after that first fusillade the short, snapping report of a pistol was like a small-voiced yet desperate defiance.

A look of consternation stamped itself on Bill Mountain's face.

"They've jumped the kid up," he muttered savagely. "That's that damned Andros' work! But how in hell he knew—"

He slid from the saddle, left his horse standing where it was and ran down the trail, lost to her sight where it angled so sharply about the overhang of cliff.

She too dismounted swiftly for some greater sense of security and listened in awe as again the rifle fire crackled and clanged, harking for the report of the smaller weapon. But now the pistol was silent.

In her turn Penelope hurried forward, but not knowing whence the shots came and being fearful of the bullets, she kept close to the embankment and stopped short of the abrupt angle in the trail, peering around the rocks in search of her vanished companion. There was no sign of him but at some little distance and across a deeply indented ravine she saw four men. Two of them were mounted while two stood at their horses' heads; all four held rifles in their hands, flashing back the sun. And all four were concerned with a spot above them on the mountainside where she required no telling that some man hid among the rocks and clumps of brush, striving to fight them off with his smaller weapon.

"The kid," Bill Mountain had said. Though he had made no reference to his brother all this while and though she could not question him, she had never ceased to ponder on those words spoken by the sandy-haired, pale-eyed man whom he had thrown out of the hotel. One who was on the run for murder done, who'd hang when they got him. . . .

Bill Mountain's brother a murderer? She didn't believe it! Not from what she already knew of Bill Mountain and certainly not on the accusation of the pale-eyed man.

She wondered what had happened to Bill Mountain. She had fully expected to see him emerge from some twist in the trail, running down upon the four men, gun in hand. One of them, she thought, was Andros. From where she stood they were just four men, alike with their rifles and big hats and horses.

One of them began firing again, his rifle angling upward as he poured several shots into the place of rocks and brush. The others craned their necks; then one of them whipped his rifle up and fired twice, the reports coming close together. She shivered and clung with both hands to the rocks, again harkening anxiously for the crack of a pistol. Up yonder where the two men poured their bullets was a region of sun and shadow and a high, potential peacefulness, and already she was afraid that a man lay there dead or dying.

But if he were dead already those others would not keep on shooting. Perhaps they had him down and strove to make sure of him as he crawled towards shelter.

Then, when she had never expected to hear it again, a revolver barked from the mountainside and one of the men dropped his rifle and clutched at his arm, cursing in rage and pain. The rifles that had grown silent a moment resumed their clanging din.

After a long while Penelope heard something behind her and wheeled about nervously. A thin trickle of small stones came pouring down into the trail from a steep bank and after this forerunner of his approach a man slid down, feet first, and brought up with a jolt within a couple of yards of her.

The stranger was a youngster, not over nineteen or twenty, and strikingly handsome; his face was fine and dark, his eyes large and very bright and expressive, wild eyes just now; dark chestnut curls were matted against a wet brow.

"Bill sent me—he made me come! Damn them!—He said you are a friend. I'm taking his horse—"

"You're hurt!"

The boy made a quick gesture; one hand was pressed to his side and his shirt was bloody.

"Listen!" he muttered.

She listened and heard the rifles at it once more, then a lull and a single revolver shot.

"That's Bill. He's taken my place. He's holding them."

His lips began to tremble and he had difficulty in speaking clearly.

"Can't you hide somewhere?" whispered Penelope. "What are you going to do?"

"I'm going—Bill made me promise! Oh, God," he exclaimed bitterly, "I want to stay and fight it out—but Bill made me promise."

He turned and went, walking heavily, to where the horses stood. Slowly he pulled himself up into Bill Mountain's saddle and for a moment sat motionless, head down and irresolute. Then with a sudden gesture, he jerked his head up, jammed his heels into the horse's flanks and rode back up the trail.

Above the clattering of shod hoofs Penelope heard a fresh fusillade of rifle fire. Again she listened for the answer which would tell her that Bill Mountain was still unharmed by that deadly hail. But when the rifle fire died away a heavy silence shut down. She went again to the turn in the trail and saw the four men, all of them on foot now, only three holding guns in their hands, the fourth busy tying his arm up in a red handkerchief.

Before any one of them stirred, while she was wondering bleakly whether at last they'd got their man, though not the man they had thought to get, she heard again the rattle and thud of loose stones behind her. When this time it was Bill Mountain who dropped down into the trail an involuntary "Thank God!" burst from her.

CHAPTER 5

Bill Mountain made himself a cigarette and she marvelled at him. His eyes were blazing and his face white with rage, yet his hands were steady. Ignoring her utterly he smoked a moment, a heavy frown dragging his brows down. He dropped his cigarette, trod on it and pulled his hat forward over his eyes.

"Stand back, close to the bank," he said and went along the trail to that point of vantage whence she had looked on the four men. He had holstered his gun under his arm but now pulled it out and carried it loosely in his hand.

"Andros!" he shouted. "Come and get it!"

His voice started up the echoes among the rocky ravines and while those echoes still were tossed back and forth one of the four rifles added its din and bullets spattered on the rock from which he had called. But he had seen the sun flash on the weapon and had stepped back out of sight. The rifle fire ceased and another voice started the echoes flying. It was Andros, sounding puzzled, shouting:

"That you, Bill Mountain?"

"Back up around the next bend in the trail, Penelope," said Bill Mountain sharply. "Then climb up off the trail and keep under cover. If they get me, you carry the word down into the valley. Find Ben Hodge; tell him they jumped the kid up and that he's hurt and I've sent him to hole-up at the head of Black Tail meadow. Got that?"

"Y-yes," said Penelope faintly, finding speech difficult. Then she got a grip on herself and cleared her throat, saying swiftly: "Don't be a fool! They are four to one. You come back with me."

Bill Mountain again called down the trail:

"Come and get it, Andros. You bet it's Bill Mountain."

"Feel like doing a suicide act, you fool?" jeered Andros. "There are four of us, every man with a rifle."

"One of you already has a bullet of mine in him," Bill shouted back. "Come ahead the rest of you and collect some more lead." He paused, then called coolly: "I'll wait here where I can pick you off one at the time. You'll last longer that way."

Andros in his turn took time for thought. Then he sang out:

"I'm coming ahead alone, Bill. I want to talk, that's all."

"Come shooting," Bill shouted back. "When I can see the whites of your eyes, that's my cue."

"No, I'm not coming shooting. I'm leaving my gun here with one of the boys."

Penelope, drawing near on tiptoes, afraid that

Bill Mountain would hear and thrust her back, watched the man riding up trail towards them. He was a big man, thick-shouldered, slim-waisted and carried himself even in the saddle with an air of arrogance. Whereas two of his following wore chaps and one overalls, Buck Andros was costumed in boots, breeches and shirt which would have been the last whisper on a city bridle path. He was a man who all his life had commanded other men and who, Penelope judged cannily as he came closer, had been a high favourite with women. Handsome and keen and assured, he could swagger a bit on occasion—and could no doubt find it equally easy to be blandly affable or mercilessly cruel.

"Hello, Bill," he said casually, and those hard bright eyes of his ran on and for an instant rested penetratingly on the smaller figure at Bill Mountain's back.

"You boys happen to be trespassing on my land, Andros," said Bill gravely. "Lost anything that belongs to you?"

"No," replied Andros as gravely. "But we found something that belongs to the state. On foot, huh? Where's your horse?"

"What horse?" asked Bill.

"You and your little lady friend aren't riding double, are you, Bill?" Andros eased himself in the saddle and again regarded Penelope with a long critical stare. Then he said more briskly:

"And you popped a bullet into one of my men, did you? Which means that you sneaked into the brush, got your brother out on the run, gave him your horse and kept us busy long enough for him to hit for the high places?" He shrugged heavily, backed his horse up far enough to have a spot underfoot broad enough to turn without danger of going over the cliff, and rode back down the trail. "I'll be seeing you, Bill," he called back carelessly.

He rejoined his men, spoke with them earnestly a moment, then with the three at his heels passed out of sight returning to the valley. Bill Mountain turned and frowned at Penelope standing close to him.

"If those fools had started to shoot or if Andros had gone for his belt gun, don't you know you might have been killed?"

"They didn't start though," she reminded him.

"Darn you, Penelope!" But a smile of approval lighted his eyes. When he spoke again it was in his lazy deliberate way. "You're a downright cool little rascal, or I'm a liar."

"If what Mr. Bradshaw tells me is true," said Penelope, "you're an awful liar anyhow!"

"Wait a shake and I'll go get the horse," he said. When he rejoined her he found her looking soberly out across the lovely valley still far below. "Don't look so much like the vale o' peace, after all, huh?"

"Will you tell me about your brother?"

"Later, yes. Now we'd better step along; we've got quite a stretch before us."

So in silence they made their way down the winding trail. Andros and his companions had passed out of sight and a drowsy hush brooded again in the mountain passes. They were nearly an hour reaching the level floor of Montana Valley. Part of the way Penelope had ridden, Bill Mountain clumping along at her horse's side. She thought, looking down upon him, that his shoulders sagged a little and she wondered whether with the fatigue of unaccustomed walking or with the sort of responsibility which bears down soul and body together. With one thing and another he was carrying a bigger load than was intended for any one man.

"Will you tell me something?" she said suddenly.

"Anything you want to know. Blaze away, Penny-lope."

"Then why is it, Mr. Bill Mountain, that most of the time you talk like an unlettered son of the soil, and that at other times you seem to forget yourself and talk like a Harvard professor or something like that?"

"That's the hell of a question to ask a man," he laughed at her. He took off his hat and rumpled a head of hair which was already at odds with itself, a heavy unruly shock as thick as a collie dog's. "Well, let's say it's this way: I'm a rough-neck as none can gainsay. On top of that I've been to school, as I told you. Add to this information the fact that I run with a rough-neck crowd most of the time, and at other times have to make myself understood by men like Lew Houston who's not only a banker but a man of more culture than you'd think—and there you are!"

"There I am," nodded Penelope. "You meet a stranger—like me, for example—and you don't care a hang whether that stranger thinks you an ignoramus or a simpleton!"

"Here's a piece of luck!" he said abruptly and pointed out across the valley. "I was just thinking you'd have to ride ahead and send a horse back to me; I wouldn't walk the rest of it for a gold mine. Now we ride together."

Where he pointed she saw three riders coming up out of an aspen grove in a hollow, and at first mistook them for Andros and his following. Bill Mountain made her jump with the piercing yell he sent out to them; he waved his hat and the three came racing. As they pulled their horses up she saw that one of them was the gay young rascal, Tonito, whom she had seen in San Carlos; the two others were like him and might have been his elder brothers.

"Senor!" cried Tonito excitedly in Spanish, "that son of a dog Andros—"

"*Bueno*, Tonito. It's all right. I know. Now I want a horse." Tonito piled off in a flash; landing on his feet, his hat was already in his hand and he made Penelope a very pretty bow and flooded her with his smile. "*Gracias*, Tonito," said Bill Mountain and settled in the saddle with a long sigh. "Gosh, it's good to be riding again." He leaned forward to pat his horse's neck. "You boys c'n double-up an' ride back to the house. Hang aroun' till I show up."

It was a delightful ride through a valley overflowing with sunshine and fruitfulness. They passed down a gentle slope studded with big live oaks which Penelope had not supposed grew at this altitude; they encountered Montana Creek streaming smoothly along between low willow-clothed banks; they crossed a mile of high grazing land and so approached the Goose Neck. Here Penelope would gladly have lingered entranced, listening to the waters pouring down among rocks, looking up at a blue sky through big yellow pines, drinking soulwise of rare still beauty.

"I love it," she whispered, addressing herself. But he heard and looked his approval of her.

"You can't help it," he said fervently. "It's a thing to live and die for, isn't it? You'd fight for it, wouldn't you?"

"I begin to understand," said Penelope.

"Half a mile more of gradual climb," he told

her, "brings us to the floor of White Water Valley. It's at a slightly higher elevation than Montana Valley, neither so big nor so rich, but it's a gem and its water is worth a million.

"Yonder," he pointed out when they had ridden the half mile, "is your kingdom and your present abode, Penny-lope. God send you happy days."

At first she saw the one house only, a low, sprawling red-crowned adobe basking in the sunshine. There were several people on the wide veranda watching them. Next she saw, peeping out from a cottonwood grove, a handful of small neat square houses.

Bill Mountain was making her acquainted with the people on the veranda.

"Ladies an' gents," he was saying genially, "here comes the one an' only Penny-lope Loring, high boss o' the White Water Valley school. Penny-lope, light down an' be at home. Shake han's with Mr. Ben Hodge; Ben's general foreman o' the Montana outfit an' a frien' of mine. Next, shake with Consuela; full name Consuela Maria Isidria Yleta. Consuela's your chappyrone, housekeeper, cook an' secon' mother. Shake with Eugenio Chavez, commonly known as Poco-poco. Shake with Billy Garcia there; Billy'll rake the stars out'n heaven for you if you'll give him a smile, huh, Billy? Josefa, where you been?" A shy, half grown Indian girl with a broom held behind her as though she wanted to hide it, peeped out of the deep doorway. “Come shake han’s with the new school ma’am.”

Penelope, a little flustered, shook hands all round. Ben Hodge, dry and brown, a man of forty-five with steady eyes that looked as hard as diamonds and a big black-and-grey moustache, was the single member of the little crowd to show any signs of Anglo-Saxon blood. The rest were the indeterminate folk of certain regions of New Mexico, dark-skinned, white-toothed, limpid eyed, and no one knew how much of their blood had come in the long and long ago from Spain. Their ancestry along the way had trafficked with the Pueblos.

“Howdy, Miss,” said Ben Hodge, and shook hands warmly. Furthermore those hard eyes of his warmed and softened; he looked her over from head to foot, smiled into her lively grey eyes and gave her hand another friendlier grip. “I might have known,” he added, “what you’d look like after having Bill’s letter describing you.”

“So Mr. Mountain wrote you a letter—and described me?” laughed Penelope and ran up the steps to the veranda. “Will you save it and sometime let me read it?—And this is my school?”

She entered followed awesomely by Consuela and Eugenio and Billy and Josefa. Bill Mountain signalled Ben Hodge and drew him aside.

“I guess we’ll have to patrol High Gate for the rest of the day, Ben,” he said. “Andros and three of his killers jumped the kid out of his hide-out. He's wounded; not bad, but it's no fooling. The kid's all right for the present; he's tucked away at the Three Sisters, and Buck Andros is off his track. Just the same, you understand, Ben? Get half a dozen of the boys out with rifles and have them patrol the trail until I come. I won't be long."

"Sure, Bill," said Ben, and went for his horse.

Penelope, sniffing fresh paint, entered a big square room; long tables, freshly made of planks, were accompanied by long benches made of similar planks; you knew which was table and which was bench by noting the comparative heights! At one end of the room was a chair in front of it a small pine table covered with blue oilcloth. From these signs and tokens she knew this was the school room!

"*Habla usted espagnol*, *Senorita*?" asked Consuela timidly.

Penelope smiled down at a very thick-set, flat-faced, yet vastly good-humoured woman, and nodded.

"*Un poquito*, *Consuela*," she replied. "Not beautifully, as you do, but a little. I studied it at school and I had a friend once who came from Mexico City and at first spoke nothing but Spanish."

Consuela was delighted. Not that she did not speak English well enough herself, only that

Spanish was so much easier. She began telling about everything: There had been so little time and there was so much to do! Soon there would be a nice new school building, with everything fine. This way was the senorita's bedroom, nice and clean; *quidado*! that is fresh paint by the door, not to touch. The curtains came from the other house; new curtains would come from town. The bed was fine and *muy limpia*, *no?* The flowers in the vase, little Eugenio brought them from the creek. And here was a sunny little dining room, and here the *cocina* with wood ready for the fire; Billy had got the wood. And here was a bathroom, all the senorita's own. And back yonder, that was where Consuela and Josefa slept; and yonder was Billy's room. It was all clean, was it not? Consuela knew that Senor Montana would understand that they had done everything very fast; he—

"*Who?*" said Penelope.

"Senor Montana, of course!"

"Look here, Consuela," said Penelope in English, having no time for Spanish now. "What has Senor Montana to do with this?"

"But, everything!" said a wondering Consuela.

Penelope further amazed her by turning and running back through the house and to the front door. She saw Ben Hodge riding away, and Bill Mountain standing by his horse and looking thoughtfully after him. She ran down the steps and he turned toward her.

"You—who are you, anyway?" she asked him. "Are you or are you not Bill Mountain?"

"Yes'm," he said.

"And at the same time you don't happen to be Don Montana, do you?"

He removed his hat with a wide gesture and made her his first bow.

"*Si, Senorita,*" he answered.

"And all this while you made me think—"

She bogged down there and he did not help her. When she came to put it in words, if she had blundered into an error the blundering was exclusively her own. She dropped her eyes and pondered the matter. Her own thoughts brought a faint tinge of pink into her cheeks. She had been rather absurd and now she knew it. "Don Montana!" The name did not fit him at all; it fitted rather some vague but splendid, dashing young Spaniard who did not exist. Already the imaginary Don Montana was fading away—yet as mists gathered about him and he retired into the limbo of nothingness, where dreams are born, he seemed to be making her an elegant bow of farewell—

She looked up suddenly and laughed.

"The truth is that you didn't make me think anything, but that I somehow gathered the impression that you were two men. Bill Mountain for one; a thoroughly romantic young Southerner for the other. Just the same," she added, trying to look severe, "when I asked you to tell me about Don Montana, you jumped at the chance to lead me astray!"

He laughed at her conception of him in the romantic role. As he toed into the stirrup and wreathed a hand in his horse's mane, he said lightly:

"I'll go dig you up a han'some *novio*, Pennylope. Meantime, look your house over; anything that's missin' will come along soon's you speak up. Tell Consuela. An' be ready about sunset to drop in on us at Montana. You'll eat supper with us an' spen' the night. Good luck, Pen—By the Lord, that's what you are! My good luck Penny, for sure! Well, so long."

Giving her no chance to answer he galloped off. She turned and went slowly back to the house.

"Now, Consuela," she said, "tell me all about everything."

Consuela smiled expansively. Asking Consuela to "tell you everything" was very much like requesting a fish to swim for you. You came to the right place.

CHAPTER 6

"Do you know, Mr. Montana—" Penelope began.

"My friends call me Bill," he smiled at her over a cigarette.

"Are we friends already?"

"You just bet we are! Don't you let anybody speak out of turn to tell you we're not. And now what's this that I know?"

"I was quite right all along. In thinking you two men at the same time, I mean."

"You mean all this?" He waved his cigarette to indicate their surroundings.

She nodded in a tentative sort of way; partly she meant all that, partly she meant other things. A certain insight of him she had had an hour earlier when Ben Hodge called in White Water Valley to escort her down to the old Montana home. He had brought a perfect jewel of a little saddle mare for her to ride, and Bill Mountain's apologies along with it for not calling for her himself. Bill, it appeared, was very urgently occupied and could not come but would see her at the house.

Riding the four miles in the sunset and first dusk, Ben Hodge told her much of Bill Mountain that Consuela had missed. The Montanas, he said, were aristocrats and had been for God knew how many centuries. One of them, a world wanderer, had come this way over a hundred years ago. He had looked down into Montana Valley, he had taken his hat off reverently, he had said a little prayer, he had vowed, God willing, that here he would live all his days and here the good clean earth, when he died, should receive him. Whatever other vows he had made and broken, this one he kept.

Since that time the Montanas had been a proud family in New Mexico. They took, one after another, American girls for wives, but always did they make certain first that those American girls were of a fine strain; they thus left to their issue an increasingly strong line of American ancestry and a correspondingly diminishing line of Castilian. But they remained Montanas, "just," said Ben simply, "as kings remain kings." This Ben Hodge had a simple soul within a hard exterior; for the family he felt a high esteem and a profound loyalty. They were lords of creation.

Then came Bill. To be sure, he was a Montana to the backbone. "Make him mad," said Bill with a grin, "and he's all Montana. Move him deeply, and the Montana crops out."

But Bill was something else also; he was a man of so warm a heart that he always wanted to open that heart and invite the whole world in. He did not relish being aloof on a high place and having to look down on people who were close together among themselves but, because of his position, isolated from him. He had friends everywhere; Ben stressed the word: *friends.* They were not all in the same rank of society; there were distinguished and well born men, there were lowly fellows who were just as good. Bill had travelled three hundred miles to the sick bed of a very humble Mexican. The Mexican called him Bill—or Beel, which was as close as he could get to it.

"Bill was four years at college in the East," said Ben. "You wouldn't think it, would you? Suppose that when he came back he had gone about among the fellows using college-talk on 'em? All his life he has been a man of two vocabularies; it's as easy for him, when all is smooth sailing and nothing happens to rough the water and throw him off his keel, to talk like an ignorant cowpunch as to speak correctly."

"I begin to think," Penelope smiled at him, "that you've rather a fondness for this Montana Mountain person!"

Ben grinned sheepishly. That he loved Bill Mountain like a son, brother and friend all rolled into one was obvious.

When they arrived at the end of their ride Penelope looked about her with lively interest. Already it was growing dark and much must be left for daylight, yet she gathered an impression of a fine old many-roomed, wide-verandahed home, of a spacious old-fashioned flower garden softly retiring into the night behind its high white walls, and of many buildings and corrals a little further away. It was all like a small isolated town dominated by the old home on a gently timbered knoll.

A young Indian came running for the horses. Ben escorted her up to the broad steps where they were met by the housekeeper, a matronly woman who like nearly everyone here appeared to have sprung from a crossing of the Latin and some other blood; only in the case of Mrs. Richards the other strain was Anglo-Saxon and appeared to predominate. She smilingly made Penelope welcome and led the girl into the house.

"Oh!" cried Penelope when she had no more than crossed the threshold. "It is the loveliest place in the world!"

"Yes," said Bill Mountain who came into the big living-room from a rear door just in time to hear her exclamation. "It is the loveliest place in the world, Penelope, and I'll always be grateful that I came in time to hear you say it and to welcome you." He made a sweeping gesture with his arm. In the old Spanish way, which was a way both of simple beauty and sincerity, he said: "While you will honour it with your presence it is yours, Penelope."

That loveliness which so impressed her was the sort of thing which can exist only in an old ancestral home which grows ripe and mellow, as gradually through the years it draws to itself that which is perfect and complementary and thus in the slow course of time fulfils itself. It was a very large room softly illuminated by several lamps with harmoniously coloured shades, with furniture already becoming antique which gave the effect of having grown here from the seed, with an enormous fireplace black with the smoke of other days wherein a small oak fire burned, and with rugs of which she was told later. Indian rugs, to the last one of them, made on the Montana Rancho, that rare sort of Indian rugs which are not manufactured in eastern cities. Bill Mountain could tell her a story connected with every one of them, beginning with the well worn first one before the hearth which had been placed where it now lay at the command of the first New Mexico Montana.

Only after her sweeping glance about her did she look with fresh interest at Bill Mountain himself. He had found time to bathe and shave and change; he wore white flannels, a soft white shirt unbuttoned at the throat, black and white sports shoes—and he had brushed his unruly hair so that it almost behaved itself.

"Mrs. Richards will show you your room," he said. "If you like to change for dinner there's lots of time—Oh, that's fixed up," he said in interruption as she began to remind him that a change just now was a luxury beyond her means; "your bags got here ten minutes ago."

"Are you a magician?" she laughed at him.

"I've got some of the best horses and best riders in New Mexico," he returned.

Her bedroom was as delightful as the rest of the house, a corner room with the deep windows she loved so, and just outside the shadowy garden, a place all cosiness and friendly intimacy and exquisite taste. As she looked into it she thought of the Montana women folk—during the hundred years how many of them, gay and sad, had sat in those cushioned windows? The walls were plain, there was one picture—

She stared at it, coming to a dead halt. It was a small oil painting representing a desert stretch under a thin young moon. She came closer, hearing never a word Mrs. Richards was saying; suddenly she whirled and bolted from the room.

"That picture—in the room you are giving me—did you know?" she asked brokenly when she came before Bill Mountain again.

He nodded.

"I had a talk with Bradshaw this morning. He told me you were Clinton Loring's girl. I thought you'd like it in your room."

"It was the best thing papa ever did, I think," she said, and he saw that her lips were trembling. "I was only a little girl—we all three were together then—"

He patted her shoulder gently.

"I'm mighty glad I had it, Penelope," he said.

"You're a dear," said Penelope, and hurried out.

Mrs. Richards, when all was explained to her, emulated Bill Mountain in giving her a pat and impulsively went a step further, adding a squeeze for full measure. Thereafter she showed Penelope her bags, her bathroom and tiny dressing-room, and left her to her own devices.

It was a very bright-eyed Penelope who twenty minutes later emerged, a Penelope in one of the happiest little dresses which ever travelled across a counter in Albuquerque. She and Bill Mountain and Ben Hodge went out to dinner.

It was all the way she knew by now that it would be: a dozen tall candles making a subdued glimmering among the fine silver service, traditionally old, on a gigantic oak table; soft-footed Indian girls, white clad, serving deftly; ruby wine in sparkling glasses, and the table bountifully set.

"Before we sit down," said Bill, "it just dawns on me that I can give a bit of happiness. Penelope, will you do an old friend a favour? Of course you will." He took her arm and turned her towards the door. "Come this way. Back in a minute, Ben."

He led her wondering along a corridor in which were set many arched doorways and at last to a room where he stopped.

"Bringing you a visitor, Monito," he called as he opened the door.

"Monito means 'Little Monkey,' " said Penelope.

He stood aside for her to go in. There in a big

bed lay the boy she had seen on the cliffs, the "outlaw" whom Buck Andros and his men hunted and shot at. White faced and gaunt and harried, he looked at her with an eager flash in his dark eyes.

"Oh, I am glad you came!" he said quickly. "Really, Miss Loring, I am not such an awful coward as you must think. You saw me running from them to-day, but Bill made me. When you come to know Bill—"

She went to the bed and took his hand.

"I am glad you are here," she said gently. "And I'm not thinking anything of the sort.—Just now, as we were about to sit down at the table, I thought of you way up there in the mountains." She turned to Bill Mountain who was smiling at them from the doorway. "I did not know that I was the one you were going to give that 'bit of happiness' when you brought me here."

"No, no; I am the one," cried the boy.

"Is it safe to have him here at the house?" she asked of Bill.

"To-night, yes. Safer than having him exposed to the cold with that scratch he got himself, eh, Nino?"

"I do not want trouble to come here," said the boy.

"There'll be no trouble, Tony, old man. All precautions have been taken."

"You appear to have many names for your

brother," smiled Penelope. "How am I to know him, as the kid, Monito, Nino or Tony?"

"He is a young gentleman of many names," said Bill. "Miss Loring, may I present my amusing brother, Juan José Antonio de Montana?"

"Will you call me Juan, Miss Loring?" asked the boy eagerly. "Or even Juanito later on, if you should like me a little bit?"

"Your brother has told me that we are all friends here at Montana. So you are Juanito and I am Penelope."

When they returned to Ben and the dining-room and before they sat down Bill Mountain explained to Penelope what he had referred to when he said that all precautions had been taken. There were, it appeared, but four practicable entrances into this high valley, one from the north led in from the Goose Neck, the one from the west she had already travelled, a third came in from the east at the Puerta del Sol, and the fourth was along the roadway down the valley and south to the railroad. Two men watched all night at each trail, and about the house Tonito and two of his brothers lolled in the shadows, and kept their eyes open.

"Do you have an army at hand, then?" exclaimed Penelope.

"Didn't you know," Ben spoke up, "that we're a snug little kingdom up here?"

She looked at him curiously; perhaps she had

known! Down there in little San Carlos had she not had the inspiration of mountain kings—all clothed in purple—

"With so many knowing that your brother is here—is it not dangerous?" she asked. "Or do more than a very few know?"

"I've no doubt that by now," Bill smiled at her, "all know."

"And this is not a case wherein 'In numbers there is danger'?"

"They love the kid," he said simply. "And they're loyal. They'd go to hell for a Montana."

"Has it dawned on you, Bill," said Ben drily, "that Andros went straight to Juanito's hideout? Straight as a string!"

Bill's eyes flashed angrily and for an instant his lips were tightly compressed.

"Somehow, now and then, a rotten egg gets into a clean nest," he said. "Yes, someone of us fell for a handful of gold. We'll not let Juan know that, though; it would hurt him terribly. And it will not happen again."

"You know who it was?" asked Ben sharply.

"No. But I passed the word around, Ben; by this time all my people know that one of their number betrayed us and them. Don't you think that among themselves they'll have a way of finding out who it was? And don't you think that we can leave it to them to clean their own nest? But now we drop sober considerations and sit down. Penelope—*salud y pesetas*!"

Later Penelope was left alone for a little while in the living room, Bill Mountain going to look in on his brother, Ben Hodge adjourning to the nearby cottage where, along with the ranch office, he had his sleeping quarters. The moon was newly arisen above the mountains behind the house and streaming through a window made a lane of light inviting her; this lane extended through the wide double doors connecting the living room and a smaller chamber in which she glimpsed a piano; she followed the moon-path and stepped out into the crisp clear night.

There was a sound of a light tread and a figure materialized from among shadows and approached her. It was the graceful Tonito, drawn towards beauty as inevitably as any moth hastening to the light. He spoke swiftly in murmurous Spanish.

"God makes it fine in a garden when the night is serene and there is a moon," said Tonito.

He had actually brushed the pathway with his hat which now, his extravagant devoir done, he replaced with a flourish.

"Yes, Tonito. It is a night for happiness and for music, isn't it? I heard you singing in San Carlos; some time you are going to sing for me, *no?*"

Tonito was nothing if not obliging when it was the case of a lady.

"If I but had a guitar—never mind," he said,

and mildly startled her by beginning forthwith to croon softly:

> "*Angel de amor, tu pasion no la comprendo,*
> *Si la comprendo, no la puedo espresar,*
> *Voy enceler tu languido gemido,*
> *Alla en la tumba, par poder descansar.*"

Penelope laughed softly; Tonito could be very sentimentally tragic.

"It is beautiful. *Mil gracias*, Tonito."

Tonito wanted to point out to her the beauties of the garden. There were roses yonder that came a thousand years ago from the Alhambra; she had heard of that place, *no,* very grand in Spain? There was an apple tree which the grandpapa of Don Bill Montana had put there with his own hand. Its name was Don Astasio. There was a geranium that smelled sweeter than all the other flowers in the world. There was a vine so old that it was as big as a tree and extended over half the valley, making all summer long a shade as in a big cave. Sure! It was like heaven here, it was high in the air but warmer than any other high place because the sun always shone and the steep hills stopped the cold winds.

When Penelope said that she must go in Tonito surrendered her to the house with an audible sigh; he went off singing under his breath "*Angel de amor, tu pasion no la comprendo*," while she returned to the living-room. There she came upon Don Bill smoking before the fire, long legs extended, hands clasped behind his head.

"It seems somehow a terrible, almost wicked thing, to talk about business," said Penelope, "but I'm afraid that I have done nothing but enjoy myself since I got here. About starting a school—I am all ignorance on the subject—"

"First thoughts are best," he told her when he had drawn up a chair for her. "Business should always be saved for to-morrow. Meantime Ben is learning all about the business angle of launching a new shrine to Minerva; he'll talk with you about it in a day or so. You understand, don't you, that we'll have a new building as fast as we can get one up? You can make out I suppose with the front room at your house?"

"My house!" laughed Penelope. Then she looked at him gravely. "Do you really expect me to go along the way you have started me? In the matter of my ménage, I mean?"

"You don't like Consuela?" he asked. "Or the youngsters?"

"Why, they're delicious! But let me see: am I to maintain a staff? Consuela and Josefa and Billy and Eugenio?"

"You are," he said emphatically. "You'll pay for their food; we have a store here which supplies us with everything at cost, so you can afford that. You'll want someone to cook for you, won't you? That's Consuela. You'll want a maid around? Behold Josefa. You'll want a house boy and a boy to saddle your horse, get wood and run errands? *Bueno.* There are Billy and Eugenio already, I'll bet a hat, vying with each other for the regard of the new *Angel de amor*."

"You heard Tonito?"

"Tonito is an impudent rascal who is always in love, always very fickle, I warn you, and who has a heart of gold."

He might have discoursed further on Tonito of whom he was very fond, but just then there came a sharp knocking at the door. He rose swiftly and hurried out and Penelope heard one of his Indians speaking to him excitedly. Bill Mountain, the moment he got the gist of what the man was saying, cut short a lot of profuse explanatory matter.

"It's all right, Gaucho," he said sternly. "He's alone, you say? Send him in."

He returned to Penelope, leaving the door wide open; he had grown grim about the mouth and his eyes were bright and hard with anger, not at all like the eyes of a moment ago which had been warm when he spoke of Tonito.

"We've got a caller," he said curtly. "Lucky for him I've given the boys, poor devils, very strict orders against shooting anybody."

"Is it Buck Andros?" she asked quickly.

He nodded.

CHAPTER 7

"What the devil do you suppose the man wants?" muttered Bill Mountain, standing with his back to the fireplace and glaring at Penelope as though he were blaming her for Andros' coming. "Well, he's got his nerve!"

"To tell the truth his asking to see you surprises me no more than your receiving him!"

"I'd rather see him in hell, I admit."

"I'll go to my room—"

"You'll do nothing of the sort!" he blazed out at her. "Do you think I'm going to allow a man like Buck Andros to drive a guest of mine from the room? No, sit still."

Penelope sank back in her chair and let her eyes drift to the door. Already they could hear brisk steps coming along the front path, then running lightly up the steps.

"Hello, Bill," said Andros from the open door.

He stepped in, stood a moment looking very intently upon his host, then permitted himself the luxury of making a detailed study of that host's companion. He narrowed his dark eyes almost imperceptibly as she had seen artist friends of her father's do when, heads tipped this way and that way, they studied a picture, coolly and critically. A faint half smile touched the man's handsome lips when he had done and he allowed his eyes full liberty to express his approval.

Bill Mountain stood leaning back against the mantel, lounging idly with his hands in his pockets and watching Andros.

"Going to introduce me, Bill?" asked Andros.

"You came on business, didn't you?" asked Montana coolly.

Andros laughed tolerantly and his eyes flashed up with sheer devilishness as they swerved to a meeting with Penelope's.

"I've heard of you, Miss Loring," he said pleasantly. "I'm sorry that Bill won't introduce me; I'm John Andros. We mountain folk are all neighbourly; I hope you'll let me ride over to see you?"

Penelope thought: "He's a 'lady-killer.' " Also she thought: "He is almost wickedly handsome!" And while she was thinking these things she realized that he was resourceful, without fear, perhaps without scruple and certainly not a man to put down by any severe remark a girl of twenty-two could think of on the spur of the minute.

Reluctantly Andros withdrew his eyes from Penelope.

"I am glad I took a little chance and rode over," he said slowly. "It was worth it. And what I've come to say you want spoken before your little friend, Montana? No secrets, I suppose?"

"No secrets."

"Fine. It's about your kid brother, of course. I know that you've got him here in the house."

If Bill was surprised or concerned he did not show it though a look of alarm leaped into Penelope's eyes.

"Yes?" he said.

"And I know something else," said Andros. "He got in the way of at least one bullet to-day. It's my bet that he is pretty badly hurt; certainly he is in no condition to take to the mountains again. You wouldn't have brought him in, you know, if it hadn't been that his wound necessitated it."

This time Bill did not even say "Yes?" He merely waited.

"You're not asking me to sit down, are you?" asked Andros.

"I give you my word that I hadn't even thought of it!"

Andros took a cigarette from the table and stood tapping it against a thumb nail.

"If the boy is taken," he continued thoughtfully, "he'll have to go down to Santa Fé to stand trial." He finished tapping his cigarette and lighted it, bethinking him to say, "You don't mind, Miss Loring? Thanks." Again he let his eyes pay her his bold tribute. With a sigh and a slow expulsion of smoke he returned to the matter in hand. "If he ever goes down to Santa Fé they'll hang him, you know, Bill."

"Do you know why I don't drop you dead in your tracks, Andros?" Montana asked gravely with an air of a man who set the question to himself no less than to the other fellow.

"Of course I know; I know you like a book," Andros answered. "It would only make a bad mess a lot worse as we both know. If it meant just cutting the sticks out from under you, why I don't believe you'd care. But you and I know that if it wasn't for you keeping your head and watching every step, there'd be nobody around to take care of the kid. He is your brother and that fact seems to mean a good deal to men like you." He shrugged and made a little gesture with his cigarette. "By the way," he continued, "I'm not exactly a nervous chap, but is that mestizo at the window altogether dependable? Hadn't you better tell him to get his finger off the trigger as long as we're all friendly here?"

Montana did not turn but Penelope looked swiftly over her shoulder and saw a shadowy figure looking in from the garden.

"It's only Tonito," said Montana. "Yes, he is altogether dependable."

"I'm glad to hear it. Some of these Spanish-Indian breeds are apt to lose their heads over a trifle. Now here's my proposition: Already I've got you licked to a frazzle on the White Water Valley property and it's only a question of time until you're out and I've got a clear title. It's that element of time that I want to dispose of. I want a free hand now instead of a year from now. Since you're licked anyhow it's not much that I'm asking you to do. Acknowledge my rights, crawl back into your shell and stay there—and I'll let up on your brother."

"Otherwise?" Bill asked him.

"Otherwise the kid hangs. One of my men is on his way out to Pueblo Junction now. He'll go straight to the telephone office and sit with his eye on the clock. If by midnight I haven't called him up from your place here and told him to keep his mouth shut he'll put in a long distance call for Santa Fé and spill all he knows to the district attorney down there. And Juan Montana will be wearing bracelets before sundown to-morrow."

"But in case I should surrender the valley and its water to you—"

"I'll call my man back. After that what you and your brother do is of no interest to me."

"You interest me strangely," said Bill Mountain thoughtfully. "White Water has cost us more than fifty thousand dollars. My father and I have expended twice that much more in development. And you suggest that I pitch all that away for nothing?"

"For your kid brother's life." Andros studied him shrewdly. "It's not worth that much? Well, I guess you're right. But I thought that possibly your old-fashioned sentimentality—"

"You make a slight misstatement," Montana corrected him. "It is not Juan's life you are giving me. Merely your word to let him go." He shook his head. "It seems that you set a damn sight higher value upon your word than I do."

"You won't deal then?" asked Andros coolly. "Well, I didn't suppose you would. But a man never knows and it was worth the chance. *Bueno.* Being a law-abiding citizen," and he allowed himself a rarely diabolical grin, "I'm out to pull the kid down. Not just spite work, Bill. It's no side issue, you know. The only thing you've got to bank your claims on is the word of a dead Montana. Up here in the mountains his word was gold. But time passes and men forget. Let me drag a Montana through the courts with all the publicity of a murder trial, let me secure a conviction and hang him—You get the idea? I simply knock hell—I'm sorry, Miss Loring!—Well, Bill, it shows the Montanas up in a new light, doesn't it?"

"You use all the tools that come to hand," Montana observed contemptuously.

"I do. When I fight I use fists, teeth and boots." He drew on his gloves. "I'm glad I dropped in," he concluded looking at Penelope. "I hope I'll see a lot of you, Miss Loring. Do you know that I'm afraid that as I ride home in the moonlight I'll not be thinking at all of business, as I should, but of you? Good night. Good night, Bill."

In silence they watched Andros go out. Then Bill Mountain stepped to the window and opened it. "Tonito!" he said sharply. "Listen well, my friend. He is going now and he must go in safety. Tell your brothers; ride with him and make sure that no hand is lifted against him. That would only make me fresh trouble. Remember. *Y vaya con Dios.*"

In the lamp-lighted window Tonito's dusky face was tense and eager and his night-black eyes flashed ominously. He even opened his mouth for a vehement veto of the Montana dictate.

"Hear me, Tonito?" snapped Bill Mountain. "Do as I say. Go now."

Tonito sighed. "It is you who know what is best, Don Bill," he said reluctantly, and was gone.

Montana closed the window and returned to his chair by the fireplace.

"You see us at our worst, Penelope," he said with a rather grim smile. "We're not always fighting like mountain cats up here."

"He will do all that he threatened?"

"He will try. But there is no present need for alarm. You see, if he did not lie when he said he has sent a man out to Pueblo Junction, that man will strike into my road at the lower end of Montana Valley and he'll get no further to-night. Even though he has sent his man in some other direction I think that he'll never get as far as either El Paso de los Indios or the Sun Gate." He glanced at the clock on the mantel. "It's early; only nine. Before long I'll expect one of the boys to ride in and report."

Penelope got up and went to the fire, warming her hands and looking into the flames.

"You don't seem afraid! I am!—Your brother is such a nice looking boy and—Oh, it's hard to believe!"

"I'll tell you Juan's little story," he said quietly. "We lost our mother when Juan was a baby. Only two years later we lost our two sisters. There were left only my father and Juan and I. We grew, you will understand, very close to one another. My father and I did what we could for our Monito; we spoiled him, I dare say, and we babied him a good deal, but he was fine and true inside and he came out all right. He's a great kid, Juan is. Also he is tremendously impulsive and lets himself go.

"*Bueno.* Behold Juan grown up, almost twenty years old. He had attended the School of Mines at Socorro; he had made his own friends. One of them during vacation he brought here. He was older than Juan, he was plausible and he was the sort of man who should have been strangled in the cradle.

"For Pasmore's entertainment—that was the name of Juan's friend—"

"Floyd Pasmore!" she exclaimed.

"He is the one. You would have heard of it of course."

"Yes. The papers were so full of it."

"The thing began here. Juan gave a dance to amuse this Pasmore. We are always giving *bailes* up here on the slightest provocation; under normal circumstances there would have been one to celebrate the opening of your school. Poor little Luisa was that night the happiest and prettiest of all the girls. She was only sixteen and she sparkled. What followed was an old, old story; one of the oldest in the world." He shrugged and stared into the fire, silent for a moment. He smiled somewhat gravely as he added: "I've a great friend in old Dan Westcott; you must know him some time. Dan says that if it wasn't for just two things in this world we wouldn't need sheriffs, for all trouble comes from them. Running water for one, says Dan, the most important; women next. Fights over water rights, trouble over women—that's the whole of it, if you'll believe Dan Westcott."

"What a lovely world you men would have if Mr. Dan were allowed a free hand to do away with the two troublesome factors."

"Dan says they're just alike—"

"He is an old bachelor, isn't he?" interrupted Penelope. And added, when Montana nodded: "Some time I must make him tell me all about his love affair. I suppose she married the one man he hated most."

"I was telling you of Luisa. She and Juan were

the dearest friends; they had been playmates all her life and a big part of Juan's. He came later to transfer to her all the love which he had felt for our sisters; on her part, she adored Juan as a little pagan girl might adore the sun.

"Floyd Pasmore was something quite different. He gave none of us the slightest inkling of his interest; how he hid it all from even Juan I don't know. But he went off to Santa Fé and lured that poor sweet little kid after him. In time she returned here as a wounded wild thing returns to its lair. Pasmore at the end had laughed at her as though the whole thing were deliciously funny. Luisa died within three days. It couldn't have been of a broken heart, you know, for long ago the theory that one can die of such a cause has been exploded. So she must have died just because she wanted to die.

"Luisa had as many admirers among her own people as there were young men to admire. Yet of them all Juan was her sincerest friend. And Juan, when he knew, went straight to Santa Fé. He held himself utterly responsible for everything that had happened. He told Luisa's mother and he told others that he was going to kill Pasmore. He was very careful, of course, that I should hear nothing of it.

"You see thus far? Juan went down to Santa Fé to kill a man who very decidedly needed killing.

After that killing was most thoroughly done Juan came home—"

"But—" began Penelope eagerly, sensing the truth.

"Exactly. The old story as I warned you, even to an ancient change rung in on it. Juan didn't do the thing; whether at the last moment he would have gone through with it, *quien sabe*? He found that he had been forestalled. You may imagine a revulsion of feeling? He came home sick with horror."

"Oh, I'm glad!" Her eyes were shining. "Glad that Juan hasn't that on his soul."

"You believe then?" Bill asked.

"Why, of course!"

"Of course. I know that Juan did not kill the man because of two things: First, Juan has told me. Second, Pasmore was shot in the back. And now you know because I have told you."

He rose and stood looking down toward her upturned face, and she experienced the sensation of being not so much looked at as through. His thoughts were far afield.

But presently they were withdrawn from whatever far distances they had travelled.

"You have had a long day and though I trust you had a siesta during the afternoon, still you must be ready for bed," he said lightly. "On your way, would you care to look in on Juan and say good night?"

"Very much." But when she too had risen she appeared hesitant; he seemed so assured that everything was all right for the night at least, and hers was a growing uneasiness.

"Well?" he asked. "What is it, Penelope?"

"Andros seemed to be so sure your brother was here," she blurted out. "Has that struck you?"

"Yes," he admitted reluctantly.

"Someone told him?" she whispered.

"I am afraid so." He looked sad, she thought, instead of angry. Yet the anger was there, too, burning darkly like flames obscured by smoke. "It would seem that old Dan left out the third of life's troublemakers. Judas wants his gold."

They quitted the living-room in a profound and gloomy silence, but by the time they had arrived at that part of the long corridor where Juan's door was they were chatting gaily and Penelope was even laughing in a delicious way characteristic of her when she felt thrillingly alive. By common tacit consent they would carry no shadows with them into Juan's room.

CHAPTER 8

That shadow which was not permitted to fall across Juan's threshold extended over the rest of the house and was already darkening the little homes of the simple folk who in their loyal hearts were children of the Montanas. Bill Mountain himself, although he had seemed the most carefree man on earth when he said his good nights to Juan and Penelope, brooded alone in the living-room while he awaited upon circumstance. He drew the shades down over the windows, extinguished the lamp, put a small log in the fireplace and thereafter sat motionless before the hearth and, after the fashion of man since he had his first fires, bent his gloomy gaze on the bright quick flames and strove to read the future in them.

He ran no risk of falling into the common error of misjudging his enemy. He knew Andros from top to toe and saw in him the sort of predatory creature which might have resulted from the mating of a lion with a fox. He was courageous, bold, daring and he was no less shrewd; he was forceful, resourceful, and utterly unscrupulous. He was the sort of man who would attack openly and fearlessly or would stab in the back and not be squeamish in the matter.

"And when, as to-night, he seems to be putting all his cards on the table," pondered Bill Mountain, "he may still have an ace in the hole."

One of the household servants, a slim Indian boy of sixteen, entered silently from the hall; it would seem that he made no sound whatever but the man at the fireplace turned sharply. The flickering firelight played upon the boy's eager face and set his black eyes glistening.

"What is it, Ray?"

"It is my grandfather, senor," answered Raimundo. "He is at the back door, he and some of the other men. He asks to see you."

He held poised, as alert as a squirrel, and wanted only a nod to send him scurrying with word to the caller that the senor would see them. Presently five men, all aboriginal southwestern Americans with scarcely more than a dash of Mexican blood, came into the room. They moved with a queer caution, never at ease in the house of the master, lifting their heavily booted feet with care lest they mar a floor or sully a rug; all but one held their hats in two hands before them and kept up a nervous fingering of the brims during the brief interview. The one who differed from the rest, Raimundo's grandfather, came naturally into his position at their fore; he held himself stiffly erect, his hat in one hand at his side. Though not even he was at his ease here, still he mastered his discomfort. That unstudied dignity which belongs to primitive men was about him like a cloak.

Montana greeted them gravely and with a courtesy which was their due and came from his heart, and invited them to chairs. Not a man of them moved; they constituted a small group in the middle of the floor with their leader a pace in front.

"Well, José?" asked Montana.

José was not to be hurried into speech. He stood looking at his overlord stonily. He was an old man, but spare and straight; his steady black eyes were as keen as those of any of his following, yet his beardless face was crossed and crisscrossed by wrinkles so deep that in the uncertain light they looked like a mesh of black lines etched on a copper mask. He had dressed for the visit; that was to be seen at a glance. He paid his highest respects when he crossed the threshold of the Montanas with cleanliness of person and a fresh shirt of large orange and black squares; the handkerchief knotted about his thin old neck was unspotted crimson and had been freshened with a dash of violet toilet water.

"I think I know," said Montana bluntly. Always he and his people spoke in Spanish. "We are going to talk; you had better sit down, José."

"No," said José, in a slightly husky voice. "We are not worthy now, senor, to sit in your house. Never again shall I or one of my people sit here until our shame has been wiped out. Never until we are clean again will any of us come here after to-night and never will one of us take the first step to make you notice that we are living. That is sworn among us, senor."

Montana nodded his understanding. Then he rose and drew nearer them, saying:

"*Bueno*, José. Then I too stand." Impulsively he put both of his big hard hands on the old man's shoulders. "You are not to blame; I know that, José. You, Estavan, you Gaucho, you Feliz, you Arnoldo—I know you all for my friends and Juan's. And you, José!" He let his hands fall away slowly and smiled. "If I lost faith in you, José, I'd know that God had withdrawn from the world."

Old José stared straight at him; never a shadow quivered in a single wrinkle—but in his eyes a flash came and went like unexpected summer lightning, leaving no sign but only a memory after its passing.

Old José spoke again in that oddly husky voice of his.

"Your message came to us, senor. Among ourselves we have talked of it and of no other thing." He came to a sudden halt; it was a way he had of speaking a thought, of pausing abruptly, of thinking over what he had said, then of what he was going to say next, and when he was ready of speaking again abruptly. During his short silence his eyes were fixed steady and unwinking on Montana's. "It is hard to understand, senor."

"Yes, José, it is very hard."

"And there can be no mistake?"

"There is no mistake. Listen, *amigo mio*: To-day Buck Andros went straight to the place where Juan hid; he and his men I tell you went to the place like men stalking a deer that they knew was in a certain spot. That is one thing. Another is this: To-night Andros came here. He knew that Juan was in the house. He could not have seen when I brought Juan here for he and his men were at a distance; Arnoldo here knows that. Arnoldo was one who watched; he can tell you that not only was it dark before I started home with Juan, but also that Andros and his men were three miles away."

Not Arnoldo alone but the three others at old José's back nodded their heads.

José put up a lean leathery hand and brushed back the long hair, once jet black but now streaked with glistening white threads, pushing it away from his brow, smoothing and smoothing it. He stood a little while longer, looking at the master. Then he turned and led the way out of the room, the others following him, clutching their hats.

"Good night, boys," said Montana.

They walked straight on, lifting their feet carefully, carefully setting them down; they did not turn, they did not answer his good night. Their burden rested heavy on their souls. Always, for a good twenty years at least, old José had called him "Don Bill." To-night his "senor" set them somehow far apart.

With sudden inspiration he called sharply after them. They twisted their heads about without turning their bodies, stopped and looked at him sombrely. He hurried across the room to them.

"Juan is not yet asleep," he said. "Come; you are going to see him!"

José looked at him over a thin shoulder. The others looked only at José. Then the old man faced again toward the door and led the way out into the night. He had spoken his piece; he had said once, "We are not worthy." There remained nothing further to say. The last man out closed the door with the utmost care; there was not even the click of the bolt as his fingers released the knob.

Montana drew a deep breath as he returned to the fireplace.

Half an hour later when he heard a voice in the yard his first thought was that here came Tonito with a report on Andros' withdrawal, or if not Tonito then one of the boys guarding the lower road. But as he rose to go to the door the voice came more distinctly and he recognised it with a start as that of old Dan Westcott, the sheriff. Dan was one of the best of friends, and therefore should always be welcome. Yet it remained also that Dan was sheriff. Certainly Bill would have been just as pleased had the old fellow picked upon some other night to make a call.

The voice sharpened perceptibly:

"Hey there! Watch your step, hombre! Happen you don't know it I'll tell you that to drop or mebbe crack either one of them jugs is to commit what they call the unpard'nable sin. Step sof', *amigo*."

Bill threw the door open and stepped aside. Old Dan Westcott, herding before him a lanky man in chaps who carried a gallon earthen jug in each hand, made his entrance. The blaze in the fireplace sufficed to show Bill who Westcott's companion was, yet almost he felt the need of a lamp to make sure.

"Hello, Bill," said old Dan. And to the man who stood awkwardly gripping his burden, "Set 'em down now, Herbie. Easy."

The lanky man obeyed with alacrity and pulled his hat off, less for the convention than to mop a hot brow. Bill stared at him wonderingly.

"Herbie Gadge!" he muttered. Frowning he looked at his old friend. "Since when have you an' Herbie Gadge been trailin' your luck together, Dan?" he asked drawlingly. "Got him workin' for you?"

"Like you see, Bill," said Westcott.

"I guess you hadn't heard, Dan; Herbie took

a couple shots at me las' night down to San Carlos."

The two regarded Gadge with interest. Now that his hat was off he revealed himself to be a man not over thirty yet with a head as bald as an egg, a head by the way which was curiously egg shaped, the smaller end at the top, the jaw almost foolishly round. Pop-eyed, small mouthed and flap-eared, he was a man whom Bill had found it hard to take seriously—until last night.

"Me an' Herbie," said old Dan, "got together on what you might call division o' labour. I'm trustin' him with my two jugs an' he's lettin' me carry his gun."

Herbie Gadge did the best he could to master his nervousness and muttered anxiously:

"You ain't got no call to bully me, Dan. I got a right to go where I please. You let me go now."

Dan pursed his lips and considered.

"It's like this, Bill," he explained. "I been down to the Junction; I'd run out o' licker an' that's why the two jugs. Comin' back I run into some o' your boys down to the lower end. They had jus' got their ropes on Herbie here, foun' him sneakin' south an' headed him back. I stopped an' chinned, that bein' my way when moseyin' on a moonlight night, an' they tol' me a thing or two. They did mention, I rec'lec' now, how you'n Herbie had done some wild shootin' down San Carlos way." He tipped his old head to the side and peered with bright eyes at the man whom he had brought along. "I ain't arrested him yet, but I could, Bill, chargin' him with attemptin' to commit massacree. How 'bout it? Want to bring a charge ag'in him?"

"No," said Bill shortly. "You know I don't, Dan."

"Then shall I turn him loose? Thought you'd be the bes' jedge. Your boys says," he added off-handedly, "that he was on his way out to the Junction to do some long telephonin'."

Bill Mountain considered swiftly.

"No, I don't think we'll turn him loose quite so soon," he said. "Wait a shake here, Dan, you an' Herbie." He left the room and they lost sight of him as he turned down the corridor. He returned before either had stirred. "I've sent for Ben Hodge," he said.

Gadge, seeing that no hand was being raised against him, began to sputter, swearing that he'd have the law on them, that Dan could be kicked out of his sheriff's office, that a free man had a right to go where he pleased—that since he wasn't under arrest he was going now. He even made a step towards the door but, though neither man spoke a single word, he came to a halt. All that he got from old Dan was a sort of girlish giggle.

Hodge came hurrying, spoke aside briefly with Bill Mountain, nodded his understanding and full acquiescence and escorted the expostulating but overawed Gadge out of the room.

"Squat, Dan," Bill Mountain invited. "I'll light a lamp. I was jus' settin' here, thinkin' things over."

"I'll squat," said Dan and shoved a chair towards the hearth. "No lamp, Bill. Can't beat this sorta light, kin you, when two fellers wants to squat an' chin? Shucks, I'm all full o' moonlight an' romance topped off by a couple jolts o' my new licker, an' this dreamy firelight, all gummed up with po'try, jus' suits me. Gimme a cigarette an' tell me."

They smoked and looked into the fire and for a little while were silent. Bill Mountain, alert for every chance sound, was troubled. To be sure Dan Westcott was a staunch old friend—but it remained that he was the sheriff as well with certain grim duties, and Bill had never known him to fail in one of them. With all his heart he wished that his old friend had chosen some other night for his visit.

CHAPTER 9

Bill Mountain glanced out of the corners of his eyes to take old Dan in. What a fine rare old rascal he was! Growing old, as Dan confessed, past seventy now, but hale. Like a ripe pine, full of vigour, casting a straight shadow. He had been a handsome young devil those many years ago, something of a spur-jingler, a hot-head, a leaper at life's throat, and the old recklessness still brightened his eyes. He had buffetted his many winters which struck at the top where they crowned him with the snow of his years; there was life in his feet and you knew it from the tight handsome boots he wore. His brown old face was withered like an apple that has lasted on beyond its season, but his clean shaved lips and chin were firm.

He stirred slightly, easing himself down for the utmost comfort, and his chair creaked.

"That was my chair creakin', Bill," he said.

"Yes," said Bill.

"Thought you might think it was my bones," remarked Dan. "Thought mebbe you might be gettin' wound up to say that when a man gets so old his bones creak it's time to be puttin' a young feller in as sheriff."

"Shucks, Dan," laughed Bill. "We wouldn't

never have any sheriff but you an' you know it."

"Soun's good," said Dan. He puffed at his cigarette serenely. "Got to thinkin'—how it'd be kinda tough on you boys say when I'm a couple hundred years old—if I croaked."

Bill Mountain appeared to reflect.

"Well, in that case, Dan," he said, "we'd jus' keep the job o' sheriff vacant as a sort o' monument to your mem'ry."

"Soun's nice," said Dan.

The night had mellowed him. The moonlight, abetted by the jugs and now by the firelight, made him meditative. Again the two relapsed into silence, but the younger man kept watching his guest keenly.

"Well, what do you know, Dan?" Bill asked abruptly when it began to appear that the sheriff might brood all night with never another word.

"Nothin', same as usual," answered Dan.

Bill rose, threw on a log, sat down and said rather more sharply: "I asked, 'What do you know, Dan?' "

"Oh!" said Dan. "Well, Bill, Herbie did do a mite o' talkin' as we rid along in the moonlight. Fac' is, he let out quite a story. All lies, mebbe. Said as how I was interferin' with the law in bringin' him back, seein' how he was on his way to telephone down to Santy Fee. Course, I don't never aim to interfere with the law, Bill, bein' a law officer myse'f. But then I had to take in consideration how your boys tol' me that Herbie had broke the peace down to San Carlos, an' it seemed mebbe I'd better fetch him this way in case you wanted him jugged for attempted suicide. Thought," he added squinting up his keen blue eyes, and peering at Bill shrewdly, "as mebbe you'd be glad I done so."

Bill reached across the hearth to lay an affectionate hand on the old fellow's sleeve. Bill's father and Dan had been that sort of friends which the frontiers make sometimes; Bill, a little boy, had loved Dan like another father.

"Herbie, bein' on the subjec' of telephonin'," mused Bill, returning that sharp, shrewd look of old Dan's, "might have done some more wild talkin'?"

"Now that's so!" exclaimed Dan. "I oughtn't to fergit things like that, not at my age." He indulged in that queer giggle of his. "He did tell me a lot o' lies about Andros havin' jumped Juan up somewheres an' took a shot at him an'—" He grew sober all of a sudden and dropped his voice: "The kid wasn't hurt bad, was he, Bill?"

"No, Dan; not bad if he gets decent care. But care an' shelter from exposure are what he's got to have."

"An' Herbie, talkin' free," resumed the sheriff, "said as how Juan was here at the house."

Bill Mountain stiffened, sat silent a moment, then demanded: "Well, Dan?"

Dan was a long time in answering. His heavy white brows bunched forward and his eyes vanished under them; he watched the fire as though his life depended on marking how every little flame disported itself among the puffs and spirals of blue and white smoke.

"I'm a funny ol' devil, Bill."

"Yes, Dan, you're a funny ol' devil."

"I been sheriff so dam' long I cain't very well remember when I wasn't. Was there a time once when I was jus' a young feller, a sort o' heller who used to punch cows an' ramble free an' do as he dam' liked? Musta been pretty far back, Bill. Takes a lot o' rememberin'."

"Well?" said Bill.

"A sheriff's got certain things he's got to do," resumed the old man still brooding over the fire. He leaned closer to it and began to chafe his hands slowly. "Sometimes, Bill, I feel like I was one o' them boys in a circus that's ridin' two horses at the same time, standin' with a foot on each, an' they keep on gettin' fu'ther an' fu'ther apart.—Now talkin' about the kid; I don't rightly know where he is, do I? Gadge is such a dam' liar! If—if I was to see Juan standin' right here—Well, Bill, man to man, I ask you? It's hell, ain't it?"

"Yes," said Bill. "That's the name of it, Dan. Yet we both know he didn't kill Pasmore. And we know that if they take the kid they'll hang him. Buck Andros will see to that."

"There's times," said Dan with a wry face, "when I wish somebody else was sheriff."

"They're not going to take Juan, Dan," said Bill steadily.

The old eyes squinted at him more shrewdly than ever.

"It's a losin' game buckin' the law, Bill. Which is to say if the law reached out its hand an' clamped it on Juan an' you got your back up—"

"I know, Dan. Just the same the law's not goin' to have him. No need friends shouldn't understan' each other, is there?"

It was a question not meant to be answered and Dan smoked in silence.

"Look here, Dan," said Bill, again first to come to the end of his patience. "It's gettin' on; you've got a long ride home—"

Dan Westcott peered slyly at him.

"I was figgerin' on your puttin' me up for the night, Bill."

Bill Mountain grew restless; he got up and moved about, kicked the log into place and stood leaning on the mantel, frowning down upon the thin white hairs of the old sheriff's head. He'd have given a lot just then to know what thoughts were ticking away there.

"No word from your man down to Santy Fee, Bill?" asked Westcott without looking up.

"No. I don't think he's tryin'. Good God, Dan," he exploded. "I don't even know that he believes what I've told him; he may be takin' my pay because it's easy money an' thinkin' all the time that Juan did the thing!"

"Nope," said Dan. "When you hired Clay Patten you hired a good man. I had a talk with him, too. He knows Juan never kilt Pasmore."

"Are we ever to know who did?"

"If they give us time, yes. Pshaw, Bill, I've knowed a case where a man went to the pen for a killin' he pulled over Socorro way forty year before!—Lord, Lordy, I'd die laughin' could we somehow pin it on Buck Andros!"

Bill looked down at him curiously.

"Yet we both know Andros didn't kill Pasmore. Andros and Pasmore were friends—"

"Which would make no never-mind with Andros," snorted the old fellow. Then he sighed. "Yep, we know, which is mos' dam' unfort'nate, that Andros didn't do it." He jerked his head up and his eyes glittered with some secret eagerness. "I got a hunch though, Bill. No, I don't see it doin' me much good so far, but hunches come seldom an' it pays to work each an' every one out. If you wanted to gam'le I'd bet you pretty considerable as how Buck Andros knows who did do the killin'!—Whoa! I ain't answerin' that one." He rose slowly; the chair creaked and he looked quizzically at Bill and chuckled when Bill smiled soberly. "Now," said Dan briskly, "here's this: If I knowed for sure Juan was at han', I'd do my sworn duty an' arrest him. I've heard he's here. So my han' is sorta forced to make what they call an ex'austive search—Steady, Bill! Keep your shirt on an' watch me."

He walked across the room and peered under a table; he went to a door, lighted a match on the seat of his trousers and looked into the dining-room; he then glanced out into the hall and came back to the fire, lowering himself into his chair.

"Havin' shown myse'f to my sat'sfaction that Herbie Gadge lied like a horse-thief same's usual, an' Juan ain't nowheres aroun'," he observed, "I c'n squat again with a clear conscience. Bill, tell me."

Bill relaxed and flashed a look of gratitude at his circuitous old friend. Then complying with that friend's request he sketched the events of last night in San Carlos, touching briefly on Penelope. He told of the encounter with Andros on the mountain, and again mentioned Penelope. "She's Clinton Loring's girl, by the way—"

Old Dan dreamily whistled a few bars of The Last Rose of Summer before he made any remark. He said, "H'm," a time or two, and then:

"Clint Lorin's girl, you say? Now I used to know Clint; I've et at his house an', by gum, Bill, I've hel' this same Penny-lope on my lap an' let her lis'en to the ticks in my ol' watch, an' I bet she blew on it an' the lid popped open!—Penny-lope Lorin'! Clint's girl!—Hmm." He prolonged his “Hmm” until it was like the humming of a bee. “Well, well, well! Think o’ that! Penny-lope under this same roof with me—after all them years.” Of a sudden he came up out of his chair. “I got to renew ol’ acquaintance, Bill. Right this minute!”

Bill looked narrowly into the bright and innocent blue eyes and wondered what on earth the old fellow was up to now.

“She’s in bed long ago, Dan; asleep after a hard day—”

Dan brushed by him saying tartly:

“Well, I guess she’ll be glad to pop up an’ shake an’ ol’ frien’ by the han’. Now, you stick right where you are! Me, I ain’t goin’ to bust any o’ the polite conventions: I’m goin’ to knock Ma Richards out, an’ she’s goin’ to chappyrone me—me an’ Penny-lope,” he concluded with his giggle. “I know where Ma Richards’ room is so you jus’ stick where you are—rememberin’, Bill,” he added with deliberate emphasis, “that you might still have folks poppin’ in yet to-night, an’ you ought to be handy to receive ’em.”

He was gone perhaps twenty minutes. Bill Mountain, puzzling over Dan and his ways, heard subdued voices; then a door closed and he heard nothing more. Presently Dan stuck his head in at the door, said, “G’night, Bill; I know the way to my room.—Seen Penny-lope; mos’ lost my mind over her, too. Well, if after a good sleep I c'n shake off about fifty years, *quien sabe*?" And Dan withdrew.

Bill sat on. The room grew dark as the fire died down until there were only intermittent sputters of flame. There'd be no sleep for him to-night. He'd await a report from Tonito, send that youngster to bed since he'd had not much sleep last night, and would still sit on. There was so little telling what might happen, and his uneasiness grew from moment to moment. He told himself that with the interception of Herbie Gadge, the present danger had been shunted aside. But the deeper he pondered the more chary he was of taking anything for granted; he did not mean for an instant to minimize Andros' shrewdness and determination and enmity. Gadge, for aught he knew, might be but one of several messengers; it was not like Andros, with the game all but in his hands, to stake everything on one play.

The assurance that his fears were not unfounded was not long in coming. Flying hoof-beats rang in a wild tattoo bursting out like sudden explosions against the silence where a horseman speeding across the turfy field turned into the hard-packed road. Where that headlong rider led others followed almost at his heels so that the thud of many hoofs sounded like a sudden clap of thunder.

Bill Mountain snatched open the drawer of a

fireside table and drew out the weapon which he had kept close at hand all night. Already the running horses were in the yard; above the din they made rose a piercing yell of warning from Tonito: "Don Bill! Don Bill!—It is a posse—Andros and other men—Webb Clark, the deputy sheriff!"

Other voices boomed out, seeking to roar him down, loudest of all Andros' voice, mocking and exultant, crying:

"Keep your hair on, Bill! Juan's our meat now. We're the Law! Come ahead, boys."

"Damn the law," shouted Bill. "If you come, come shooting!"

Tonito first of all burst into the room shouting: "It is me, Don Bill—Tonito." Close behind him came several men. Tonito, weaponless, flung himself sideways as the first shot was fired. That was Andros, taking Bill Mountain at his word, shooting as he came, firing almost at random since the big room was dark save for a faint and quivering glow from the dying fire. Yet Bill Mountain knew who three of those lean swift shadows were at Buck Andros' back, three gunflashing young desperadoes who would kill at the drop of the hat. They sprang to right and left, clear of the door, as they entered. Pistol shots, red flares and the acrid smell of powder filled the room. Bill Mountain, grim and steady, rained his bullets among them, praying to get Andros first.

Webb Clark, old Dan's deputy, had been shouldered aside by the more eager ones but now came running in, bellowing commands.

"In the name o' the law!" he shouted. "In the name o' the law! Damn you, Bill, ain't you got any sense? You're resistin' an off—"

No trigger finger was stilled at the deputy's commands. While he was speaking more than one man would have been shot to death were it not that the darkness instead of being relieved was but made the more uncertain by the tricky, mystifying flicker-flicker-flicker of the fire. As it was one of Bill's shots found a mark and one of Andros' three retainers reeled staggering backward; his falling gun clattered noisily on the hardwood floor. Lead rained all about Bill Mountain; a grunt of rage broke from him as he took a bullet in his right forearm.

Wilder than ever was the bedlam in the place. He stooped groping with his left hand for the weapon he had dropped—Andros yelled out, "Got him! Come ahead, boys!" and raced through the room to the hall. Straightening up Bill saw the blur of his figure vanishing; he saw what was like a whirlpool of humanity by the front door—there was a crashing sound, a thud and the noise of splintered pottery—at first he had the wild idea that it was a man's skull cracking! Tonito had caught up one of old Dan's jugs and hurled it into a man's face. Two men were down, clawing and battering each other; they were Tonito and the man whom he had hammered over the head.

Other leaping figures raced towards the hall door and from further off came Buck Andros' exultant voice: "Down the hall, boys! The last door on the left. Juan's in there!"

Bill Mountain, using his left hand, was firing after a speeding figure who he thought was Webb Clark when his arm was jerked down. And that was the first intimation he had that Penelope Loring had run in through the music room and was hanging on to his arm.

He shook her off, having no ears for whatever it was that she was telling him so frantically. But his right arm hung useless at his side and her two arms were strong and she was flinging all the strength of her vigorous young body against his.

"Out of my way!" he cried angrily.

"No, Bill! No! Listen to me—"

He flung her violently aside and leaped forward; every man was gone from the room save Tonito and a still figure on the floor where Tonito had hammered again with the butt of a pistol snatched from his opponent. But as Bill sprang Penelope once more caught his arm; before he could break free again a voice ringing out from the corridor put ice in his blood. There spoke old Dan Westcott singing out gleefully:

"Here ye be, Webb, right when mos' needed for once! Hello, Buck; you too! I'll reppytize the whole works of you. There's Juan's room; you'll find it locked but take your time, take your time, boys."

"Dan!" gasped Bill, and grew rigid. "Dan!"

Penelope took swift advantage of his single moment of indecision. She threw her arm about his neck and pulled his head down, *making* him listen.

CHAPTER 10

"Everything is all right, I tell you!" were those amazing words which Penelope was saying over and over. "You listen to me, Bill Mountain—"

"Let me go," he said savagely. "Dan or no Dan, law or no law, they are not going to have that kid!"

"Bill! Can't you understand? I tell you that Juan is safe away—and that dear old Dan Westcott is a blessed, blessed angel!"

"Juan safe away?" he repeated, glaring at her. "You're crazy! He's in that room—"

"He isn't! He's gone—Now you'll listen to me, won't you?" A long sigh escaped her as she let her hands fall away from him and began rubbing her arm where he had hurt her. At last, light dawning on him, he listened eagerly.

At the far end of the long corridor they could see a group of figures at Juan's door. Andros was holding a lamp in his left hand. Old Dan was saying: "Take it easy, boys. No hurry. There's iron bars over the winders an' he can't get out that way. Here, Webb; your eyes are better'n mine; see if this key'll work."

"He got Mrs. Richards up," Penelope explained hurriedly. "Then they came to me and I dressed in a hurry. Dan said, 'Looky here, I'm sheriff an' if I was to know Juan was here I'd have to do my duty an' arrest the boy. But havin' looked high an' low, I know he ain't in the house so my conscience is clear. Now if Juan happened to be outside an' had a horse saddled—an' if anything popped he was to be off an' away, who'd know? Not me?' All along Dan thought Buck Andros was up to something and that trouble was in the air. And—"

"He gave me no inkling—"

"He didn't want you to know. He was afraid that you'd not allow Juan, wounded as he is, to go; he said you had your back up and he was afraid you'd make the mistake of fighting it out no matter who demanded Juan."

"Juan's in no shape to be riding to-night—"

"Better than arrest, isn't it?" she insisted. "They'd have made him ride! Better be riding to the mountains than to jail—"

Webb got the door unlocked, shoved it open and stepped to one side. Dan Westcott, his voice sounding convincingly businesslike, called out:

"Stick 'em up, Juan! We got you. We're a posse an' you ain't got a chance. Let's have the light, Buck."

Dan and Buck Andros were the first in the room.

"There he is in bed!" Dan sang out. "Nab him!"

Bill Mountain broke away from Penelope and ran down the hall. But before he got to the open door he heard Buck Andros saying angrily:

"That's not Juan Montana! It's one of their damned meztizos!"

"Them's Juan's clothes," spoke up old Dan. "Don't I know? That's his fancy leather coat an' yon's his hat an' if them ain't his ridin' boots I'm a liar!"

Penelope like Bill had started fearfully when Andros announced that Juan lay there, though with her own eyes she had seen the boy slip out of a back door. Her mystification however was not so deep when she recalled that old Dan had suggested that Juan change to other clothes from hat to boots, and leave his discarded things in the room. But she had had no inkling that another man was to take Juan's place and not until the old sheriff spoke again did she have a clue. By that time Bill Mountain was in the room with the others and she was looking in on them. A young Indian lay in Juan's bed; as he reared up she saw the bandage swathed about his upper body.

"Made monkeys out'n ourselves, looks like," said old Dan. "This feller ain't Juan! Looks sorta like him, though, which is to say he's about the same size an' age. Shucks. Some other feller has been masqueradin' as Juan an' leadin' us astray." He brought his keen old eyes to bear on his deputy. "Webb Clark, you're a dam' jackass an' always was," he said disgustedly.

Bill Mountain could have taken Dan Westcott

in his arms then and hugged him. Webb Clark was the picture of mystification and discomfiture. With old Dan so quick to place all blame for bungling on him, he looked gloomily at Andros.

"Buck here tol' me," he muttered. "Said he had sure an' certain info'mation Juan was at this house an' in this room."

"You'd oughta come to me, 'stead o' takin' things into your own han's, Webb," remarked Dan acidly, and transferred his meditative regard to Andros whose brows were drawn gloweringly and who looked as perplexed as Webb Clark. "You, too, Buck," said Dan tartly, "you oughta come to me. I ain't goin' to say nothin' in public about Webb bunglin' things, but gosh-A'mighty, Andros, you'd oughta have sense enough to know Webb ain't had the exper'ence I've had with forty years sheriffin'. Any time you got any info'mation you better bring it along to headquarters. Hell's bells, man, jus' when I had this thing by the tail you fellers has sure made a fine mess o' things!"

"I don't notice you've been doing such a hell of a lot yourself," snorted the thoroughly disgruntled Andros. He turned to leave the room and came unexpectedly face to face with Bill Mountain. Andros was white-faced with rage at the trick that had been played on him and his voice roughened with passion as he cried hotly: "Damn you, Montana! You half-breeds may be pretty slick at this sort of game but before I am through with you I'll see you busted flat and your brother hung."

"Scat, you polecat!" said Bill Mountain, his face almost as white as Andros', his eyes blazing.

"Hi!" shrilled old Dan Westcott. "Cut it out, you fellers! The firs' man that lif's a finger, I'll let him have it! Andros, you're purty far off your own stampin' groun' anyhow. Better back off an' get a new start."

Andros looked over his shoulder to sneer at the old man.

"We all know Montana's got you in his pocket, Westcott. That's why I went to your deputy instead of to you."

"Better get t' hell out o' here," snapped old Dan. "Gather up your dead an' wounded if such there be, an' don't start in sassin' the dignity o' the law as vested in me."

Andros laughed at him and called to the deputy, saying: "Come ahead, Webb, let's go." But Westcott was of another mind and said sharply:

"Webb's goin' to stick by me a spell while we go into conf'rence an' I coach him so's he won't be makin' any more bad mistakes."

While he was speaking Buck Andros for the first time saw Penelope standing in the corridor and went out to her. Leaving the room behind him in darkness he shone the lamp light into her face. A moment he towered above her, so much taller that she had to put her head back to look up at him, his savage, buccaneering eyes staring down at a face which was bright with excitement and into eyes sparkling with gladness that his blow had fallen on empty air.

With those eyes on him Andros affected a sudden swaggering high insolence.

"Oh, you'll see me again and under different circumstances, Pretty Penelope," he told her briskly. "By the way, when you get tired wasting your charms on a man who is blind as a bat when it's a question of a pretty girl, why then send for John Andros. Good night, my dear, and sweet dreams."

He proceeded on his way still carrying the lamp, his shadow enormous on the corridor's white wall even when he had passed from sight through the living-room door.

A match flared and old Dan said crisply: "Come ahead, Webb; it's up to you an' me to see Buck an' his huntin' dogs safe off the place; I don't want as there should be any more trouble come up out'n this bone-head play you made." Lamps and candles were lighted. Tonito's form came waveringly out of the dark; he had a gun in his hand and his head was turned towards the door through which Andros had gone. Bill Mountain called him back. Mrs. Richards appeared hurrying; Ben Hodge rapped and called at a door and was let in. Dan on his way with a bewildered deputy at his heels called over his shoulder, "Ain't bad hurt, are you, Bill?" Penelope started forward with a sense of guilt; she had forgotten the wounded arm. She and Mrs. Richards made Bill go into the kitchen and grew busy with hot water and clean cloths and iodine. Their patient didn't look at them and seemed unconscious of the bleeding groove from the upper arm to elbow as he concerned himself exclusively with what Tonito had to tell.

Tonito's story was given in a few angry words. Buck Andros had played him and his two brothers for suckers, that was what! They followed him into an ambush. Tonito was warned just in time; he saw Andros light a cigarette; that was all right. But Tonito could see that the cigarette was glowing when Andros struck a second match. It was a signal and Tonito shouted a warning and pulled his gun out. But already the men hiding jumped up and Tonito heard the swish of a rope. It nearly got him; both his brothers were jerked from their saddles. He whirled and ran for it to bring word to Don Bill, but the accursed rope had jerked his gun away. But for that, as God lived, Tonito would have killed that son-of-a-dog Andros!

"Good boy, Tonito," said Bill warmly, and patted his shoulder. "Get some of the boys and see that your brothers are all right. Then to bed, old man, and make up some sleep."

Though there was little sleep that night, Penelope was astir with the sweet early morning. She awoke with the delicious feeling that life was a perfectly gorgeous affair besprinkled with all kinds of entrancing adventures which went racing by like fence posts seen from the window of a speeding train. She did not want to miss a single one of them! As she slipped out of bed she saw a glint of the early sun piercing the big trees shadowing the stone-flagged patio. She stepped under a shower of icy water which made her gasp and shrink and then laugh and tingle; she dressed swiftly in her riding things, stood a moment smiling tenderly at the single painting on her wall, and then tip-toed down the corridor to the living-room. She did not know whether the rest of the household woke or slept; she was on her way to the front porch and the fresh open morning for a first view by daylight over the valley as it revealed itself from the old home.

But in the living-room she fell to loitering. It had been set in order last night, yet not all reminders of what had occurred last night were to be summarily dismissed. For one thing that "licker" of old Dan Westcott's which had gushed out of a shattered jug had charged the place with a pungent smell which lingered on. "You may break, you may shatter the vase if you will," murmured Penelope and smiled in memory of all the fuss old Dan had made over the loss of a gallon of whisky for which he had ridden all the way out to Pueblo Junction; he'd a notion, he swore, to arrest Tonito and have ol' Jedge Peters send him to the pen for life. All of which, she knew, had been by way of growing wordy at a time when he did not want to discuss other and more important matters; he was escorting Buck Andros off the ranch, dragging Webb Clark along, and in general clearing the place of invaders without giving anyone a chance to say a word.

Other tokens of last night's hectic moments had defied the tidying of Mrs. Richards; there was a hole which a bullet had made through the window pane; on a table top was a splintered gouge. The thought came to her that no doubt these sturdy old walls in the hundred years they had stood here had witnessed many a lively and colourful happening. What a shame they couldn't be treated like camera plates and made to give up in a visible, continuous panorama each event great and small, funny and tragic, romantic and sentimental and sorrowful and glad, in the long story of the life of a family flowing on like a river! These old walls knew! They remembered and even carried signs could you but read them, knots tied in memory's handkerchief—bullets embedded in the adobes, fine lines and scratches. Right here the first Montana had stood, looking about him upon his dream materialised; he wore a sword and very high boots and, perhaps, a ruffle or two. Then had come the senoras and senoritas, the babies crawling all over the place—and, who knew? other nights like last night with something other than spilled whisky staining the floor boards.

Moving in a reverie through the room, Penelope came to a tall bookcase and began looking at the titles. Here were a full hundred volumes every one of which had to do with horses. Breeding and rearing and training; horses in sickness and health; their feeding and stabling; thoroughbreds, hunters, the American Saddle Horse and polo ponies. She opened a book at random; looking proudly out at her from a coloured reproduction of an old oil painting was that valiant old aristocrat, Flying Childers, glorious marvel of his age who never once even sniffed the odour of defeat. A conqueror, he looked the part, a superb bay who seemed arrogantly conscious of his high Eastern blood, poised upon the four white feet of victory. Beneath the picture was the legend: "Flying Childers, got by the Darley Arabian out of Betty Leeds, born 1715, died 1741."

She turned to a second bookcase where were ancient volumes, many in fine bindings, which had accumulated generation after generation, culled by dead and gone Montanas. A glance showed that these dealt with the American Southwest, its history and development. One volume held her eye and she drew it out as though she had heard its voice asking to be handled by one who, because of her love for her home state, was worthy to hold it. She experienced a little thrill of delight on opening it. It was one of the original small edition of Villaga's *Historia de la Nueva Mexico.* Fine old Villaga! Those three hundred and more years ago this land of New Mexico had so moved him, its annals had so thundered and echoed in his soul that he like a modern Homer had sung its history in epic verse!

"I thought I heard a mouse in here," said Bill Mountain from the door.

She whirled about, the book clasped to her breast.

"But this thing is priceless!" she exclaimed. "I never saw a copy of it before, though I've heard of it all my life!"

"Old Villaga?" He came on into the room; he, too, was dressed as upon yesterday and his old worn lop-sided boots still had yesterday's dust on them. She saw that he carried his right arm in a sling and was about to remark upon his wound when he continued thoughtfully: "It requires a poet, you know, to write a history like ours. And not one American out of a hundred ever even heard of the old boy! The past of New Mexico should be chanted in hexameters, or woven into a splendid tapestry all reds and golds."

"And purples!" said Penelope. "And to think of

your having read Villaga from the 1610 edition. To have read Villaga at all—"

"Why not?" he said smiling at her. "It's a question of having time for these things, you know. Down in the jungles where everybody is rushing around in a circle to keep up with the hands of the clock, there's no time for anything. Up here we have nothing but long quiet days and uneventful nights—"

"Mercy on us!" exclaimed Penelope. "Here I've witnessed three gun battles within twenty-four hours and the man talks of long empty days and uneventful nights! He carries his arm in a sling and discourses on peace!"

She put the book away and laughingly they strolled together to the dining-room from which came a faint clatter of dishes and the very aroma to crown and make perfect the morning. On their way Penelope offered demurely:

"Do you know I'm afraid you're rather mixing your rôles this morning?"

"Spell it; we have hot cakes for breakfast."

"R-ô-l-e-s. Although your speech about hexameters and tapestries really belongs to my host, Senor Montana, you do dress, it seems to me, just exactly like an old rough-neck friend of mine named Bill Mountain."

"The double life has its moments of mental strain," he confessed as he drew out her chair for her.

A gay streak of sunlight lay across the white cloth, glinting upon the silver and distilling a diamond from a glass of water, and despite any sober thoughts which must have concerned Bill Mountain the breakfast hour was a handful of gay moments. Mrs. Richards passing down the corridor looked in to say good morning. At sight of the laughing Penelope she exclaimed:

"Bill, just look at her! Have you the faintest notion that she is real? Here I feel like I'd been hammered through a knot-hole and then dragged back, and to look at her you'd swear she'd been dancing and having love made to her and then had slept a day through after it all. Just look at her!"

Thus commanded, he looked. A pair of big sparkling grey eyes came hastily to a meeting with his and then ran away, red lips that were tremulous all of a sudden for no reason on earth twitched into a faint smile which also fled in haste, a bronze curl lay softly against a rose-petalled cheek.

"She looks all right as far as I can see," said Bill, and transferred his clear gaze to Ma Richards. "What's unreal about her?"

Ma Richards came very close to answering him with a sniff—but then it had been a hard night. And after all she might as well get her lesson learned and accepted: There was no earthly use trying to make him really see a pretty girl.

Tonito passing languidly through the garden availed himself of the facilities offered by a big plate glass window and let his melting black eyes pay their adoration. He had a red rose behind his ear. As he received a bright nod and smile Tonito the graceful touched his hat; he did not take it off but his little gesture was as eloquent as his love-making eyes and said the same things. His rose fell; he stooped for it, dusted it very, very tenderly, inhaled it, touched it to his lips and flowed liquidly out of the picture-frame of the window. An impudent young rascal, but you could not rightfully hold Tonito blameworthy for that. Blame rather his ancestry, blame the croonings over his cradle—blame the sunshine itself and the moon and the birdsong and the little winds which blew across the uplands of New Mexico.

"When I promised to scare up a handsome young *novio* for you," chuckled Bill, "I didn't mean Tonito."

"Your arm must be paining you dreadfully," said Penelope. She came to his rescue as he was one-handedly and not very successfully trying to cut a strip of bacon with the edge of a fork. Abruptly she added, "You're really worrying about Juan, aren't you?"

"With decent care his wound wouldn't bother him any more than my arm troubles me," he returned. "I know that you and Mrs. Richards did the best for him that could be done, sending him off with a blanket roll and a flask and a packet of food. But the nights are pretty crisp now, and lying up in the open isn't the most desirable thing in the world. Of course he has made a bee line for Grouse Canon; I'd have guessed that even though he hadn't left word with you. There's shelter there of a sort."

"You will manage to see him to-day?"

"Not to-day. Early to-night, though. As long as there is light you can gamble on Buck Andros having men on the high places using field glasses. This morning I'll show you over the ranch if you'd be interested. You're going to pick out a couple of horses for yourself."

"A house of my own—a house full of servants—at the very least a couple of saddle horses—" Penelope sighed in mock dismay. "Well, when I do wake up I'll know that while it lasted it was a perfectly gorgeous dream! And nothing to do but ride around and look at the ranch! I suppose that I can have Consuela run the school for me while I find other amusements?"

"Oh, there's no hurry about the school," he said lightly. "You will tell Ben later on what books are wanted; you'll have to wait until they come—"

"School starts immediately," said Penelope, very businesslike. "My responsibilities maintaining a menage grow enormous and the salary cannot start until work does. I'll lecture to my pupils, using Villaga as a text! You'll let me copy some of the reverberating lines? I'll have my whole school chant them for you when in your capacity of school trustee you visit us."

"It's an idea. Well, if you insist—"

"I do," said Penelope.

"Then to-morrow you can ring the bell—if we can find you a bell to ring. Some more coffee? Want to go see some of my horses then?"

They were rising when Ben Hodge came in. He greeted Penelope like an old friend and then reported to Bill that already Herbie Gadge, released from custody and frothing over with swear-words for which he really should have his mouth washed out with yellow kitchen soap was on his way. Bill was explaining about Herbie Gadge to Penelope as they went outside when a stony-faced Indian who had been waiting at the edge of the garden, came stolidly forward, touched his hat and delivered a curt message which sounded like a sullen command. It was from that weathered old patriarch, José, who last night had held himself unworthy to sit in the home of the Montanas so long as the shame of his people bore them down.

"*Bueno*, Tomas," said Bill as curtly as the other had spoken. "Tell him I am coming. Also, the senorita comes with me." Tomas grunted and departed; Bill looked down gravely into Penelope's upturned face. "Yes, you're coming along. It will be something I think you'll remember."

She flashed a swift look of enquiry at him and marvelled that his expression could in an instant become so rigidly implacable.

"I—I don't think I'll go," she said uncertainly. She drew away from him; somehow, vague as it all was, he frightened her. Her mind was alert and shrewd, her imagination lively. From the few words which the Indian messenger had spoken she knew that Montana's people were losing no time in dealing with the traitor in their midst.

"I'd like you to come," he said very soberly. "Also my people would like it. You came among them, a stranger, at a time when they felt themselves unclean. It will be their wish, as it is mine, that you see them when, purged and purified, they can lift their heads again."

At once hesitant yet conscious of the obligation he laid upon her and of a pricking curiosity which would not be altogether denied, she walked at his side down the steps, through the garden and along a little path which led under the live oaks to a clutter of adobe buildings. She scarcely had eyes for a view which at another time would have claimed all her attention, the green valley itself, the river down its middle and in the nearer foreground the stables and hay barns and the proud heads of many beautiful horses watching her over the corrals. All this was for later on; now she saw only the Indian homes, clean white walls and roofs of warm tile glowing in the sun; strings of red peppers glimpsed through open doors; ropes of onions and a colourful Indian blanket sunning; and in a group before these little homes a crowd of people very still in the clean young morning.

That utterly silent group of people, men, women and children of whom there must have been no less than three score, all so intensely still, laid a queer spell upon her. They did not look at her and Bill approaching and they did not look at one another; she had the uncanny feeling that their eyes, though open, saw nothing and that they were not breathing.

When at last a man moved she looked at him with a curiosity which grew swiftly into fascination. He was an old man, the oldest of them all, the father of some of the grown men and women about him, the grandfather of youths and maidens, the great-grandfather of some of the little brown, black-eyed babies clinging to adult legs and, alone of all, round-eyed with an interest which observed everything; an old man with a gaunt copper mask for a face with an etching of criss-crossed dark lines. He was bare-headed; his long straight hair was very black save for streaks of white in it and about his forehead was a narrow strap of glistening red leather. About him was an indefinable and indescribable air of dignity. Old José had been a chief in the long ago when a chief was a king.

He had been but awaiting Montana's coming. Now he stood out in front of his people and spoke to them in his husky voice, addressing them in their latter day tongue of Spanish.

"So great a deed of shame," said old José, "could come only from the heart of the most wicked of men. Men like that do not weep over what they have done. A man like that cannot weep."

He stopped in his oddly abrupt fashion. There was a faint stir among those who heard; it was like a ripple going through them. Out of a deep silence a woman's voice spoke shrilly; she too said: "A man like that cannot weep." She was an old woman, thick and stout and dark, her fat shoulders swathed in a red shawl. A man of middle age spoke gravely: "A man like that cannot weep." They were all deliberate; there was no sense of haste in their midst; when one of them spoke it was only out of a silence which once more shut down when he had done. Penelope's eyes drifted from face to face; she saw Tonito, stolid like the rest, with his red rose still behind his ear, forgotten now. Beyond him she saw a young girl and thought of the little Luisa whom Pasmore had lured away and who came back home to die, for this girl too was slim and duskily pretty with mysterious velvety eyes.

After a little while old José said: "I know!" Again there was that faint movement like a ripple and, when all was still again, many awed voices said, "He knows!"

"Stand in a circle," commanded José.

They drifted into their places as though his speech had been a little wind blowing them and formed a great circle, even the little ones dragged into their places. What enormous eyes those little ones had, eyes glued upon the old man who was the centre of that ring. Penelope grew conscious first of Bill's hand on her arm, then of the fact that he and she were a part of the circle of his people. She saw that the Indian girl was beyond him, only two or three places removed; she saw that at her side stood a man she had not marked until now—and instinctively she flinched away from him. He was a twisted man, a man with a face warped awry and with one shoulder higher than the other and with a heavy crooked nose. Yet it was not because of these things that she winced. It was because of something which she had seen in his eyes, something which flashed up and died down and which she could not understand. She saw the whites of his eyes as he rolled them.

"I know," said old José a second time. Again several hushed voices muttered, "He knows."

He squatted on his heels and made a quick brisk fire of dead leaves and twigs fallen from the oaks. When he brought forth something which he had kept until now hidden inside his shirt another one of those queer little ripples went shivering around the ring of tense and expectant humanity. "It is the fire-stick!" someone said awesomely. José still squatting held it over the fire; it was a short stick not over twelve or eighteen inches long with an odd-looking lump the size of a man's two fists at the end of it, and it was this knobby end which was held close to the blaze. It made Penelope think of a clumsy, over-fat tamale, all bound in husks. With the flames licking it, it did not burst into blaze but began to emit a thick cloud of smoke and a spicy, pungent smell.

"The wicked one cannot weep," said José and rose slowly to stand very erect, his eyes staring straight ahead of him. This time no one echoed his words.

Her fascination growing all the while Penelope saw him move suddenly and thrust the smoking thing close to a man's face so that the smoke was all about his mouth and eyes. The man strove to keep his eyes wide open yet they blinked in spite of him; almost immediately they began to water and the tears rising to assuage the stinging flowed freely down his dark visage. José, with never the quiver of a muscle of his old coppery face, moved slowly, now this way and now that, thrusting his fire-stick challengingly into one face after another, and men and women with the pungent smoke in their eyes blinked and the protecting tears came fast enough.

Of a sudden Penelope relaxed and the reaction came; fascination fled and along with it that emotion next door to awe which she had caught from the Indians. She could have laughed at the absurdity of the whole affair; if anything on earth was a scientific certainty it was that any individual, into whose face the stick was thrust, would weep freely enough, be he ever so villainous. Her lips twitched. She glanced covertly at Bill. His face was as rigid as ever and very stern.

Then she looked back hurriedly at old José and jerked her head up with a start; for the instant she thought that he was coming straight at her, meaning to subject her to the ridiculous ordeal. If he had dared she'd slap his nasty-smelling old heathen contraption out of the way and show him her back.

The fire-stick was not directed at her but was held close to the chin of the twisted man at her side, the fellow into whose eyes she had seen that queer flash come. Those eyes were wild eyes now, staring like a frightened horse's, all whites. The smoke crept about his features, it clung to his thick hair and rose from it in little wisps like streamers of vapour she had seen among mountain crags. It obscured his staring eyes, hid them entirely, then thinned and broke and lifted. And his eyes were harsh and dry, glaring sere balls of horror.

A sort of strangling scream broke from the twisted mouth. The man whirled and tried to run. Penelope saw men leap upon him from every side. At the moment, as he went down under them, she saw only one face clearly. It was Tonito's. He stood not ten feet from her, a look of death in his face. The red rose was still behind his ear, but there was no thought of red roses in Tonito's heart.

She caught Bill's arm, excited and afraid yet most of all concerned with that look on Tonito's face.

"Look at him!" she whispered. "What is it?"

"It's one of Tonito's brothers," he told her. "I'm damned sorry. Better come away now."

"What are they going to do with him?" she demanded fearfully.

He shrugged. Already they were doing it. A struggling form went down under a mass of humanity which covered him like a swarm of angry bees. They began tearing his clothes off his back; a man, yelling as he came, all of them done with restraint and awe now, flourished a long bull-whip. It hissed through the air and snapped like a pistol shot.

Penelope covered her face with her hands, then spun about to have her back to it all and put her hands on her ears, striving to shut out a long agonised scream.

"You must stop them! Bill Mountain, for God's sake stop them!"

"Come away," he said sternly. "He is getting no more than he asked for. They'll leave him alive—and he'll go and never come back. For these people whose tenure is of a hundred years at Montana exile is worse than death."

Another scream rose above his words. She started to run from the place, then, white-faced and with flashing eyes, she stopped and faced Montana. What she was about to say to him, whether angry command or pleading, died in her throat at the look in his eyes. They were pitilessly hard.

Suddenly it grew very silent. They had tied the twisted man's hands at his back, fiercely tight; old José made a little cross of two charred sticks and tied it about his neck. With bloodied back the traitor was given his freedom to depart and went stumbling away through a lane made by the two lines of his people, his no longer, who watched him with unblinking stony eyes. After that second scream there had come never so much as a moan or curse or prayer from him. He went hurrying away, his back bowed as under a tremendous weight, his head down, his eyes on the ground. No one addressed him; a few of the very young alone spat after him.

"Where will he go?" asked Penelope faintly, feeling a little sick.

"To Buck Andros, I suppose. Where else? At any rate he'll never come back. It would be death to do so. Nor, do I think, are we going to be troubled by any more treachery. Now we're going to look at the horses."

She was eager to go. But going she looked back over her shoulder. Not at the wretched man stumbling away into exile from his people and from all the world he knew, but at Tonito. Poor gay Tonito of the red rose, no longer gay.

CHAPTER 11

Swinging along at Bill's side Penelope experienced for a moment or two the curious sensation of floating between two distinct existences. Last night remained very real to her with its blaze of guns and the smell of powder, and its hatred and bitterness and feral anger. Then the scene which she had just witnessed belonged with its stark savagery to last night which had fathered it. All that constituted one phase of actuality. . . . And now?

It was the breath-taking beauty flooding all about her that briefly created within her that troublous sense of being between two realities. The thing behind her was still so near that its shadow was over her; how could she so soon reconcile it with this new reality whose name was sheer beauty? Could both exist so close together?

Montana Valley, truly seen now for the first time, was a gem locked away in the fastnesses of the mountains. Emerald fields rippled away out of sight and the bright sunshine upon them and the sweet clean morning breeze blowing over them streaked and mottled them with many shades of green. The creek wandered between willow fringed banks and flashed the sun; irrigation ditches flowed with silver and sparkled, while the darkly forested slopes constituted regions of shadowy mysteries. The whole place seemed to have come but recently from God's fingers, or rather to be lying still in His palm, and where man began to carry the work on as is a part of the great scheme of things, the human touch had been in harmony with the divine.

For where the gentle slopes edging the valley asked for orchards, the orchards burst forth in long cultivated lines of yet another shade of dusky green, and among the cool leaves one knew that the apples swelled and reddened; and in the basin were checkered fields of lusty verdant alfalfa, and other squares of golden grain and the straw-yellow acres of stubble fields. Out of a field of corn the faces of a flock of little Indian children peeped as from a forest. The air was filled with the scent of lusty green growth and that lustier smell of the good wet earth where the life-giving water ran.

All this was beauty of a soul-searching order yet it was to Penelope the lesser of two beauties; that other was the beauty of horses. Beyond the big barns and the red tiled stables were the corrals and paddocks and smaller pasture fields and still further off were the race track and the polo field, and at one sweep of her sparkling eyes Penelope saw more downright beauty than she had ever dreamed of capturing in one picture frame, even so vast a one as this.

The glory of superb horses was like a heaven-sent fulfilment of the promise of the fertile upland valley. Penelope's eyes grew round with wonder and admiration and then it was that last night and the earlier morning began to waver in a mist and become things of the past, while the present moment brightened and her bemused spirit came winging back into the rich actuality of the Now.

"Oh, that perfect dream of a horse!—and that one!—and that one there!—"

She looked up swiftly into Montana's face; his jaw was set, his mouth remained grim for his thoughts still clung elsewhere, but already his eyes too had brightened.

Perfection, though it seeks many moulds, perhaps comes through no medium closer to achievement than in horses. Here in their different high enclosures were animals of several orders, racing stock and saddle horse, Percherons and polo ponies, with never a single member of their elect group which was as not nearly without flaw as many years of breeding could ensure. Here were horses with lineages jealously guarded like the lineages of kings. And like kings and queens and like little lordlings and princesses they carried themselves. Pride arched many a curving crest.

A lusty young stallion looking out over his fence trumpeted his challenge to the world. He breathed of fire and power; he knew himself for a devil of a fellow who had but to pound the ground with his forefoot to make the earth tremble. Not a day over three years old, not a superfluous ounce upon him, yet his bulk represented two thousand pounds of weight and he carried it like a ballet dancer. Though he could not know that his blood-stream ran back across the centuries with never a single unworthy mesalliance, yet nevertheless he must have felt it. The blood itself knew that he was Crusader and that twelve hundred years before a man-king had bestridden his forefather, a horse-king, at Poitiers. His skin was satiny, grey-clad, and the overflowing vigour within him tingled at his very hair roots.

"You're looking for a couple of saddle horses for yourself, you know," said Bill and was smiling by this time. "Crusader there would make just one bite of you. I've some pretty nifty examples of the American Saddle Horse over yonder—"

"Oh! That one!" cried an ecstatic Penelope.

"That's funny," he said. In the field beyond the nearer small paddock half a dozen young saddle animals, running free, were galloping towards them; at their fore ran a satiny young mare, her sleek sorrel hide flashing the sun, her cream-coloured mane and tail floating airily like spun silk. "Her name is Penelope, too!"

Penelope the girl laughed.

"Thank heaven Mr. Bradshaw warned me!"

Just then there came into sight around the corner of one of the stables two mounted polo teams, young Indians in the saddles with gleaming boots, jerseys and caps, with their sticks laid across their shoulders. They swung blithely through a gate and cantered off toward the playing field. Their ponies, Bill Mountain's pride, struck a new and delightful note in horse-flesh.

"They are going to play?" asked Penelope.

"When next season opens every one of them is to be a tournament pony; the boys riding them are good players as well as mighty fine horsemen."

"But the ponies! They know and they love it! They are going into it like a football squad!"

"Sure they love it," he said gravely. "One Sunday morning, a couple of weeks ago, what do you suppose happened? One of the boys had left the gate open or else Caprice—she's that handy little rascal in the lead—or maybe Pocahontas; she's the red-bay beauty five places behind Caprice—one of these two, I'd bet a man, got the gate opened. I came out on to the porch just in time to see them take their places, two full teams of 'em, and start the game. They struck the ball with their hoofs or nosed it along and—"

Again Penelope answered him with her laugh.

"If you hadn't told me this one, I might have believed the first story, about the saddle horse I picked out being named Penelope."

Bill remained as grave as a judge; he almost looked hurt, she thought, at her refusal to take him seriously. He turned, saw Tonito coming head down and with moody scuffling boots, and called to him. Tonito jerked up his head and approached more swiftly but it was a troubled face which he brought to them. Bill appeared to note nothing of this, clapped Tonito on the shoulder and said:

"A couple of horses, Tonito, *amigo.* Wanderer for me and, let's see—you might rope and saddle Penelope for Miss Loring."

"*Bueno*, *senor*," said Tonito and departed. A moment later Penelope the girl saw an unerring rope drop its wide loop over the high head of that other Penelope!

"So you were telling me the truth after all!"

"Both times," said Bill soberly.

They mounted and rode together and for a little while Penelope forgot the occurrence of yesterday and last night and this early morning, and revelled in the present. She watched the work-out on the polo field, she expended her admiration on Dixie and Waxy and Highflyer, three of the most beautiful of the racing thoroughbreds and she fell in love with her namesake, a gaited animal full of spirit yet perfectly trained. Along with the past she forgot that she had been engaged to open and conduct a school at White Water.

"I've had a perfectly glorious morning," she

said at lunch time, flushed and sparkling with happiness. "And I've grace enough to be ashamed of myself; I know that you have had so much on your mind—"

"I've got to get through the day somehow, you know," he said.

It flashed on her that Buck Andros would have made a far more gallant speech. Yet who would ever look to Bill Mountain for gallantry?

"But now I must remember what I am here for. I am going right up to my school; will you have word sent around that the children are all to come in the morning? I'll plan some sort of work for them."

Penelope rode alone to White Water on her namesake—Bill had told her of that famous Penelope of long and long ago whose progeny had been rich in Derby and St. Leger winners—and would have been the happiest girl in the world were it not for her concern for that poor boy Juan and her quick sympathy for Tonito of the lost gaiety. Why need there be sorrow and suffering in a world like this? For the second time within twenty-four hours she thought of the line: "Where all but the spirit of man is divine." At the end of her ride Consuela was awaiting her and both Billy and Eugenio came running, vying for the privilege of taking her horse, and Penelope had a sense of homecoming and warm friendly welcome.

Bill Mountain "got through the day somehow." Tempted sorely as the hours passed to ride to Juan by daylight he saw where wisdom lay and adhered to his determination to go with caution. Again he was paying Andros full credit for shrewdness and boldness and determination; Andros, if he knew nothing else definitely, did know that Juan had been wounded and was somewhere at no very great distance. Trust him then, from a hiding place among the mountains, to keep watch over the ranch all day. Bill's eyes travelled to never a high place within miles that he did not envision Andros or one of his men ensconced there, field glass at work.

But the instant the sun dipped behind the black ridge of the forested western slope he bestirred himself. There would be a moon and it was in the first dark before moonrise that he wanted to be on his way. He made a small blanket roll, thinking that Juan could do with the additional covers, with a food-pack in its core. He buckled on two shoulder holsters and chose a small sporting rifle from his gun room; stiff and sore as his right arm was it could be made to do service if need compelled. Then he sent for Tonito.

"The poor devil is heart-broken," he told Ben Hodge who was aiding him in his preparations. "When he realised that it was an own brother of his who had double-crossed the kid the light just went out in him, Ben."

"So you're taking him along with you?" demanded Ben. "Just to show him—"

"I'd trust Tonito until hell froze solid," said Bill sharply.

"You've trusted all your people, like that, haven't you? I'm not saying that Tonito isn't as faithful a cuss as—"

"No, don't say it, Ben. Now suppose you have a couple of horses saddled and brought up at the back? It's dark enough."

Ben departed and presently Tonito came to Bill on the front porch. Already it was too dark to make out expressions, yet Tonito's slow, scuffling walk and the unaccustomed droop to his shoulders, even the way his hat was pulled down in front, told the story.

"I'm riding out to see Juan," said Bill crisply. "I'm only half a man with this lame arm of mine, Tonito. Go get yourself a rifle and ride along with me."

Tonito was a very long while answering. He remained on a lower step and kept scraping with the toe of his boot. He did not jerk his head up with his old jaunty air and looked anywhere except into Bill's eyes when he spoke. He was sorry, he said, and seemed only sullen; if the senor did not mind Tonito would not go. There were other boys who would ride with him, better men than Tonito, too. And without awaiting answer or permission Tonito stepped back, and, moving swiftly now, was gone into the gathering dark almost at a run. About to call him back, Bill thought better of it; there was so little gauging all that worked in another man's soul.

Ben Hodge himself returned with the two horses, a coal-black and a dark bay neither of which sported so much as a splotch of white to betray them. When Bill said a casual, "Come ahead, Ben, let's go ridin'," Ben hurried in high satisfaction for a rifle, and the two turned northward.

"Thought you said Juan was holed-up in Grouse Canon?" said Ben.

"Right. But we'll go up through the Goose Neck, make a bend towards Andros' boundary line, and circle back along the old trail. It won't take over twenty minutes longer and there's such a thing as Andros' surprise parties coming too thick together."

As they came abreast of Penelope's new home, looking bright and cheery with its lamp-yellowed windows, they heard the thrum of a guitar and soft voices singing, the voices of Consuela and Josefa, with those of the two boys Eugenio and Billy chiming in less boldly. They sang:

"*Adios*, *Suzanita*!
Y adios bonita!
El lunes te vengo a ver
O el martes de mananita!"

And then Consuela said laughing, "*Ahora*!" and Penelope's voice joined with the others.

"School's begun," said Ben as they rode on. "Miss Loring's got to learn all about Suzanita and her pretty *boquita.* Quite a girl there, huh, Bill? How's she strike you?"

"Right as rain," said Bill.

"That's the hell of a way to say it," growled Hodge. "She is as sweet as a pretty ripe peach peeking out through green leaves. It's no business a girl like her having to work for a living."

"No?"

"Why don't you make eyes at her, Bill? That's what Montana needs, a nice little *senora* to queen it and make a home for you. Didn't you ever think of that?"

Bill laughing in high amusement.

"I'll have to tell Penelope! Gosh, what a laugh for her!"

"And a slap in the face for you," grunted Ben, "if you go at it that way."

"A slap's what I'd be asking for! Don't be a damn' jackass, Ben."

" 'S all right," growled Ben. "The only jackass in this crowd is one that does all his brayin' when you open that mug you're talking about."

"Let's scatter, Ben," said Bill a moment later. "I'll swing off here along the west trail and then for a couple of miles along the Andros line. You poke on ahead and I'll cut in on you up at the foot of the cliffs the other side the high pasture. If we keep our eyes open we might see something."

"You never can tell," agreed Ben, and rode on, humming: "*Adios*, *Suzanita*, *Y adios bonita*."

Before they had ridden fifty yards they were lost to each other, the light of the stars failing to pick them out among the scattering pines which fringed the upper valley and swept upward in ever sturdier ranks towards the edges of the basin. Bill struck across a grassy field on which his horse's hoofs made but little sound and turned down into the willows along the banks of White Water River. He did not cross at the ford where, were there any spying eyes watching for him he would be expected to splash water, but rode down a steep bank at a safe distance below the customary crossing. Though he pulled his feet out of the stirrups and thrust his legs up along his horse's neck it meant a wetting, yet compared to a bullet through the body a dash of cold water was welcome. Climbing the far bank, moving guardedly through the willows there, he again turned slightly westward before he resumed his northerly course.

He gained and followed thus the low ridge marking the boundary line between White Water Valley and the Andros lands, taking due care not to climb so high as to cast a silhouette against the sky nor yet to drop so low down as to pass out of the strip of timber which here dwindled and thinned on the lower slopes. By this time he had drawn his injured arm out of its sling; though it pained him no little he saw wisdom in moving it gently and in working the fingers of his hand.

Through the tree trunks he caught now and then the faint rippling glint of the stream; nothing else visible stirred. He rode with increasing caution, stopping frequently to stare in all directions and most of all to listen. He had no expectation of seeing anything, yet there was always the chance of hearing a hoof clang against a stone, or even an unguarded voice, and horses before now had been known to betray themselves and their riders by whinnying. True enough, Buck Andros at this moment might be sitting at home with his boot heels cocked up on a table and his idle hands clasped behind his head and his eyes frowning over a next move. But that picture of an astute and extremely alert enemy did not form nearly so clearly as another one in which Andros, like Bill himself, rode with a hand on the grip of his gun.

At a moment when he was straining his ears against the faintest sound it was his eyes after all which made a thoroughly puzzling discovery. Straight ahead of him where there was a rocky cleft in the hills he caught a flash of light. Now light, thought Bill, was the last thing on earth any prowler would be showing. Some impatient devil lighting a cigarette perhaps? No; it was a brighter light than that and though it had vanished almost the instant he saw it it came again, a small steady blaze.

He dismounted, dropped his horse's reins to the ground, hung his spurs over the saddle horn lest their clank and jingle give him away, tucked his rifle under his left arm and went forward swiftly. He kept to the pines, and within five minutes came to understand the reason of the fire and to see who it was that used it.

Standing with his back to the light was a man with his hands bound behind him. Down on both knees, working hard with the knots which had been drawn so savagely tight that morning was the second man. And this second man was Tonito.

So this was Tonito's reason for not riding with him to see Juan. Tonito had a brother of his own, the twisted fellow Amador. Prompted by swift anger, Bill's first impulse was to boot the two of them off the ranch. Amador had had his fling and his own people had made him a free gift of all the rest of the world provided only he never again set foot on Montana land where he invited death by returning.

But in the end Bill frowningly withdrew. The fact that Amador had remained all day long with his hands bound—and he must have suffered intolerably—set him puzzling. Certainly the fellow had gone the shortest way to Andros; that he was up here now near the Andros place was amply significant. And Andros, who on occasion could be as cruel as a knife blade, had simply laughed in his face and kicked him out as being no longer of use.

Yet explain Tonito? Well, they were brothers. Had Tonito guessed what sort of treatment Amador would find when he went to the man to whom he had sold himself? Of course the suspicion would have arisen in many minds, perhaps in most minds, that Tonito himself was as deep in the mire of treachery as his brother. The thought did not even suggest itself to Bill Mountain.

He remounted and swung eastward through the thinning pines towards the head of the small upper lake. He was circling the faintly stirring water with its shivery reflections of the stars, with ahead of him the black bulk of the cliffs under which he was to re-establish connection with his foreman, when he was startled by a spurt of light and this time there was no need to question its nature. It was the orange-red flash from a gun fired from the top of the cliffs, and almost immediately the sound of the shot reached him. A second shot answered it from among the lower shadows where Ben should be by now. He turned straight across the clearing, used his spurs and came with a rush to where Ben was.

"Spill out of the saddle and crawl close under the rocks, Bill," said Ben. "You're welcome. There are more of them than there are of me. Riding the old trail, high up. Half a dozen anyhow."

"Headed which way, Ben?"

"Headed east. Towards Grouse Canon. Watch for 'em as they go through the notch. I caught a first glimpse of them coming up on top of the ridge and thought I could duck in here without their seeing me. My horse struck a spark out of a rock and that gave me away. They'll be sitting tight right now, watching for us to make a move.—Don't think they know where Juan is this time, do you, Bill?"

"No," said Bill curt and sharp. "How could they? It's just that fox Andros taking a chance; he has figured out the most likely places, that's all."

"Fox is right. He has cut in between us and Juan. We're corked up like a bug in a bottle, Bill. They'll have a man watching the trail; the minute we rode into it we'd be asking for all we got. He'd have all the fun; it would be like breaking eggs with a stick. What's our play, Bill?"

From Bill presently came a sound oddly like a grunt of satisfaction.

"True enough as far as you go, old horse. But the old trail plays no favourites. We're headed off, yes, but those birds up there have got to expose themselves against the skyline when they ride through the gap. It's shifty shooting by starlight, I'll grant you, but with luck we can make 'em think it over. They've got a steep climb yet to make, they'll have to take it single file—and I'll stand a drink for every saddle we can empty."

"Think Juan can hear the shooting?"

"Not ours, maybe; we're too low down. But theirs, yes. Which Andros maybe knows; that might be why only one shot was plugged at you and why I didn't draw any lead riding to you."

"I don't like squatting and doing nothing but just wait," said Ben.

Bill was a long time answering. He, like his friend and foreman, had no fondness for marking time at a moment like this.

"Ben, old man," he said soberly. "We're going to hand Buck Andros a delicate hint that his days and nights of trespassing have grown monotonous. But right now and right here I don't like the battle line-up. We've checked him for the moment; he's hiding in the shadows and doing all the watching. Another thing: I don't believe for a second that he can find his way straight to Juan. So you and I hit saddle leather again, ride like the devil down the valley as far as Mule Deer Spring, and cut straight across to Grouse Canon. The chances are fair that Andros, seeing us dig out here, will squat where he is a while, wondering and trying to figure it all out and wasting time. We'll have the longer ride but better going, and if we don't beat him to it we ought to pop in on him before he's jumped Juan up. Good medicine? What say?"

"Let's go," said Ben.

The instant that they were in their saddles they

were off and away. From high up on the cliffs came the rattle of rifle fire and a dozen bullets went screaming above their heads. Ben turned in the saddle to jeer at the marksmen, but his yell broke off in an angry "Ouch!"

"Not hit, are you, Ben?"

"Scared only," snapped Ben. "That bullet came so damn close I'll bet it raised a blister."

Bill laughed at him. The bullets ceased screaming about them and they settled down to hard riding.

CHAPTER 12

The first inkling of what was afoot was given Penelope by a sudden voice in the silence, its intonation startling her before she caught a word. She was in her own room, a delightful nest furnished from the old Montana home, and though ready for bed had been drawn to the companionable blaze which Consuela had set crackling in her bedroom fireplace. Bubbling over with life which of late had become so zestful an affair, she was impelled to sit by the fire and think of it all. She should be sleepy—but she drew on a wisp of a negligee, got her writing pad and disposed herself cosily to talk it all over with Patty:

"I've got so much to tell you! I've simply landed in the Valley of Adventure. Right at the start, you've got to get Bill right! I got only a glimpse of him, and the wrong glimpse at that, down in San Carlos. The air is clear in our Up Yonder Country, and we see things as they are. He is *big,* Patty. He is—spacious! He *is* like a mountain, one of those noble old fellows that, the more you look at, the more splendid things you see. (Now don't be a goose.) I gave you quite the wrong impression in my first letter; he has the finest eyes, dark and quick and *seeing* and expressive. When he smiles—"

Thus far had Penelope's racing pen sped when Ben Hodge's voice put a full stop to her letter-writing. She ran to her window and heard everything.

Ben had swung in here at White Water while Bill Mountain turned off into Mule Deer Canyon and pushed on into the mountains to head off Andros and his men. Ben gave his orders hurriedly since he too was impatient to be hammering along the canyon trail. There were several families in the tiny settlement under the trees behind Penelope's school; the men were to arm themselves and follow on and one of the boys was to carry word down to Montana Valley. With these brief instructions given and men sent scurrying, Ben used his spurs and split the air for Mule Deer trail. Hoofbeats ahead of him, dying away between the mountain flanks, told him with what haste his employer sped on ahead.

The moon was rising only now and no ray from it penetrated where Bill Mountain rode. It was dark under the pines in the high-walled ravine but he and his horse knew the way and made daylight speed. It was slower work further on as the trail steepened, but he was comforted by the thought that Andros and his night-prowlers must traverse as difficult ways. As the moon floated clear of the eastern ridges horse and rider broke the skyline on Mule Deer ridge. Ben Hodge, labouring upward far behind, caught one glimpse of the centaur-silhouette.

Once on the ridge Bill Mountain again swung along at a gallop, giving his horse its head. Some two miles off to the north-east he saw the bald pinnacle of Anastasio's Mountain glinting where a shaft of light struck a flinty fault which gleamed like dark metal. Where that old Titan loomed above a region of cliff and gorge were Grouse Canon and Juan.

From an open space whence he could look down a long barren slope bright with the moonlight he saw far off the hurrying figures which he knew to be Andros and his men. Drawn near Grouse Canon, Bill did not turn down into the hollow to find Juan; instead he dismounted, tied his horse in a small grove of mountain cedars, and made his way along the rocky ridge on foot. He knew where the riders would of necessity come; he arrived at the spot well ahead of them and nested down among the boulders. When Andros, riding a horse's length in advance of the others came within range Bill Mountain sent the first warning bullet hissing over his head. Andros came to a dead halt, his men stopping in a clump behind him.

Bill Mountain supplemented the bullet's message with the shout:

"If you bunch up close together that way I can

get two-three at one shot maybe: Scatter, you rats; I'm starting in!"

Andros rapped out a sharp command, and his men reined about and scurried off to a safer distance. Andros himself did not move.

"I mean it, Andros," Bill called out to him. "From now on we're death to trespassers on Montana land."

Andros surprised him by swinging down from his saddle. For a moment his form was hidden behind the bulk of his horse and Bill fully expected a shot over the animal's back. But Andros had something else in mind. A second later he stood out, clearly revealed, holding his rifle high over his head.

"See it?" said Andros. "Well, here goes." He threw the weapon from him as far as he could and Bill both saw the flash of moonlight upon the barrel and heard the clang as it struck among the rocks. "I want to talk with you, Bill," said Andros then. "I'm coming ahead." He took the first swift step forward.

"Hold it!" Bill called back warningly. "I'm done talking with you, neighbour. Rifle or no rifle, I'm going to plug you dead centre if you don't back up."

Andros laughed at him, retorting good-humouredly:

"You can't do it, Bill. You can't plug an unarmed man. It's not in you. I could do it and would jump at the chance. Different breed of cattle, huh? Well, that gives me an advantage I'd say. And here I come. With my hands up, too!"

He continued to advance steadily and the light was sufficient to show how both his arms were high above his head. They stuck up rigidly like two sticks balanced on his shoulders.

"Because a man throws away one gun it doesn't mean that he's no longer heeled," said Bill thoughtfully. "Watch how you walk, Andros. It would be unlucky for you if you stumbled over a stone; I'd think you were going for your belt gun and, bingo, I'd let you have it!"

"Shucks," said Andros, as cool and good-humoured as ever. He stopped and said, "Well, here goes my forty-five, too. Please teacher can I take my hand down long enough to pitch it into the discard?"

He was being watched narrowly; he was close enough now for each gesture to be plain, so close that almost the expression on his face could be read. He lifted his revolver out of its holster and pitched it several feet aside of the trail. It began to look as though Andros came in peace.

Yet Bill Mountain did not trust him. After last night's talk there should be small unfinished business between them that could be in any way advanced by further words. So, watchful for trickery, he laid his rifle aside and replaced it with one of those weapons from a shoulder holster in which he put greater confidence in an argument at close quarters. It suggested itself to him that all that Andros wanted was to spy out the land, to seek to ascertain whether Bill was all alone or backed up perhaps by Juan and still others. Bill himself was confident that Juan was nearby, perhaps even now hearing their voices and making a guarded way up from the canon, and that Ben Hodge and some of the White Water men were well on their way. Therefore he assured himself that Andros would not learn much and that what little he did glean would only lead him into error. Nevertheless he meant to take no chances.

"You'll keep your hands up," he said sharply. "And you'll stop right where you are! It's close enough for a talk. Maybe you're right and I haven't the heart to plug you dead centre as I promised, but so help me I'll cripple you if you come a single step closer."

"Oh, all right," said Andros, still good-humouredly, and stopped. "Only if I meant to start something do you think I'd send my men back and tie into it all alone? I tell you, I just want a couple of words."

"Let's have 'em then."

"Right. You see, I've got something else to do besides chase all over the world after that hang-dog brother of yours. After all Juan's a sort of side-issue. I've got a proposition to make you."

He lowered his hands only enough to clasp them behind his head. The simple gesture was innocuous enough—until it quite completed itself. And the completion did not come until Andros had spoken a few more words. He said: "You see, Bill, both you and I have a lot more at stake than—" Then it came. Andros, before he had started to walk forward, had shoved a second pistol into the neck-band of his shirt, its butt sticking up behind his head. When he appeared to clasp his hands behind his head he was all set for instantaneous action. That action was as swift and true as the snap of a steel trap.

Both men fired. There were but the two shots which came so close together that at a little distance they sounded like one. Andros' men sat irresolute a moment, then began gradually to move forward. Ben Hodge, panting up the ridge, began laying down a barrage of rifle fire. Juan from the shadows fifty yards above the spot where Bill and Andros had engaged each other, emulated Ben Hodge and for a moment the two rifles set the echoes wild with their crisp, vicious reports.

Andros' men scattered and one of them yelled: "Buck! Buck! What's the game?" They were at a loss, since there had been no time for Andros to coach them. Also, in the saddles and on the upland, they constituted targets hard to miss while they could catch no glimpse of the men among the rocks who were pouring lead among them.

While they hesitated the sound of rushing hoofs told where the men from White Water rode in haste on their bare-backed range horses. Ben shouted to them and to Juan; he called to Bill and when he had no answer he turned all his interest upon Andros' men. They began to draw off, though reluctantly. Ben, cursing them with tears running down his face, yet held a rifle in the steadiest of hands. When he saw a man double forward and slip loosely out of the saddle, Ben laughed at the sight and still laughing, still with tears on his weathered face, he kept on shooting. He knew that Bill Mountain was out of the fight and there was no need to ask why.

Andros' horse, caught between two fires, started to run. The whipping stirrups and lashing bridle reins bred panic and the animal went plunging out of sight down a steep slope. Ben Hodge laughed at that too—the sight of Andros' empty saddle.

"He's dead," choked Juan. He knelt and his eyes flashed wildly in the moonlight as he looked up at Ben Hodge. "Andros has killed Bill."

"And Bill killed Andros," said Ben. "They were not ten feet apart."

Juan leaped up and climbed to the top of a big boulder in full sight of all.

"Come on, you dirty dogs," he yelled excitedly

and began firing across the broken lands at the shadowy figures of Andros' hesitant men. "It is Juan Montana, the man that you want. Come and get him! Come on, I tell you, come on!"

A rain of bullets poured about him. Ben caught him savagely by the arm, jerking him back.

"Come down, you damn fool!" he snapped. "Bill's not dead—not so soon. Keep your hair on. We've got to get him home and see what we can do for him. You've gone off your head, man."

"Bill? Not dead?" whispered Juan. He threw himself down on his knees again. "Bill! Bill, old man. It's Juanito calling you. Bill—"

Bill Mountain's eyes opened and he said weakly, "All right, kid." He managed to move his hand and pressed it against the wound in his chest.

Juan said unsteadily: "Sure it's all right, Bill. We're taking you home—we'll have a doctor in no time—"

"Andros?" muttered Bill. He thought that he was going out, and a man liked to know whether he was to have company.

"You drilled him clean, Bill," said Ben Hodge.

Bill tried to grunt his satisfaction with the news and a sort of twisted smile twitched his lips.

"Dead?" he asked.

Ben hurried where Andros lay and brought back the report:

"Not yet, Bill. But you nailed the snake proper.

Now take it easy; a lot of the boys are almost here and we'll have you home in two shakes."

Bill began muttering. Both Ben and Juan leaned very close.

"Doctor—" he muttered. "Andros—ask him—"

Ben, who knew his beloved boss so well, understood; at any other moment Ben would have rebelled like a bronco bucking stiff-legged. But now he only swore under his breath and obeyed the command. He went again to Andros who, lying on his back, looked up at him somewhat blankly.

"Want to lie here and die?" snapped Ben. "We're taking Bill home and getting a doctor. He's inviting you. Or you can have your men cart you back to your own dump. That strikes me as the thing to do."

Andros stared at him a long time. It was with a tremendous effort that he made his faint, gasping reply.

"I'd die before my boys could—Montana's closer—sure, Ben—take me along—"

They took him up gently, for after all they thought that he was dying, and placed him close to Bill behind the boulder. Explanations were shouted to his men; they took Ben Hodge's word for everything, threw down their guns and came to lend a hand. It was a full two miles down to White Water and a truck.

Penelope heard the men returning. There was

one who raced on ahead of the others and who tarried only long enough at White Water to cry out the dreadful news: the Senor Montana and that Andros had met and both were dying if not dead already. Yet he was speeding on to the old home to telephone for a doctor.

The others, a slow, sorrowful procession, came later. She saw lanterns gathering about the truck. Consuela, weeping, was running with a mattress while Eugenio and Josefa hurried after her with armfuls of blankets. Penelope, already dressed and anxiously awaiting news, ran with them. She stood with the back of her hand pressed tight against her lips, her eyes made round with agony, as a limp form was lifted tenderly by many men to the bed in the truck. She saw Juan then; in the soft light of moon and lanterns his eyes seemed deep, dark liquid pools.

"Juan—tell me—"

"Senorita!" He caught at her arm and held her in a nervous grip. "It is my brother Bill—you understand? All because of me! They are taking him home—they are sending for a doctor! Good God, how slow everything is! There is no time—"

A man climbed to the seat of the truck. Another joined him. This other was Ben Hodge. Juan, who had dropped his horse's reins to come to Penelope, now sprang into the truck bed, sitting down at Bill's side. Penelope climbed up after him but instead of sitting she stood erect and put her hand on Ben Hodge's shoulder.

"Tell me," she whispered.

"Oh, it's you, Miss Loring? Bill's hurt pretty bad. I've sent a man on to try to get a doctor and a nurse." Her fingers had clutched convulsively and he laid his big hand gently on them. "We'll pull him through and don't you worry," he said crisply. "It takes one hell of a lot of killing to wipe out a man like Bill."

"I'm going with you. I can help. I'm not a nurse but—I'll send for Patty! We'll have her with us to-morrow! Patty Lane's the best nurse in Albuquerque."

"Sit tight," said Ben. "We're going."

Then she too crouched down and the truck started, moving slowly. She on one side and Juan on the other of the quiet blanketed form, the two looked fearfully at each other. For the first time she saw Andros, though at the time she didn't know who he was; both she and Juan ignored him, bending low over Bill Mountain's white upturned face.

"Pray for him, Penelope," whispered Juan.

His hand groped for hers. She squeezed it tight. She could not answer him otherwise but Juan knew that she was praying.

CHAPTER 13

Penelope came face to face with the most breathtaking fact in the world. Sudden comprehension was like an electric current. She felt a thrill go tingling through her from head to foot, she knew that her cheeks had turned crimson—she harboured for that one instant the panicky thought that it was common knowledge that she had gone rosy to the tips of her toes. She ran out of the room. It was pure flight, headlong and somewhat blindly blundering at that; she careened full tilt into an amazed Mrs. Richards, gasped something quite incoherent, and bolted for her room, that room which she had occupied the first night in Montana Valley.

That first time it had been an artist's dream captured on canvas which had drawn her; this time it was a higher Artist's dream framed in a mirror to which she sped. She looked at herself with all the intentness she could have brought to bear upon a girl whom she had never seen before but in whom she had some profound interest. It is no very great exaggeration to state that it was a little stranger who glowed back at her in reflection.

Those were Penelope Loring's eyes, as big and sweet and softly grey as there could be any excuse for any girl having, yet they were different. They had never looked back at her—or at anyone—like that! They shone like stars on a soft warm summer night. That was Penelope Loring's saucy red mouth, but there was a different smile upon it making it tenderer and more downright alluring and provocative than it had ever been until this amazing and delicious moment. She had never been so lovely and she knew it, and something sang within her that this was a new, freshly born loveliness which had come to stay. She pressed the back of her fingers against her flushed face, cuddling her cheek against them, and kept on smiling.

Mrs. Richards tapped hesitantly at her door.

"Is anything the matter, Miss Loring? Juan says that you ran out of the room and—"

Penelope answered her laughingly. Mrs. Richards cocked her head aside and perked up her brows at such spontaneous gaiety.

"It's nothing—I just remembered something—tell Juan I'll be back before he can roll a cigarette."

She had been giving Juan a glass of water. It was now a week since Bill Mountain and Buck Andros had been brought to the house, dying as all thought. Juan, too, had been a bad case what with the exertion of his flight from under the noses of Andros and the deputy sheriff and the shifting of his bandage and the blood loss with minor complications which it brought about. Juan, as well as the others, was still in bed. As she played nurse—it was late afternoon and the short school day was over—Juan had dropped a remark or two which were not intrinsically of such stuff as makes history.

"You are so adorable, Penelope," he had said, looking up at her and smiling.

"That's nice," Penelope had returned, as lightly as you please.

"My brother," added Juan, as one quoting the highest authority, "says that you are the one and only honest-to-God girl in the world."

And that was the remark that did make history. Water was slopped over from a full glass to Juan's bed and Penelope heard the music of the spheres.

Was this the way love came? Not according to all the rules of the game. It should burst out at first sight or, missing that, it should be the slow blossoming of time, of years maybe and of an extended acquaintance with the gradual commingling of little interests upgathering into big. It had no earthly business sneaking up on one this way and then jumping out all unexpectedly like some stupid practical joker saying "Boo!" at you! And why hadn't she known before?

She had been too overcharged with dread, for one thing; too weary and anxious; too much on the run to help when there was any help to be given; too heavy with sleep when the lulls came.

A clicking of high heels sounded in the hall and Penelope snatched wildly at a book, made a leap for the bed and did her best to give an imitation of a girl absorbed in last spring's best seller. The door opened without any formality of a knock, and Patty Lane breezed in with the remark on her lips: "Golly, girl, but my feet hurt." She went to the mirror and began tightening a honey-coloured curl about her finger. Penelope looked up at her swiftly, glanced down at her book and said indifferently:

"How is he now, Patty?"

Patty spun about and made a face at her.

"So you've gone and done it, Pen. I said you would."

"Gone and done what?" asked Penelope innocently.

"Climbed to a high place," said Patty, "and made your swan dive. Took a long breath, gave yourself a shake and went overboard head first ker-splash into the puddle of love!"

Penelope flooded her with derisive laughter.

"Laugh, darn you, laugh," said Patty serenely. "Think you can fool one of my wide experience? Where do you keep your powder puff? My nose gets as shiny up here in the mountains as a glass eye in the moonlight."

Saucy and pert and very piquant was Patty Lane, petite and blue-eyed with a mutinous red mouth, alert from her high heels to the tips of her nicely kept and extremely capable finger tips.

"You're not in your uniform," said Penelope.

"Look at what I'm up against!" sniffed Patty. "You're a wickedly distracting little beauty and I've got a pug nose! Think I'm going to go marching about in a blue and white starchy looking rig with you floating about in that sleezy rag that doesn't pretend to hide the fact that you are as God made you. You wrecker! You know darned well that a glimpse of you would send Venus yelling for somebody to lend her an overcoat and yet you make remarks if I climb out of a uniform and drape myself in something that maybe will draw attention from my pug."

"You and your pug nose! It's pert, if you want the name for it and the property of a pert and perfectly upsetting little flirt, Patty Lane, and you know it. What's more you're a Red Indian—"

"Dew tell," grinned Patty.

"—and if I catch you trying to add his scalp to your string—"

"You're a funny kid." Patty sat down on the foot of the bed, kicked her shoes across the room and began massaging her feet. "As long as you were all set for a high dive why did you have to pick out a great lumbering, gawky cowboy that—"

"He's not lumbering!" cried Penelope warmly. "He isn't gawky. He's no cowboy, either—he's a *caballero*! I don't know what you are talking about anyway. And I'm no more in love than—"

"Than Juliette was when she swallowed the druggist's prescription. As if I didn't know the minute I heard your voice over the long distance telephone!" She mimicked: " 'Oh, Patty, Patty, hurry, hurry, *hurry! Listen,* Patty! Can't you hear me? Can't you *understand?* It's a matter of life and—*No, no, no!* I can't say it! He *mustn't* die! He mustn't, he mustn't, *he mustn't!* He is so *wonderful!* Oh, *Patty—*' "

"And," said Penelope reproachfully, "you made me beg and beg, saying something perfectly maddening about another case—"

"Maddening or not," retorted Patty, "I've got to go on that other case the minute I get word and you know it. It's my best chum, next to you, and her first baby, and we promised each other when we were probationers to stand by."

Penelope looking dreamily through an open window which gave upon the garden, wasn't listening. Why hadn't she herself known all along? It seemed now much more than a mere week ago—but then it had been no ordinary week at all—since the jolting truck had brought him home. She had been so desperately fearful! A man whom she had never seen, a commonplace, stolid fellow named George Ladd came in, dressed in faded overalls and dirty boots, smelling of the stable, and took charge. How her heart sank when she took him all in and she learned who and what he was. Bill Montana's veterinarian! And to think that Bill's life depended upon his stodgy hands and his knowledge of the anatomy of horses! She had wanted to caution him, to be at his side every instant so that she could watch and guard against clumsiness. And George Ladd had snapped at her and shoved her out of the way, rolling up his sleeves on thick reddish arms—and had laboured so skilfully and to such glorious effect that in her eyes he was no longer stolid and stupid but quite a shining person, and brought stable smells as sweet as new mown hay.

As he had striven with Bill Montana so did he work with Buck Andros and with Juan. Then the doctor had come; he had been located at a thirty mile distant ranch where he was aiding in the advent of twins—quite as though the world weren't already sufficiently populated! Why did people have to choose a time like this to have babies? The physician, a tall red-headed young fellow whom they called Doc and whose name turned out to be Crawford, talked things over with the phlegmatic George Ladd, nodded his approval and went to work where Ladd had left off. For three days and nights the man hardly ate or slept; he snapped people's heads off as only dictators of his profession can; he gimleted at the new nurse, Patty Lane, with a frosty eye; he drove her like a slave and scolded her like a bad child; he jeered at her when she grew white under the strain and later on patted her on her fluffy head; he sized Penelope up with a dissecting sort of eye, cut shrewdly through the outer husks of a rather distracting pulchritude and arrived at the canny decision that she was a young person of nerve and stamina, whereupon he made use of her services equally with Patty's.

"My God, what a physique that man has, and what nerves!" he said when, after probing mercilessly for a fragment of clothing which had been driven along into the wound he came out of Bill Montana's room.

"And therefore," said Penelope steadily, "you're going to be able to pull him through!"

Dr. Crawford glared at her but it was only abstractedly; he was tugging moodily at his long lower lip.

"Some men are harder to kill than others. It's like this: You take a dinner plate and shoot a hole in it and it all goes to smash, doesn't it? But you take a piece of sole-leather, poke nineteen bullet holes in it and it hangs together."

"So does a piece of fine silk," said Penelope.

He looked at her in his surgeonly way, always laying back outer flaps of tissue, probing.

"Get me a drink of whisky," he commanded curtly. He was hollow-eyed and irascible from sleeplessness, fatigue and strain. "Then come along to lend a hand while I see about John

Andros. It's like Bill Mountain to try and kill a man, then drag him home and try to heal him. After the dirty trick Andros pulled on him, too!"

When three days later he made them write down his detailed instructions and then he took his departure, he was more like a gigantic red wasp than ever; no man had ever laboured harder.

"They've got their chances, both of them," he said angrily, quite as though this were in despite of all his efforts to the contrary and he hated to admit defeat. "If you girls have got any sense and do your jobs right both the damned fools may live long enough to shoot each other again and put some more money in my pocket. Juan's out of the woods already. Send for me if you want me; in any case I'll drop in day after to-morrow. Good-bye, Miss Loring; you've got the making of a corking nurse in you. Bye-bye, Patty Pert; you'd make a swell blacksmith's assistant."

Patty showed him the tip of a red tongue. But gazing thoughtfully after him she admitted: "He's a marvel, the devil! Why do you suppose an artist like him is satisfied with turning into a country hick?"

"Hick?" said Penelope. "With you, I suppose a hick is any man who has too much sense to be content with being one of the scramble down in the jungles."

"Jungles?" demanded Patty. "Oh, yeah?"

Every day Buck Andros' foreman Dave Rance,

came for a report. He was a swaggering, insolent young desperado, with cruelly hard blue eyes which had a way of paying the most impudent of compliments when they went roving over either of the girls. This Dave Rance cooled his heels on the front porch until Ben Hodge was at liberty; then the two of them went together to Andros' room where Ben remained during the two or three minute visit. Ben was taking no chances; he did not believe that Andros knew that Juan was in the house; but he did know that Andros was never to be trusted, even though it still was a question whether he would live or die.

"Thanks to my old friend, Don Bill Quixote," said Andros before the end of the week, "I'm going to make the grade with bells on. It would be funny, eh, Ben, if I got well and Bill pegged out!"

"You'd hang as sure as water runs down hill," Ben assured him grimly.

"Let's hope old Bill pulls through then—And I was dead sure I was nailing the son-of-a-gun square through the heart."

Close enough to the heart had both men shot and the two wounds were almost identical in all particulars. Both had shot a trifle high so that the bullets had torn into the upper chest almost midway between the arch of the aorta and the point of the left shoulder. Given a little less magnificence of physique on both their parts and a shade longer delay in that first-aid treatment at the deft hands of George Ladd and a subsequent skill lacking the artistry which was Dr. Crawford's, the Montana-Andros feud must inevitably have been at an end before now.

"As you go out, Ben," said Andros, "ask Miss Loring to step in."

Ben Hodge, tightening his lips, stalked out, but it was Mrs. Richards whom he dispatched to the wounded man's room. Andros, however, would have none of her and damned her out of his sight. In the end he had his way and Penelope came. All that he wanted was a glass of water but he swore he would die of thirst before he took it from any hand but hers. He called her Pretty Penelope; he began making love to her when another man would have thought only of his own perilous case.

"I loved you the minute I saw you, my dear," he said quite simply.

His words brought no warmth of colour to her cheeks, but instead there were times when they turned her cold and white to the lips.

"There is no earthly reason why you should talk like this to me, Mr. Andros," she told him frigidly. "It doesn't amuse me in the least."

"It isn't meant to amuse," he returned swiftly. "Look into my eyes, girl!"

She did and looked away hurriedly. At the moment his eyes were honest enough, though she had thought there was no sincerity in his warped soul. He was not pretending, he was playing no part, he was not flirting with her as he had flirted with so many girls. For once the man was in dead earnest and in his eyes there was a look which there is no counterfeiting.

With Patty he did amuse himself and Patty coquetted with him to her singing heart's content.

"He's the handsomest thing unhung," Patty informed Penelope quite as though her friend had no eyes of her own. "And I don't believe he's half the bad hombre that you all try to make out. You're just goofy over your mountain man, and because he and Buck have got hot-headed and tried to blot each other out you nail all the wickedness to Buck Andros. He's rather a dear. Maybe I'll just let myself go—there are other things than just being a nurse all one's life."

Penelope tweaked her arm and said indignantly: "If I thought that you meant a word of that!"

"And why not?" demanded Patty airily. "A girl's got to fall sometime, hasn't she? Of course, there's Juan—I adore him, don't you? If I don't get called away pretty soon on my other case, well—" She laughed and began humming: "It's Springtime in the Rockies."

Penelope began to look troubled. She hoped that Patty would adore Juan; it was so much safer than getting too deeply interested in Buck Andros.

“Time to feed the animals,” said Patty with a glance at the watch on a shapely wrist.

Penelope went thoughtfully to the kitchen. Outside she saw old José standing like a statue, his unwinking eyes fixed upon Bill Mountain’s window. There he would stand by the hour. During the first few days and nights there had always been a crowd of Bill’s people watching the house, and even when the time came that the men reluctantly went once more about their work there lingered on the women and children, a silent and tense gathering, awaiting patiently any word from the house. The scant tidings which came out to them were carried on running feet: “He is not any worse!” “He is drinking some water now!” “Maybe he is a little bit stronger!” “He is hungry and that is a fine sign!” Alone of them all old José never asked a question, never gave any sign in his copper-mask face and now, with the others beginning to think of other things, stuck at his post. Penelope began to love the old fellow for his devotion. At five o’clock he would come to the house and be admitted to Bill’s room. Bill would glance at the bedside chair and old José would make a ceremony of sitting down. It was a part of a small drama re-enacting itself daily. At times José would say two words, at others he would come and go in absolute silence.

The broth on the stove began to hiss; Penelope came up out of her abstraction, filled a cup and carried it to Bill's room. The sight of him plucked at her heart strings, he was so gaunt and weak, his eyes seemed so inordinately large, his cheeks so hollow under the growth of black beard. Only his mouth was the same and it smiled at her.

"I knew you were coming," said Bill. "I can tell your step a mile off."

"A full mile? Are you sure you're not confusing my tread with Crusader's?"

She fed him with a spoon and he was faintly amused.

"I've given you the devil of a deal, dragging you up into all this trouble of ours," he said when the spoon rested in the empty cup. "Why do you go to all this trouble? You ought to make Mrs. Richards or Patty do the dirty work. They're paid for it."

"I enjoy waiting on you," said Penelope serenely, "but if you would prefer the others I'll let them bring you your broth."

"What you bring me is always nicer, tastier you know, than the stuff they feed me," he admitted.

"You know, Bill Montana, that it all comes out of the same pot," said the matter-of-fact Penelope.

He appeared surprised. That was funny. Honestly, no joshing, somehow it had always seemed to him that she had the knack of seasoning things just right!

She put the cup on the table and sat down beside him.

"You are really a prize patient," she smiled approvingly.

"Nothing of the sort. I'm just a tough old trooper who's used to a lot of rough and tumble and thrives on it."

"Valiant old trooper—the sort it's fun to nurse."

"You're an angel with all the trimmings, white wings and harp and everything." He patted her hand which touched his pillow. "And I've given you a beastly slice of life up here. You ought to be having some real fun instead of working and worrying all the time. Here I am, flat on my back, when I ought to be keeping my promise to you."

"Promise?" She perked up her brows trying to remember.

A glint of humour brightened his sunken eyes.

"I said I'd go out and get you a *novio* to strum a guitar under your window and—"

She flared out at him then.

"It's not very complimentary to a girl, Mr. Montana, to indicate that you feel it necessary to go out and rope some young man for her. Thanks, but when I want a *novio* I can pick out one for myself!"

"I'll bet you can do your own roping!" he chuckled. "Ever think of making eyes at Juan? It would be great to keep you in the family, Penny-lope."

"Juan is quite the most charming youngster I ever knew," said Penelope musingly, and when she knew he wasn't looking cut sideways at him with her eyes. "But he is just a youngster, isn't he?" She appeared to be considering with all due gravity. "The one really fascinating man on the ranch is Buck Andros, you know. Do you suppose if a thoroughgoing girl took him in hand she could make a decent citizen out of him?"

"Good God!" he gasped. He looked at her, alarmed. "Penelope, you don't mean—"

"Oh, of course not," she laughed. She patted his nerveless hand gently, took up the cup and saucer, and said over her shoulder, "Shall I look in on you to-morrow?" and carried a lot of sunshine along with her out of the room. Bill, abruptly left to his own devices, stared at the ceiling frowningly.

CHAPTER 14

Wearing a tight little sphinx-like smile Penelope went about her affairs which began with dissimulation and ended with a pensive ride to her own place at White Water. The dissimulation conducted with delicate artistry and restraint was all for Patty; that clever young woman who had been so sure that she had nosed out a love story in its earliest stages, was to be set wondering and then begin to doubt her own astuteness. Penelope liked to carry her head high and what girl could do that if she published to the world that she had turned longing eyes upon a man who thought that it would be great to keep her in the family in a safe and conservative sister-capacity?

The enigmatic smile had developed into gay inconsequential laughter when she left Patty, ran down the steps and went swinging her hat and clinking her spurs on her way to the stable for her horse. Raimundo, the houseboy, wanted to bring her horse for her, but she only thanked him, dazed him with her smile and left him gazing worshipfully after her.

Tonito came charging down upon her on horseback as she reached the first gate. It was he who would open it for her; it was too heavy for a senorita like her and would make her pretty hands all rough. Though it was habit with Tonito to open all gates from the saddle he dismounted and stood at her side. Also there was another gate; he would walk along with her and open that one, too.

"But that is not necessary, Tonito! You must go on with whatever work you were doing. You do work sometimes, don't you?"

Tonito flashed his teeth at her. He was the old Tonito again, very gay, even to a red rose behind his ear. For him to have remained sad would have been for him to cease to be Tonito. Still, when she looked into his laughing eyes, she wondered. Of late there seemed to be a soberness behind Tonito's smile.

"You see, I had anyway to go to the stable," he said so glibly. "I must change to another saddle; this one hurts my poor little horse. And so I can get you your horse." He looked at her slyly. "You like this rancho, *no?* It is fun for you everyday to come and watch the thoroughbreds and the polo ponies?"

She nodded brightly. It was more than fun, it was sheer delight. She had struck up a warm friendship with George Ladd, the veterinarian; he saw her coming now and waved his greeting. He had taken her upon pleasant tours through his demesne, explaining everything and finding her an intelligent and sympathetic listener. Ladd prided himself on his position and on the results for which he was responsible. For was not this nucleus the very core and pride of the Montana properties? Here again Penelope thought of Montana Valley as a mountaineer's kingdom with Bill Montana delegating authority in various quarters; Ben Hodge as general foreman was a sort of caliph's grand vizier and certainly George Ladd about the stables and paddocks was a downright dictatorial lordling. In his small sphere, which by the way represented a lot of money, hundreds of thousands of dollars in fine horseflesh, the veterinarian was eagle-eyed and iron-handed.

His stables were the last whisper in modernity. The horses' quarters were clean, fresh, airy rooms; Ladd himself saw to the proper ventilation and roared like a wounded lion at the wrong windows opened creating a draught. It was his job not so much to doctor animals that were sick as to keep them all in the pink of glowing health. He showed Penelope the metal-lined boxes where the feed was kept; no dirty rats allowed. He came as close as any one man could to poking his finger into every forkful of hay that went up into the high lofts, and if you could have shown him a tiny clod of earth or a pebble or a handful of spoiled hay or grain he would have turned as red as a turkey gobbler. He pointed out in his office in the largest stable, the charts hanging on the wall; therein you had the pedigree of every four-footed living creature with which he condescended to deal. There were other charts, too, recording his experiments in feeding and in dosing, and still other charts containing records of performance. Ages and weights and habits, all were down in apple-pie order.

But most of all Penelope loved to watch the horses themselves, superb creatures, fine-limbed, satin-clad, high-headed beauties each in its own way.

"There comes an old friend of yours," chuckled Ladd.

It was Daybreak, a four-year-old bright bay stallion, a perfect glory of a horse from crest to hoof. He made Penelope shiver with a queer admixture of admiration and fear. Two husky Indian stable boys were leading him to his quarters after an airing; they had him between them with two ropes through his halter ring and neither of the boys for a single instant took his watchful eyes from the stallion. Daybreak, his flawless skin gleaming, his muscles rippling visibly, rolled as watchful eyes upon them, and at any moment Penelope looked to see him whip his lead-ropes out of their hands and become in action that engine of destruction which he looked even in half repose.

"The finest of the fine, the greatest blood-horse on the ranch," said Ladd pridefully. "He's going to be the daddy of some mighty nifty running stock. Bill's pet, by the way—or one of his pets anyhow. Bill's the only man that ever rode the old son-of-a-gun. How'd you like to fork Daybreak, Miss Loring?"

"No, thanks," laughed Penelope. "I'd far rather ride Mr. Montana's other pet, dear old Dixie. She is—"

"Look out!" roared Ladd. "My God—"

The big bay stallion, requiring the most flimsy excuse to run amuck, elected for sheer terror when a thoroughly familiar stable hand threw open a door suddenly and stepped out to shake a saddle blanket. Daybreak lunged backward and with a savage jerk broke free of his halter ropes and reared high on his hind legs, his teeth bared and wild eyes rolling wickedly. As his waving forefeet came earthward again, striking the hard-packed earth with a thunder clap, the two boys who had held him leaped back from beneath the menace of his hoofs; he lashed out with his heels and then it was that George Ladd shouted his warning, fearful for Penelope. Daybreak, however, was not concerned with her; head down and muzzle outstretched he charged the two boys who fled for their lives.

One of them, shut off from the barn into which the other had shot like a rabbit down its warren, sprang to a gate and slipped through barely in time to avoid the click of the big teeth. The gate was only closing when Daybreak struck it and went through with a crash and splintering of timbers. The frightened boy swerved with a swiftness which served him well and fairly hurled himself over the fence and back into the enclosure. Daybreak, trumpeting terror and defiance, shot straight out across the field.

And then Penelope saw two little brown babies coming hand in hand from the creek, waving their bunches of flowers. They saw the horse, stood riveted to the ground a moment, then screamed and fled. Even in that breathless instant she had cause to remember Bill Mountain's words when he had said, "I have some of the best riders in New Mexico." Of their number Tonito was surely one. As his toe found the stirrup his horse was off after Daybreak at a dead run. As he struck the saddle his rope was in his hand. A noose leaped into being, whistled about his head, widened and leaped through the air upon its unerring way to whip tight about Daybreak's rebellious neck. Others ran to his aid with other ropes, and presently they returned leading their captive and laughing.

"One more happy ending story," said George Ladd when Daybreak had been returned to his stall, examined for cuts and found without a scratch. "Busted a gate and didn't take a dent in his hide."

"He came close to wholesale murder," Penelope reminded him, "and all you think of is a possible bruise on him!"

"Guess you're right about picking Dixie for a friend," he conceded drily. "Daybreak's sure hell-on-four-legs."

Dixie was looking at her over a high fence and Penelope crossed a yard to stroke the velvet nose and to talk with this little lame mother of many splendid children. Dixie was now retired; she grew old and was one of the pensioners who had a rich field and a fine snug barn all to themselves. With the first cold days, Dixie at their fore, these would make their annual pilgrimage to another Montana ranch, one fifty miles away where a warm belt lay along the foothills.

"Bill's doing fine to-day, they tell me," said Ladd as she rejoined him. "Takes notice about things again, don't he?"

"Every day I tell him all the stable gossip," she informed him. "That's why I had to have a word or two with Dixie; they send love messages back and forth, you know."

He saw her mounted on the milk-white mare which Tonito had saddled for her—she was riding Lady May to-day—watched her ride away and then turned to look curiously at the bareheaded Tonito.

"What the devil were you doing here, anyhow?" he asked curtly. "Seems to me, young feller, that I spot you loafing around the stables a hell of a lot here of late!"

"Me?" asked Tonito innocently. "Oh no, senor.

Only this time I come to change my bridle, my poor little horse's mouth was getting sore."

Penelope, homeward bound, looked in on Ben Hodge at his office.

"Glad you rode by," he said as he came out. "I've got another letter from the country school superintendent and all is well-o. It seems we got off wrong-end-to in starting school first and then thinking about such matters as forming a school district, electing trustees and raising funds—"

"Bill Montana told me down in San Carlos that he was a trustee! Though I did have sense enough to realise when I got here that a school was just in the throes of being born, I didn't suppose—"

"Bill's such an awful liar," laughed Ben. "Any way, we're all according to Hoyle now and Bill of course will be elected chief. Funny cuss, ain't he?" He eyed her shrewdly. Just like Patty, thought Penelope, swiftly on guard.

"Now that you mention it, he is a funny cuss!" she laughed at him.

"Know what Bill needs most of anything?" asked Ben. He came down the steps and began wreathing his hand in her horse's mane.

"If Doctor Crawford knows what he's talking about—"

"Shucks. I don't mean that." He grinned at her as at the oldest of old friends. "There ought to be a nice little Mrs. Bill Montana knocking his head off before breakfast every morning. Why don't you roll those big innocent eyes at him, Penelope?"

Ben must have begun to suspect himself of being a wit, so gay and mirthful was Penelope's laughter at his suggestion.

"I'm only a girl, Ben," she reminded him when at last she fell to wiping her eyes. "If you want to domesticate Mr. Bill Montana that way you've got to scare up a Houyhnhnms for him!"

"Whoa!" cried Ben Hodge. "That's a new one on me."

" 'Whoa' is quite the right word to use when speaking to a Houyhnhnms," laughed Penelope. "You haven't forgotten your Gulliver's Travels, have you, Ben? Surely you'll remember that strange country where the people—"

"Were all horses with a name like a whinny!" Ben too began to laugh. "Guess you're right. Bill, the fool, never saw a girl in his life, but I thought—"

"*Adios*," smiled Penelope, and flashed away on Lady May looking as cool as apple blossoms in the shade.

As she rode by the house Mrs. Richards hastened down the front steps, fluttering her apron and hoo-hooing to her.

"Land sakes, child," exclaimed the housekeeper when Penelope had reined Lady May in at the garden wall. "You're a picture! All pink and white and shining on that frisky white horse!"

"Am I?" said Penelope gaily. "And that's why you stopped me?"

"Bill says you went off without telling him good night."

"I thought of something I had to do; I did go in a hurry. But I left my good nights with Patty."

"You and Bill haven't had a spat or anything have you?" asked Mrs. Richards hopefully.

"Mercy no! What put that into your head?"

"If I was you," said Mrs. Richards gravely, "I'd take time to say my own good nights. Bill's a sick man yet, remember; folks that way sometimes get notions. I think he'd like it—You weren't hurrying so you could ride along with *him,* were you?"

That stressed "him" certainly did not refer to Bill Mountain. Further Mrs. Richards was looking across the fields where someone had caught her eye. Penelope turned to see who it was and even at a distance recognised Andros' impudent and cocksure foreman, Dave Rance, arriving to make his daily call.

"Certainly not!" retorted Penelope, and her eyes darkened angrily; only yesterday Dave Rance had leered at her and suggested that some day he might ride along home with her. To-day he came at a later hour than usual and happened rather accurately to judge the time of her departure. "I'd ride with a wolf first," she concluded bluntly.

"Coming in, aren't you?" asked Mrs. Richards.

"Bill does want to see you about something or other."

"Yes, just for a minute." She dismounted, tied Lady May at the gate and the two turned to the house. As she entered Bill's room she heard Mrs. Richards sending Raimundo running for Ben Hodge whose orders were so strict in regard to any visitor to Buck Andros.

"Going?" said Bill, noting her hat and gauntlets. His eyes brightened but she sensed that they had been moody when she came in. "Lucky Penny! To be able to climb on top of a horse and ride! I'd give an arm to be up out of this and riding along with you!"

"At the rate you're improving it will be no time at all until you're in the saddle again." She smiled encouragingly. "I was down at the stables just now and a lot of your friends wished to be remembered. Old Crusader says, 'Tell Bill to hurry up and drop in on us.' Daybreak says, 'Regards to Bill and tell him if he doesn't come down pretty pronto and tell those polo ponies where to head in I'll bite 'em in the neck.' Dixie, the old darling, just sent love and kisses. She's the loveliest thing I ever saw."

She brought him a lot of bright gossipy items, making mention of Tonito and of George Ladd but saying nothing of the insubordination of Daybreak. As she ran on she noted how intently he was regarding her and for an instant had the uncanny feeling that he had read her mind and knew of the Daybreak affair too.

"What is it?" she asked, breaking off with her chatter. "You look at me—differently."

"I was just noticing," he said, smiling at her. "That's a nifty little riding outfit you're wearing to-day."

"This?" She began to laugh. "What ails the man! Why, Bill Mountain, this is the same rig I wore the day I came here, the only riding togs I've got, in fact!"

"That's funny," said Bill.

A moment later she insisted that she had much to do, said her smiling good night and left him. Instead of going back through the house she quitted the corridor by the back door which led to the rear garden and thus, instead of avoiding Dave Rance, as she planned, came face to face with him. The room allotted to Andros was at the far end of the hallway and Rance, having made his minute-long call with Hodge in impatient attendance, had gone outside in lockstep with Hodge at another door. But to-day he had left his horse behind the house and Penelope saw him striding towards her through the garden.

Just then Andros' window opened and Patty put her head out, looking mysteriously urgent. She drew Rance's attention with a sibilant whisper and at first Penelope thought to be the witness to a bit of empty flirtation. But Patty for once was strangely sober; a folded paper in her hand was thrust out, swiftly pocketed by Rance and she disappeared. The whole thing was almost as quick a process as the batting of an eye.

Penelope's first impulse on seeing Dave Rance was to turn back into the house, pointedly avoiding a man whom she detested. There was something, however, in Patty's act, an atmosphere rather than the deed itself, which kept her where she was, a tense spectator. Patty was so surreptitious about it all and so deeply in earnest.

Rance's eyes lighted up.

"How's the pretty little schoolma'am?" he asked, grinning at her, and came forward, his hand out. "Ready to ride, huh? So'm I! Let's go."

"That paper—" began Penelope, her wits at their nimblest, thinking of Ben Hodge's close espionage based on suspicions which he had every reason to harbour.

"Ain't gettin' jealous, are you?" laughed Rance. "Jus' because little Patty han's me a love-note?"

"A love-note?" Penelope's brows shot up and her eyes hardened.

Rance, the sort of man who for one reason and another was as full of conceit as a wet sponge is full of water, misunderstood. Why shouldn't a pretty girl grow jealous if he looked at another? Such things had happened with him before now.

"God!—You little beauty!" he said. Before she guessed his purpose he caught her in his arms.

Penelope gasped in consternation and as he tried to kiss her she turned her face aside and struck him across the mouth. Even so his arms only tightened and his lips brushed her cheek. She fought savagely, beating at his face, and all the while his relentless arms were crushing her and it seemed to her that the fool thought she was only pretending, that she wanted nothing better than his embraces. Panic-stricken she began to scream.

They were but a few steps from Andros' room and Andros was the first to hear. Over Dave Rance's shoulder Penelope saw Andros at the window, haggard and gaunt with eyes like a madman's.

"Rance!" he roared. "Damn you, Rance!"

Penelope broke free and stood panting, scrubbing at her sullied cheek with the back of her hand, her eyes bright with anger, her face scarlet. Dave Rance whirled about at Andros' call and stood glowering.

"Well, Buck, what's eatin' you?" he demanded doggedly. "Thought you was supposed to be sick in bed."

Andros, clutching at the window frame to save himself from falling, said thickly:

"You—you put your hands on her! For that, Dave Rance, I am going to kill you."

Rance laughed at him but slowly his face paled, only a smear of red remaining where Penelope had struck.

"Aw, hell, Buck," he said.

"I am going to kill you, so help me God," said Andros, and overpowered by weakness began sagging.

Then Ben Hodge came running about the corner of the house and Penelope hurried to him.

"He has a note," she said brokenly. "I saw it, Ben." She started to say that Patty had given it to him; instead she added hurriedly: "I saw it handed to him out of John Andros' window."

"Bully for you, Penelope," said Ben, and added grimly: "No harm done yet, I guess? He hasn't had time to read it? I'll get it."

He got it by the simple expedient of jabbing the muzzle of a forty-five into Dave Rance's ribs and making his wants known. He read it at a glance and then escorted Rance to his horse and said after him:

"You're not to come back, Rance. No Andros man is. If Andros lives I'll send him over the first day he can travel. If he dies, I'll let you know. Now get t' hell out of here."

Rance rode off as jauntily as he could manage, yet was obviously glad to be gone. Ben came back to Penelope and handed her the note. It said merely:

> "Juan is in the house. Get word to Webb Clark right away. Have him raid the place.
>
> "J. A."

Penelope, very much shaken, went into the house. She would stay here to-night after all rather than risk another meeting with Dave Rance. And she did want to talk with Patty.

CHAPTER 15

Bill Mountain commanded that Ben Hodge be sent for immediately.

"What's happened, Ben?" he demanded as his foreman brought a blank face into the room.

"Shucks, Bill," Ben told him with a fine assumption of carelessness, "you've got ears as long as a jackass. Well, too bad to disappoint you but nothing much happened. I had a word or two with Dave Rance and told him not to come back. I caught Andros trying to give him a high sign. That can't go on."

"What about Penelope?"

"She was the first to spot the by-play—"

"Come clean, Ben!" said Bill irritably. "Something else happened. What was it?"

"She saw Andros slip a note out of his window to Rance," said Ben. "She called and I came running. I got it before Rance could even look at it." His casual air began to forsake him; the angry blood fought for a place in his tanned cheeks and his eyes hardened. "That yellow dog that ought to have been left to die where you shot him hasn't got the sense of gratitude you'd expect to find in a tarantula. Somehow he found out that Juan was here, and tried to put Rance wise."

"Sure he didn't get the word across to Rance?"

"Dead sure. And there'll be no more of Andros' men coming over here to get it."

Bill nodded. Yet his eyes kept probing at Hodge and it was clear that he was not satisfied on all points.

"You're holding something back, Ben!"

"Nary. That's the whole story, far as I know it."

"It's nothing of the kind! Ask Penelope if she'll look in on me once more. She hasn't gone yet, has she? Go see, Ben."

Penelope sent word to him that she would come in a minute: she was changing from her riding things having decided after all to stay overnight. It seemed to Bill that she was longer than usual at her toilette; the fact was that she was subject to hot flushes of anger which at the moment played havoc with that smiling serenity one was supposed to carry into the rooms of the bedridden.

"You see," she said gaily when she came to Bill Mountain, "a girl is every bit as changeable as she is supposed to be. You did invite me to stay over until morning, didn't you?"

"Tell me what happened just now," he said, looking fixedly at her.

Like Ben Hodge she strove to dodge the issue, but it was no use.

"Damn it," he cut her off angrily, "if I can't have the truth told me here I'll get up and have it. I heard your scream and it gave me the shivers.

I barged out of bed and made a stab at getting to the door; by then it was all over and I toppled like a drunk. You were scared to death. Did Andros make some sort of a false move at you?"

In the end Penelope decided that it was better to tell him the truth than have him juggling feverishly with all sorts of wild conjectures. But her cheeks flamed as she told him.

"Dave Rance tried to hold you and kiss you! My God!" he raged. "A thing like him to touch you. And me flat on my damned back!"

He seemed to hold himself entirely blameworthy; it was all his fault that she was here and that such vermin as Rance and Andros trailed their slime about her. He was so deeply moved that Penelope felt a little pang at her heart and went swiftly to him, taking his nervous hand in both of hers.

"Don't be silly, Bill," she begged him. "It's all right. He didn't—Why he hardly touched me, and I slapped his face for him good and hard. Let's forget it."

He flung her hands away and reared up in bed, he glared at her out of the most terribly stern and angry eyes she had ever seen and she fell back from him, frightened.

"Damn Andros!" he shouted at her as though he damned her too along with him. "What right had he to take a hand? It was my place, mine I tell you! And here I lay like a broken-backed dog.

Send Ben back to me; I'll have Andros dragged off the ranch with a log chain tied to his legs. Send Ben to me, I tell you!"

Ben had been listening in the corridor and appeared while Bill was still roaring for him. With a firm hand he forced the sick man to lie quiet, then he and Penelope together strove to placate a patient who in a few moments had succeeded in undoing a week's work of faithful nursing. Penelope bit her lips and bent her head, trying to keep the tears back; her little adventure while doing her no harm had succeeded in getting two badly wounded men out of bed, had misplaced Bill's bandages, started a hemorrhage and thrown him into a fever. Patty, who had had so great a part in creating this condition, came in looking professionally capable, administered a hot drink and a sedative and thus made some small amends. It was her deft hands which examined the bandage and replaced it.

They left Bill lying white and grim-jawed, his eyes shut as he simulated sleep, and tip-toed into the hall.

"Darned babies, that's what they are," sniffed Patty, and fell to tapping a cigarette against a gleaming thumb nail. "All sick men. About as much reason as a two-year-old." She lighted her cigarette, glanced at Penelope through the smoke and encountered a pair of eyes filled with condemnation. Up shot Patty's amber brows. "Well, sister," she exclaimed, "what's your trouble?"

Penelope beckoned her out into the patio. "How could you do a thing like that, Patty?" she asked in a troubled voice.

"Me?" asked the innocent Patty. "Was I the girl who stuck a peach and cream face up to Dave Rance and asked to be kissed?"

"I don't refer to that and you know it!" said Penelope indignantly. "I've never asked any attentions from that thug and that's another thing you know. But that letter—to think that you would act like that! Patty, what made you?"

Patty flushed up and her big blue eyes gleamed defiance.

"Well, what of it?" she demanded. "There are two sides to everything, if anybody should ask you, my dear. One of them is Buck Andros' side. Here he's corked up in the house of his enemies, down and out with a bullet through him and he can't have a word in private with one of his men but old Nosey Ben Hodge must be earing in on it. Now I'm not claiming that Buck Andros is anybody's little white pet angel but what man of this outfit is? I guess he's no worse than the rest."

"He is!" said Penelope wrathfully. "He's a sneak and a murderer—he tried to kill Bill in the most cowardly trickery—"

"If you listen to Bill, yes! But how about listening to Buck's side of it?"

Penelope caught her savagely by the arm.

"Do you know what was in that note?" she demanded hotly.

"And don't care—and I'll thank you not to pinch my arm off like a crab," said Patty.

"It was a letter telling that Juan is here. Buck Andros would have died but for Bill's bringing him here and giving him every chance and now he turns square around and tries to betray Bill's brother—Oh, the man is an unthinkable beast!"

"If he was dying," retorted Patty, making a great ado over rubbing her arm, "who was it shot him? If Buck did peach on Juan, well then what has Juan been up to that he's dodging the law? If you're so darned anxious to call people murderers—how about Juan?"

Penelope stared at her incredulously. But she knew her Patty of old and began to understand. Patty, the best natured of individuals under nearly all circumstances, did own a blazing temper which now and then broke bounds; Penelope thought of Daybreak's sudden rebellion. The whole truth of the matter, and Penelope was astute enough to guess it, was that Patty had committed an act of which she was heartily ashamed now that she glimpsed its consequences, and that outburst of hers was shame's mask. Penelope ran her arm about her friend's stiff shoulders and the result partook of magic; the shoulders slumped, a cigarette was flung violently down on the tile floor, there was a sob and Patty burst out crying.

"I'm such a darned little fool, Pen; I didn't know—that Buck Andros is a dirty devil and I'll—I'll put rat poison in his broth. He t-told me that he was just writing ab-bout some ranch business and d-didn't want Ben Hodge to know all his private affairs. The liar! I'll never go near him again."

But like many another nurse who has quitted a patient's room vowing she'd never go back into it she did return and it was perhaps Patty's skilled hands which kept the man from dying. He, like Bill Mountain, had overtaxed himself and had brought on a relapse which came close to being his undoing. That night was one of hushed voices and hurrying feet, of almost constant ministration and of sleeplessness and anxiety for the household. The only one to know nothing of it was Juan who had been taking his siesta and slept soundly through the afternoon episode.

After a night of strain and many cups of coffee Penelope returned listlessly to White Water and to her little school. The children, a dozen or so of them, bright eyed and noisy and overflowing with animal spirits, were a handful and taxed her. She set some of the bigger girls to helping the little ones, gave them generous recesses and managed to live through one of the longest days of her life.

Convalescence which had been so rudely retarded was gradually resumed. Dr. Crawford came, scolded, ordered and went, and admitted that mountaineers took a lot of killing. Returning a week later he declared both men out of the woods and on the up-trail, provided they didn't fly into a passion and go to breaking heads before he gave them their clearance papers.

Penelope called every afternoon but always returned to her own place for the night. During her few bright minutes at Bill's bedside, neither of them made any reference to what had happened. Of Andros she was determined to see nothing; she hoped never to be forced to speak with him again as long as she lived.

During these days there was always someone dropping in at the ranch house to pay a friendly call; frequently enough, having come to see their neighbour, Bill Mountain, they remained to fall more or less seriously in love with one or both of the two girls. Oliver Duckworth rode over from his ranch on the far slope of the mountains; Jerry and Tom Hunter, two bronzed, level-eyed young ranchers from Green Valley, took turns in coming over every three or four days; a bald-headed old prospector from Mesa Alta proved himself to be the most accommodating of fellows. He offered Bill his services freely, volunteering to go strangle Andros in his bed, and he lost no time at all in offering Penelope a half share in his fabulous mine—as yet undiscovered—if she'd but take him along with it. Penelope refusing him with thanks he took up the matter with Patty.

"Toddle back to see me, old timer, after you've found your bonanza," Patty laughed at him. "What you want to learn is to cut your bait before you go fishing."

When old Dan Westcott put in an appearance he made a point of stopping at the stable for a five minute chat with George Ladd before going up to the house; George taking a hint that was as broad as any one of his barn doors sent a boy running with word that the law, as impersonated in the old sheriff, was at hand, and Juan Montana had best have his door shut.

"It's this-away," said Dan soberly. "I been sheriff quite a spell an' I know the law; I ain't got any call to go searchin' a man's house unless I got a search warrant or happen to know that the man I'm after is lurkin' on said premises. Now in the case of Juan Montana, I heard a rumour las' week that the boy was seen headin' for the Mexican border an' goin' fast. That idea that he'd hang aroun' here, knowin' I'm after him, makes me laugh. I expec' he's a thousan' miles on his way by now."

He explained his theory to Bill and got a hearty handshake for payment whereupon he grinned and tucked in the corners of his crafty old mouth.

"You'll be jinglin' spurs in no time a-tall, kid," he said, and went to look in on Andros. He enjoyed standing in Andros' doorway and smiling benignly on him.

"You're a hell of a feller," he chuckled, "thinkin' you could beat Bill Mountain shootin'! Better learn your lesson an' leave him alone after this, Buck. He'll get mad some day an' ruin you. Right now if he wanted to go to law he could have you arrested for two-three things, trespass an' assault with a deadly weapon an' not mindin' your business better. You know how it is, Buck; if he swore out a complaint I'd have to gather you in an' cart you over to the hoosegow right now."

"You!" jeered Andros contemptuously. "You doddering old fool, you couldn't gather a bunch of wild flowers."

Old Dan pushed his broad hat back and cocked his thumbs into his belt from which depended two old revolvers whose black walnut grips were slick and shiny from his calloused old hands.

"It's only by the grace o' God an' Bill Mountain's *caballero* spirit that you're alive," he said stonily, "an' either one o' them sweet factors is apt to peter out mos' any time. Now bein' an observant sort o' cuss I've noticed as how Bill mos' usually stomps on his own rats, but the Good Lord has a way of pickin' Him a proxy. So be it as He picks me, Buck Andros, I'll give praise where praise belongs an' try to keep a steady han' as I line up my sights."

To Bill he said almost tearfully, "Why 'n

hell don't you let me cart him off to gaol, Bill? He's as full o' poison as a bottle o' strychnine. On the way I'd let him grab a gun, an' I'd kill him deader'n a mackerel for resistin' an officer. Might save a lot o' bother that way."

"Thanks, Dan old sport," said Bill. "But it looks as though this were his fight and mine." And Dan Westcott, knowing that it could not be otherwise, swore at him affectionately and went his way.

As he quitted the house the sheriff was hailed by Ben Hodge.

"Patten's here," said Ben. "Just drove up from Pueblo."

"Who?" said Dan, still woolgathering.

"Clay Patten. The man Bill has at work on the Pasmore killing."

"Oh, him! Sure, I know. What's he here for? Got anything on anybody?"

"He wants to see Bill, that's all I know. It struck me that you might stick around until we find out what brings him."

"Lead me to him," said Dan gruffly. "I know Patten from halo to hoof."

Clay Patten's halo was a round shiny bald spot fringed with thin pale hair. He was a small urbane individual with a tight mouth and shrewd blue eyes, and it was hard guessing his age; he might be thirty or fifty. The certain thing about him was that he knew his way about. No man ever short-changed Clay Patten.

"No, Dan. I'm not doing any talking right now," he said the instant he saw the light in Westcott's eye. He shook hands, then returned to the chair which he had shoved into a corner of Ben's office. "I just blew in for a little chat with Mr. Montana."

"Suits me not to do any talkin' about the Pasmore business," said Dan, though it suited him not in the least. "But speakin' general of other matters, haven't got any line yet, have you, on the missin' heiress? Meanin' Johnny Lane's girl?"

"I find it pays," said Patten, "to do one thing at a time. This second matter I have passed along to my partner. It's real pleasant weather we're having lately, isn't it?"

Presently he went up to the house for his talk with Bill Mountain. The sheriff and Ben Hodge watched him go and watched for his return; old Dan was first to catch sight of him and went straightway to learn what he could from Bill himself.

"What did he have to say, Bill?" he asked.

Bill, looking inordinately tall stretched out on his bed, and very gaunt, lifted clouded eyes to him.

"If it wasn't for you, ol' timer, always sayin' there's none better'n Clay Patten," he said heavily, "I'd kick him off the job an' put a good man to work. He hasn't anything definite to report; he came to ask a lot of ol' questions all over again; he wants a talk with Juan. Damn him, he wants to stick aroun' here three-four days, jus' visitin' an restin' up!"

Dan's eyes, not in the least like Bill's, grew bright with interest as he exclaimed:

"Leave him be, Bill! Let him stick as long's he likes. It's a good sign." He seemed so downright satisfied with things that Bill tried to hope his confidence in Patten was not misplaced; old Dan remained only long enough to remind him that after every heavy winter there was a brand-new springtime, better'n all that went before, and then betook himself elsewhere softly whistling: "There will be a bright to-morrow, When the roses bloom again."

And so Patten was permitted to "stick around." He idled all over the place; he admired the horses; he sat on fences and regarded remote distances; he was never tired of spinning yarns with Tonito, with George Ladd, with old José, even with the children of the place who took a great liking to him.

During these days Penelope saw nothing of Buck Andros, adhering rigidly to her determination never to speak with him again. But Andros willed otherwise and in the end had his way. A score of times he had asked for her and his messages had been carried by Mrs. Richards and Patty; each time Penelope had said a quiet

"No," leaving the nurse or the housekeeper to do what polite embroidering of the plain negative appealed to them. On Mrs. Richards' part there was no embroidery; as for Patty who was young and romantic and to whom the man was vastly pleasant and rather fascinating, she softened the refusal as best she could.

But Andros began to order his door left open and kept watch. Seeing Penelope passing along the corridor he called to her, urging her to grant him one moment. Face to face with him, seeing how feverishly his eyes shone at her from a haggard, bearded face, she did not have the heart to deny him.

"What is it?" she asked from the doorway.

"Miss Loring," he pleaded with her, "it's not much that I am asking. Will you listen to two words from me?"

It was the first time since the night of her arrival that he had addressed her as Miss Loring; almost at the outset, in that boldly presumptuous way of his he had named her Pretty Penelope. The "Miss Loring" now decided her and she came into the room.

"Why have you avoided me so pointedly of late?" he asked more mildly than she had ever thought to hear Buck Andros speak.

"Avoided you?" said Penelope coolly. "I'd hardly put it that way, Mr. Andros. I am not your nurse, you know, and you and I have so little in common that it would be 'pointed' as you put it if I had come to see you."

"You see Montana every day," he said swiftly.

Penelope shrugged distastefully.

"Is this all that you wished to say to me?" she asked.

He pulled himself up on an elbow; the eyes he lifted to hers were those of a masterful man humbling himself.

"I have told you already that I love you, Penelope," he said earnestly. "I'll be going soon, just the minute I can make the trip, and I'm growing stronger every day. I had to speak with you before I left, for you are not to think that I am not to see you again. I used to laugh at love; I didn't understand; I thought it was all sentimental drivel. But now—why, I'd go to hell for you, Penelope!"

"Mr. Andros—"

"I tell you I love you so that nothing else counts!"

"No!" said Penelope. "You don't even know me; we've never spoken a dozen words. And certainly I could never love you—"

"You don't know what love is! Haven't I just told you that I didn't believe in such a thing? You don't know and can't know until—"

He broke off short to stare at her, puzzled by her queer little smile.

"Why do you look that way?" he asked sharply,

"What are you thinking? If you—Good God!" he exclaimed between wonderment and kindling anger, "You're not going to fall in love with that hulking Bill Montana! Penelope! Look at me. Look at me, I say!"

She faced him defiantly. But as she felt the hot blood flooding her cheek under his suspicious eyes she turned abruptly and left the room. Within her breast was so great a conflict of shame and anger that she had not dared trust her voice; the light laugh with which she wanted to answer him would not come. She slipped out of the house unseen and hurried to her horse. For Penelope Loring at that instant she experienced a seething contempt in which was a flick of downright hatred. She who had always held her head as high as any girl, looking at the other fellow with clear, level eyes, felt humiliated. Patty had guessed; Andros suspected; perhaps Bill Mountain himself, since he was not stone blind, understood her folly and was mildly amused by it.

She did not go straight home that day. It was an early Sunday afternoon and her time was her own. She rode at a gallop, pulling off her hat to let the rush of air blow her hair back and beat in her face which it seemed would never grow cool again. She abandoned the road at the Goose Neck, lured by the murmurous solitudes among the big pines, searching out their cool depths along a friendly winding trail.

In an upland meadow where a dimple in the hills was like a silent, peace-flooded grotto under the pines she dismounted and lay flat, looking upward through interlacing dusky greenery at vivid fragments of blue sky. The faint breeze streaming through the forest was like the very far-off whispering of a great ocean. Borne down by an utter loneliness greater than any she had ever known since the time of her father's death, she thought longingly of him, the best and dearest of men. She recalled his face so vividly that she seemed to see it smiling down at her, and to hear again in treasured memory his repeated words, "The thing to do with this funny old life, Little Bright Penny, is just to be brave and gay. Then everything follows." Always, as she knew him, he had been brave and gay, a man with a quaint smile, crooked and whimsical and very endearing. Thinking yearningly of him she strove to smile as he would command, and the blue bits of sky grew tremulous and seemed all misted over.

Lying lax, cradled in the grass, she tried her valiant best to think things out. She had supposed that when it came love would be upon iridescent diaphanous wings, something very bright and tender and happy. Was it instead a sort of fiendish scorpion-thing with a sting that dripped poison? And now that it was here what to do with it?

"Get your man!" She had heard laughing red

lips say that, but did they know whereof they spoke? Did a girl become a huntress, fill her quiver and shoot every shining arrow into the heart of the man she wanted? That was one thing. Another was to hide what she felt, just be brave and very gay, and go on loving where her love was not invited. Still another alternative was to throttle and kill the young love that was only now making its first outcry of the newborn. . . .

She listened as though for some message in the hushed whisperings of the pines; she watched the yellow splotches of light mottling the rough brown boles, saw them quiver and slowly shift and vanish; shadows about her lengthened and told the passing of time like gigantic clock-hands; the wild life which her coming had sent scurrying into dim retreats forgot its fears and resumed its various activities. The crested jay which had sighted her from afar had screamed its quarrelsome warning and sailed off on strong blue pinions, but in the end returned to the pine-top directly above her and peered suspiciously down at her. From a score of hiding places striped chipmunks popped into sight like tiny fur-clad bundles of taut springs which were forever flicking them into new positions or scampering flight. From a hillside came the brief, small thunder of a blue grouse's wings and down the same slope through a clearing Penelope saw a flock of wild turkeys volplaning to a dark pine grove. She sat up to watch them out of sight, dusky gleams absorbed in the deeper dark of the trees.

"Just be brave and gay and let things work themselves out? Is that the answer?" she asked of the quiet afternoon.

She mounted and rode down to the Goose Neck where, having a choice of two directions, she elected to return to the Montana home. There was no reason why she should not say her casual good nights, and her departure had partaken of the abruptness of flight. Patty Lane would be surmising, and Penelope was determined to nip that young woman's conjectures in the bud. Penelope looked at her watch; only half past three. . . .

Patty Lane was looking at her watch; exactly half past three. Time to dose John Andros whom Dr. Crawford suspected of having a liver. "I'll say he's got a liver!" muttered Patty with whom during the afternoon Andros had been unusually ill-humoured. Arriving in Andros' room, tilting bottle to spoon, she said sweetly:

"Here's your nice medicine, Mr. Andros."

It was nasty stuff to take and she knew it and was glad of it. Andros, lying on his side and looking out through his window with bleak, heavy eyes, said impatiently:

"Take the damned stuff away. I don't want it. Chuck it into the river."

"Yeah?" said Patty serenely. "Anything else you'd like?"

"Yes. Tie the bottle to your neck, then fire away."

"So you won't take it?" She began to stiffen; a hint of rebellion in her domain made Patty as severe as a battle-axe.

"No, damn you," said Andros surlily. "And just because you're Patty-the-Nurse around here—"

"Patty to my friends," said that young lady icily. "Miss Lane to you, Mr. Andros." She put down the medicine and took a thermometer from the table.

"Get ou—" Thus far Andros. Patty popped the thermometer home. He jerked it out and flung it across the room.

"That'll go on your bill," said Patty. She grew red with anger but contented herself with the words and a shrug. "If you want anything, my lord," she said over her shoulder, "you can ring; ring and be darned—"

She was half way down the hall when Andros shouted after her. She hesitated, shrugged once more and came back; it was all in the day's work and just one more bit of unreason from that most unreasonable of all created things, a sick man.

"What did you say your name was?" demanded Andros sharply.

Patty's eyes rounded at him.

"Mercy on us, is the man delirious after all?" she gasped. "Here after two weeks—"

"I know, I know," he said impatiently. "When you first came I didn't listen to names; since then I've only heard you called Patty. What did you say the rest of it was?"

"To you I'm Miss Lane," said Patty.

Abruptly his whole manner changed; he smiled at her and asked her to overlook a poor devil's nervous rages.

"I'll even take the liver-rouser," he said, and kept his word. "I'm sorry I flared up like that; I won't again. It's a promise. So your name's Patty Lane," he ran on chattily. "I used to know a fellow named Lane; a great friend of mine he was, too. Old enough to be your father. Henry Lane, that was his name—your dad's name wasn't Henry, was it?"

"No," said Patty, beginning to thaw yet not entirely forgiving and forgetting. "His name wasn't Henry."

"Of course not," said Andros. "But for just a moment—Oh, I don't know what it was, maybe the way you hold your head when you're on your high horse—"

"Anything else, Mr. Andros?"

Andros laughed good humouredly, yet there was still that oddly serious look in his eyes.

"What was your father's name, Miss Patty?"

"Just why all this interest?" Patty countered.

"What affair is it of yours what his name was?"

"Interest in you, my dear," laughed Andros. And added teasingly: "Surely you're not ashamed of it, are you?"

"Ashamed? Let me tell you, Buck Andros, no one will ever be ashamed of you if you're one tenth the man Johnny Lane was. Yes, that was his name; not John like yours, just Johnny; Johnny Lane, and maybe you can guess from that how well he was loved."

"Johnny Lane," said Andros and looked at her more shrewdly than ever. Then he began to laugh in a way which made Patty actually wonder whether the man was springing a temperature on her.

But Andros, putting himself out to be friendly and entertaining, led her thoughts into other pastures and Patty, instead of sailing out in chill dignity, sat down and remained to laugh and chat with him. When Penelope came into the house from the rear garden she heard their voices. She even caught a word or two and a little flick of contempt came into her eyes. Buck Andros' love, it rather seemed to her, was an elastic affair after all, for she gathered the impression that he was making a dead set at Patty—and could not guess that with Andros love was one thing and the opportunity to cultivate Johnny Lane's daughter was still another. She heard Andros' quick, exultant laughter and wondered at it. That he had stumbled upon a certain vital discovery in the house of his enemy and under that enemy's very nose, was the sort of thing to be sure to move the man to sardonic mirth. Yet Penelope failed to have the key.

CHAPTER 16

Later it became obvious how swiftly and shrewdly Andros had planned and how at the outset fate itself played into his hand. "'Miss Lane to you, Mr. Andros!'" The man writhed in his bed. No matter how men strove, chance it appeared made all the difference! Just now the luck was all his, but at any moment she might become Miss Lane to Bill Mountain; a careless remark dropped from a silly girl's lips had the power to bring a man's tallest ambitions crashing about his ears.

The curious fact that neither of the two men most interested in locating Johnny Lane's heiress had thought to discover her in their nurse was, under the circumstances, not the least surprising. She had arrived at a time of stress when both Montana and Andros were beyond noticing who came or went; if Penelope had introduced her friend by name none saw in her anything but a most welcome, urgently needed nurse. Penelope always called her "Patty" and the informal folk here promptly followed suit.

But now conditions changed; the shadow of near tragedy was gone from a household which began slipping back among familiar, placid ways; Mrs. Richards and Patty chatted together in the patio where the housekeeper sewed and the girl smoked cigarettes and polished her finger nails, while Andros chafed at his incapacity to grasp opportunity by the throat. Confined to his bed, shut off from all contact with his men since Dave Rance played Tomfool, he yet saw a chance to take the winning trick.

He began with Patty, placating her, extending himself to the limits of his resourcefulness in expunging any unfavourable impression and replacing it by another in which he showed himself in all his most fascinating aspects. Why the devil couldn't he have known sooner? Why couldn't he have worked on the girl from the first minute? At least he now made what amends he could, and Patty, astute as she was, began to wonder whether the man were actually falling in love with her.

When he had gone in this new direction as far as he dared, careful of overplaying his hand, he asked her if she would have Ben Hodge come to him.

"You wonder what I want with him?" he said smiling up at her. "I'm going home, my dear. I'm strong enough—and anyway I'd rather die than remain under obligations here where I am not wanted." With Patty looking at him in surprise he added simply: "I wish that you could go along with me to see that I made the trip all right."

"You are in no condition to go yet," said Patty severely. "And of course, since I am hired by Mr.

Montana, it would be all nonsense my thinking of leaving the house."

"Yes, yes, I know," sighed Andros.

Ben Hodge, acquainted with his determination, was not the man to put an obstacle in his path. If Andros chose to die on the road that was his lookout and, as Ben regarded the matter, no great loss to the world. A bed was prepared in a motor truck, a rider sent ahead to advise Andros' men of his return and to instruct them to send a truck of their own to meet the Montana car at the upper end of White Water Valley. Andros, gaunt and haggard yet grim-lipped, took his departure.

"You have saved my life, Patty," he said as his only farewell. "I'll never forget that."

The next word they had from him came with unexpected suddenness. One of his men rode a foam-flecked horse to the house only four hours after his going, saying that the trip had been too hard for him and that it was feared he was dying; Dr. Crawford had been sent for but pending the doctor's arrival which might not be expected within a dozen or twenty-four hours, would the nurse come to him? If anyone could keep him alive over the interim it must be Patty.

"Too bad for Andros then," grunted Ben Hodge. "She has gone. She left the house about an hour after he did."

In Patty's sudden departure was one of those gestures which chance so characteristically indulges in when men's plans are all in order. The long expected call which Patty had warned them might come at any minute did come at last; she crammed her few things into her bag, said a hurried farewell and was off in haste to catch a train at Pueblo Junction which would speed her some two hundred miles to the bedside of that friend of hers who was about to make the world the shining gift of a new life.

"You'll be back, Patty?" Penelope called after her. "I want you to come visit me—"

"I'll write as soon as I get there," cried Patty. Penelope knew that she wouldn't. "When the che-ild is a couple of weeks old I'll be out of a job again, I suppose. I'd love to come, Pen. Lots of luck in the big things of life, kid. Bye, everybody—"

And Andros who had made the trip to his own place without mishap, had the satisfaction of knowing that for the present all was well. He had but to make haste in his recovery and be before Bill Mountain in dealing tactfully with Johnny Lane's heiress. The cards were in his hands now, he had ample time to study the game and should be man enough to handle Patty Lane in one way or another.

As for Patty herself, surely she would have thrilled to the tips of her toes had she realized that she was the high card in a game in which men staked their lives. Being, however, as unconscious of her peculiar importance as is the ace which drops in to make a royal flush, she went serenely upon her own affairs and dropped completely out of sight. She arrived on her new case in ample time, remained to see the newly born babe grow into the lusty estate of four weeks of age, and sent Penelope the first picture postcard:

> "We're leaving to-morrow for California; the change will buck Margie up and do the kid good, too. Then, what do you think? Margie's sister out there is to have a baby too and I'm to have the case. I'll write. How did Buck Andros stand the trip? Love to everybody."

During this time and some weeks to follow Penelope saw but little of her new friends in Montana Valley. These were days in which she filled her life full of her school work and was grateful for so much to do. From White Water and Montana valleys alone sixteen children ranging in ages from five to fifteen came trooping in to the ringing of her hand-bell; from neighbouring ranches came still others, two of the boys from a ten-mile distant valley. With every grade represented from the first to the last in the grammar school curriculum, with some young minds keen and eager, and others dull and listless, she had her hands full. But, putting a fresh young enthusiasm into her labours, she extracted from them a joy in proportion.

On settling down to work in earnest she had convened her domestic staff and, after explaining as to little children, had discharged them. They must see that with only a country teacher's salary she was hardly in the position to employ four household servants! To be sure, Bill Mountain had engaged her at the absurd wage of a hundred fifty dollars—and had meant all the while, of course, to have Ben Hodge put that amount through along with the rest of the Montana budget. Penelope soon set Ben right on that matter; in time arrangements would be consummated at the county seat, a fund would be allotted to the new district and Penelope would draw her rather more modest salary. So, though reluctantly, Consuela and Josefa and Eugenio and Billy nodded their understanding and accepted their dismissal—and the next day Josefa was again sweeping and bedmaking, and Consuela was presiding smilingly in the kitchen, while Eugenio and Billy were all over the place bringing wood and drawing water.

All this was to the lively accompaniment of hammer and saw going merrily, men's voices shouting at teams and wheel barrows creaking as the new school house was building. It was topped off with a tiny belfry and soon the early morning bell-notes went billowing down the valley and upon occasion were to be heard as far afield as Montana.

Though she saw less and less of Bill Mountain, Penelope knew that he was out of bed now and beginning to creep about the house, renewing contact with his little kingdom. One day when she stood at the big new blackboard setting down an engaging account of the activities of a cat and a rat for the younger ones to copy, she grew aware of a sudden ripple of suppressed tittering at her back. Eraser in one hand, crayon uplifted in the other and a chalky smudge across a flushed cheek, she glanced over her shoulder. Sitting on top of a rear desk at the back of the room was a highly amused Bill Mountain.

Penelope could not keep the gladness out of her eyes. It was so fine to see him looking his own self, up and about the world. But she tried to look merely normally pleased as she came down the room to him.

"Howdy, ma'am," said Bill Mountain, rising and towering over her, and engulfing her hand in his own. "Bein' as how I'm trustee I'm compelled by law, you know, to drop in ever' so often an' see what's doin'. I was real pleased, ma'am, too to see you writin' so pretty on the board, an' I was wonderin' whether mebbe I couldn't come to school myse'f an' learn—"

Penelope escaped with a lithe twist, turned from

him to the many upturned and highly interested faces and announced in the most matter of fact way:

"Excused for recess, children. Ten minutes. Eyes straight in front; now turn—rise—dismissed." After they departed, twisting their heads backward, she made a face at her trustee. "Any time that you think I am going to have you spying on me, Bill Mountain," she informed him gaily, "your thinking is all wrong."

"Anyhow," he grinned at her, "I done my lawful duty, tryin'."

"May I remind you," said Penelope as soberly as she could, for she was not feeling the least bit sober inside, "that a part of my duty here is to teach the younger generation to speak English properly?"

"Didn't I say as how I mebbe ought to come to school?" he asked as soberly as he could.

It was altogether a very delightful little visit and at the end he made her promise to ride down to have dinner at Montana the next day. She really meant to go, but when the next day came she took a long lonely ride instead and sent Eugenio with her excuses and regrets. Could she have known how savagely a thoroughly disappointed and disgruntled Bill Mountain attacked a specially prepared dinner, she might have felt sorry that she had not gone. It is equally likely that she would have had a happier ride.

These were Arcadian days in the Up Yonder country. She saw golden, rippling fields invaded by clattering machines and busy men, and smelled the sweet hay sunning. Enormous wagons heaped high with their overhanging yellow loads creaked away to the big barns, leaving in their wake scattered wisps of sunshine. The reapers swept all before them in the ripe grain fields, and thereafter the broad empty acres gleamed with stubble; fat bags of wheat and barley were conveyed to the granaries. The early apples turned red among the glossy leaves and went into the lug boxes in the shade. Cider presses went to work; the sweet fragrance of crushed apples pervaded the air. Trucks in a long line made a rich-laden caravan going out to the railroad. The later apples began coming on and pumpkins turned rich golds and russets and reds making one think of Hallowe'en and Thanksgiving, and striped vari-coloured gourds plumped and ripened along the fences. And Penelope sometimes sat on her porch of an evening that was hushed and still save for faint, far sounds, and inhaled the clean air with its smells and loved the earth and its fruitfulness and peace.

Into her dreams one tranquil twilight came a rider out of the gathering dusk, Juan Montana whom she had not seen for weeks and who she thought was forty miles away in hiding at the mountain ranch of a friend.

"Juan!" she exclaimed, starting up.

He sat beside her on the steps, holding his horse's reins, smoking many cigarettes, a nervous, restive Juan whose eyes gleamed in the dimming light.

"Sometimes I think that I am going mad," he said and was very tense though he pretended to laugh and shrug. Penelope, quick to understand as she was warm and human in her sympathies, sensed the boy's agony and laid a soft impulsive hand on his arm. He covered it for a moment with his, giving it a grateful friendly squeeze; then he sat with his elbows on his knees, his chin in his hands and his eyes staring into the fading distances. "It is hell, Penelope, for a man like me," he said gloomily. "I am not myself; *por dios*, I am another man altogether, one that you do not know and have never seen! I am made for happiness, to sing and laugh and drink the free air like wine, and to be a little drunk just with the joy of being alive. That is me, Juan Montana. And instead I slink and hide and cower and run; I grow into a sneak and soon I shall be a coward. I get so lonely, shut off from all whom I love, that I weep like a girl. The pine forests that I used so to love, I am beginning to hate them; they are still and dark and bear me down like a great stillness at someone's funeral. It would be better if I went down to Santa Fé and said to them, '*Bueno*; here I am. Take me and hang me by the neck and so make an end of me.' "

There were tears in his voice, tears in his weary soul and, before he had done with the rush of his complaint, tears in Penelope's grey eyes. She did all that she could to brighten this one hour for him and in the end Juan did get himself in hand and laugh and tell her that he was just a big baby who had come running to her for comfort since comfort from her was so sweet.

"Does Bill know you have come back?" she asked anxiously.

No, Bill did not know. Juan had ridden to the house just now and had learned that his brother was away and had been absent already for some days.

"He is down in Santa Fé," said Juan. "Clay Patten sent for him. Poor old Bill! It's all so useless. They will never know who killed Floyd Pasmore. There are times," he cried explosively, "when I wish that I had done the thing! Then—"

"Juan!" she pleaded with him.

"You see!" he retorted bitterly. "It is making a crazy man of me."

She made him come into the house and Consuela gave them coffee and thin wisps of toast with jelly. Juan sighted a guitar and began playing and singing the saddest and tenderest little Spanish love song that ever invited sighs and tears, while outside Consuela and Eugenio and Billy and Josefa and some two or three others from the clutter of houses among the trees organized themselves into a guard circling the house and making sure that none came to surprise the young Senor Montana. In the end it was an outwardly gay though still reckless Juan who said his good nights and returned to the lower valley for a talk with Ben Hodge.

He came again the next afternoon, saying that he could not wait for night, vowing that he was starving for Consuela's coffee and toast and jelly.

"I am starving; it is the truth," he told Penelope earnestly. "Starving for a little bit of companionship. Maybe you are saving me from going crazy. Who knows?"

"But in the daylight, Juan! It is so dangerous."

He shrugged. Danger it seemed was everywhere and certainly he preferred being taken and thrown into jail than going mad from sheer loneliness. In the jail there would be other good fellows and they would tell one another tall lies and so pass the time humanly.

CHAPTER 17

Meantime no direct word but rumours only came to them of John Andros' doings. It was known that he, like Bill Mountain, had entirely recovered from his wound, that he went about as usual and, again, like Bill Mountain, that he was now and then away from his ranch. Where his journeying carried him none knew though at first it was suggested that he had gone gunning for his former foreman, Dave Rance. But Rance was known to be in Kingston, and continued to live there undisturbed. He was never without a gun and was never known to miss an opportunity to speak his mind of Andros as a fool who, always considering any girl fair game, had at last lost his head over one who laughed at him. Andros must have known of Rance's being in Kingston and of Rance's talk, and the very fact that he did not take the time and trouble to run the man out of the country or kill him as he had promised should have been ample indication that he was exclusively occupied with other and larger matters. The first inkling of what he was about came a few days after Juan's reappearance in the valley when old Dan Westcott received a visit from his deputy, Webb Clark.

Dan when at home occupied two rooms at the

Montgomery House where he had lived as star boarder and lodger for the past twenty-five years, and here Webb Clark found him one morning coming downstairs headed towards breakfast.

"Here I am," said Webb in a tone of voice to imply, "You wanted me an' now you got me."

"Here you be," Dan agreed drily. "Yep, here you be. Had breakfas' yet?" Webb had; an hour ago. "Good," said Dan. "That's a bully way to start out a day an' you're a bright young man an' will go far, Webb."

"You wanted me," Webb reminded him. And when Dan cocked a curious eye at him he added, "Buck Andros said you did, anyhow."

"Buck Andros?" said Dan and cocked up both brows at that. "When did you see him? Where?"

"Just now," said Webb, looking puzzled. "On the street. He was talkin' with Whipple an' another guy, stranger to me, all three bunched up in a huddle an' seemin' to be dead in earnest, too. Buck said to me I was to come here."

"Hmf," remarked Sheriff Westcott. He led the way through a deserted lobby into the dining room, Webb clumping along at his heels. "Squat," he invited, drawing out his particular chair in a corner. "I'll stan' you to a cup cawfee, Webb; cigar even, if you say so." To the waitress who greeted him smilingly he said genially, "My! but it does pep a man up an' give him an appetite jus' to look at you, Milly! I was tellin' Webb here that I was goin' to have a piece o' dry toas' with mebbe a glass milk an' now danged if you hadn't better fetch me a pot cawfee, three fried aigs, plenty bacon an' some flap-jacks. An' don't fergit the maple syrup. What sort of a lookin' man, this stranger, Webb?"

"Dumpy," said Webb. "Red faced; dinky, stiff grey moustache; jowls an' nose mos'ly; a red neck-tie, white silk shirt; pot bellied—"

Dan whistled. Also he looked at his deputy almost with respect. Webb might blunder in this and that but he could make you see a man!

"Know who he is, Dan?"

"You're damn shoutin' I know him," snapped Dan, all of a sudden grown waspish and looking worried. "Andros an' Whipple an' Harley Prentis! What'n hell's up, do you reckon? An' Andros wanted you an' me together here—Hm-m-m-m." And thus what he began like a wasp he ended like a bee.

"Harley Prentis?" muttered Webb, also mystified. "He's got no business up here."

"Shouldn't have," Dan said frowning. He sat drumming on the stained tablecloth, a far-away look in his shrewd old eyes. Of a sudden a muffled exclamation burst from him, he shoved his chair back and came to his feet with a bound. "I'm gettin' out'n this in a hurry, Webb," he said and reached for his hat where he had hung it on a peg. "Tell Andros you couldn't find me but that mos' likely I've gone up to the court house. I'm duckin' out through the kitchen—Hell's bells," he concluded disgustedly and sat down. Andros closely followed by two men had come into the lobby and already glimpsed him.

Dan greeted them genially though he did not take the trouble to rise again. When the three came straight to his table with the look of having business with him he said innocently, "Lookin' for me? Had breakfas' yet, gents?"

They drew up chairs and sat about the table; all three looked serious, yet their expressions differed: Andros was as hard as nails yet in his hardness there was a gleam of triumph which Dan did not relish, Whipple was gravely doubtful, and Harley Prentis revealed a cold predatory eagerness in his chill pale eyes. Save for themselves the room was almost deserted; at its far side were a couple of travelling men with their noses alternately in their coffee cups and their papers, and near the door an overgrown boy wolfed liver and bacon; otherwise they had the room to themselves.

"Juan Montana is back with us, Dan," said Andros abruptly.

Dan had guessed as much; further, old fox that he was, he had guessed what Andros was up to the instant that he had started speculating on the fact that he was hobnobbing with Whipple and Harley Prentis together. He foresaw the man's move and had he had about sixty seconds additional time would have bolted through the kitchen and holed-up somewhere to think things over. Yet now he said innocently:

"That so?"

"He's back in Montana Valley," said Andros, with the sort of smile the sheriff did not like.

"Hm-m-m," said Dan.

"Harley Prentis is interested in Kid Montana's arrest," continued Andros coolly, "since as district attorney—"

"Thought Whipple here was distric' attorney," said Dan.

"It's not up here but in Santa Fé that Montana will stand trial, you know," resumed Andros. "And Prentis swears he'll get a conviction if you give him the man to prosecute. He has heard rumours that we're all outlaws up here, that we're hiding Montana and even that our sheriff refuses to make the arrest. Of course, that's all a pack of lies, Dan," he jibed. "I told him that as soon as we told you where the murderer is hiding out you'd go get him."

Both Prentis and Whipple, knowing exactly how matters stood, refrained from making a remark, the local district attorney looking not particularly pleased with the situation while Prentis permitted himself to smile faintly.

Dan's breakfast arrived. He wished to heaven he hadn't ordered so many eggs, but downed them heroically; also he regretted the maple syrup and the hot cakes along with it, but ploughed stoically through his meal. He blew his coffee cool and partook of three cups; he wiped his old grizzled moustache on the back of his hand, made himself a cigarette and permitted himself the luxury of sending a thin stream of smoke into his tormentor's face.

"I got a notion, Mr. Andros," he said thoughtfully, "that you're quite a kid for playin' practical jokes." He let his eyes wander to the Santa Fé attorney's face. "Andros made monkeys out'n me an' Webb once already," he said mildly, "gettin' us to raid the Montana place, swearin' Juan was there—an' all we jumped up was a young Injun buck that had got in a fight an' they was doctorin' up."

"He's all that Webb and I found," cut in Andros angrily. "But Westcott was at the house when we got there! He had had plenty of time to get Juan out of the way."

"I had plenty of time mebbe," said Dan tolerantly. "Same's I had time to tie some ribbons in my hair an' dance a jig. I didn't do that neither, an' I didn't see hide nor hair of Johnny Montana."

"You know damned well he was there," said Andros, defying him to deny it.

Now Dan turned, still mild of face, to Whipple. "Am I a liar, Whipple?" he asked.

Whipple tried not to hesitate, yet having

hesitated answered with the greater heartiness:

"No, Dan. No man ever had the right to call you that."

"Then lis'en to me tell you that I didn't see Juan, even after I looked high an' low; an' I didn't hear him an', dammit, I didn't smell him, so how'n hell could I know he was there? I say Andros made monkeys out'n us once—"

"I think, Mr. Westcott," said the Santa Fé man drily, "that you can hardly ignore the information which Mr. Andros now brings you. He has assured us that young Montana is in the valley now and that he can lead us to him. I, of course, can do nothing, having naturally no official standing in your county. But—"

"How does Andros know where Johnny Montana is?"

"Easy," retorted Andros. "Of late I've become possessed of half a dozen pairs of the highest-powered binoculars in America, and I have set men to do nothing but watch for him. I know that kid—as well as I know you, for instance. He couldn't stick the lonesomeness of it any longer. He'll be dropping in to see Penelope Loring about three o'clock this afternoon. Should we by any chance miss him there we'll find him at home."

"As I just said," put in Prentis curtly, "you can hardly ignore information of this sort, can you, sheriff?"

No, Dan couldn't ignore it. Even should he do so, there was Webb Clark to go—and even though he kept Webb out of it, there was Whipple sworn to see that fugitives from justice were brought to trial. It was a trick taken by Andros. Old Dan rose slowly, his brows bunched in profound speculation; shrewd as he was he could hit on no plan. There'd be no chance to get a word to Juan; trust both Andros and Harley Prentis to see to that.

"I'll go get him if he's there," he said simply.

On their way through the mountains to White Water Valley Andros found occasion to say to Dan out of earshot of the others:

"Just to make it a glad day all round for you, Westcott, I don't mind telling you that I've got the Montana outfit licked to a frazzle. The deed to White Water is as good as in my pocket."

Penelope was flushed and breathless with hurrying when she came home from school that afternoon and was all eagerness as she asked of Consuela: "Has anyone come?" Consuela supposing that she referred to Juan Montana said no, the young senor was not here.

"It's someone else," said Penelope. "I had a note to-day—"

It was a hastily scrawled few lines from Patty surprising Penelope with its manner of arrival, bewildering her with its content and altogether stirring vague alarm within her. One of the school children who came from a several miles distant ranch had brought it saying that a strange lady on horseback had stopped him on a trail and given it to him. Patty, who did not write two letters in a year, had made a fine mess of this one; it suggested wild improbabilities and said nothing in the least definite beyond, in an incoherent postscript, advising Penelope that she was coming to see her some time that afternoon, begging her to keep it secret and demanding wildly to be told whether Patty Lane was the happiest girl in the world or the biggest little fool.

Penelope was still puzzling over the thing when half an hour later Juan arrived. She strove to put Patty out of her mind for the moment and, having invited Juan into the pleasant front room, began what was meant to be a severe talk with that young man. She was uneasy for him, doubly uneasy since his brother was away, and wanted him to promise not to run all this unnecessary danger. She had hardly more than begun when she heard a clatter in the kitchen, a sharp cry and Consuela came running and calling out:

"Oh, for the love of God! Men are coming! One is Buck Andros."

Juan leaped to his feet and darted to the front door. He whipped back, closing the door; his face had paled a little and his eyes were burning bright.

"There are others coming that way," he said,

and drew a deep breath. His right hand went up under his left arm-pit where he, like his brother, wore his weapon. "One is Webb Clark, one is a man I do not know."

He hesitated only the barest moment. Suddenly he darted into another room and Penelope, running after him, saw him with one leg out of the window.

"Juan! Juan!" she pleaded. "You will be killed! You must—"

"I am not to be taken alive, Penelope," said Juan savagely over his shoulder. "And I cannot hide behind you. This is the best way. Tell Bill—"

He dropped out of the window and she saw him running. He was trying to get to his horse but found the way shut off. In the yard was a sturdy little woodshed and Juan made for it just as a voice called out to him:

"We got you, Montana! Hold on there!"

Juan leaped through the shed door, pulled it shut after him and ran to the one tiny window in the place.

"Come get me!" he called. "I see Buck Andros is with you; why not send him first?"

Penelope ran out on the porch and saw several men on horseback closing in about the woodshed. She saw Andros and Webb Clark and two men whom she had never seen before. But old Dan Westcott was there, too, and she hurried to him.

She had never seen an unhappier face than Dan's at that moment.

"Steady, Penny-lope, steady," he said sternly. "He's got to take it standin' up. It's all his damfool fault; he's asked for it. Draw back an' keep clear."

He swung down from his horse and came forward on foot, the two guns at his hips looking inordinately large and deadly in her horrified eyes.

"Hol' back, you boys," he commanded. "I'm runnin' this show. Andros! Stop that!"

Andros, sighting Juan at the little window, had made haste to fire. Juan had ducked down but first had taken time to fire back.

"Damn you, Andros!" roared the sheriff. "Stop it or by God I'll burn you down!"

"Letting him go again, I suppose?" jeered Andros.

"Mind what I said," said Dan. "A man like you I warn jus' once. Keep your shirts on, the rest o' you boys."

Withdrawing his wrathful eyes from Andros he strode across the yard towards the shed, his spurs jangling noisily.

"It's me, Juan," he called out. "I'm comin'."

Juan's voice sounded a brittle note of desperation.

"I'm not going to be taken alive, Dan. I'd rather it wasn't you. Why don't you send Andros?"

"It's goin' to be me," returned Dan equably, going straight on, neither hurrying nor loitering. "Long as I'm sheriff I like to tend to my own jobs."

"I'll kill you, Dan, unless you get me first!"

"Kill if you feel that a-way, kid. I don't knows I'd care much. Anyhow, I ain't pulling a gun on you. Better take it easy, Juanito. Here I am."

There was no way to fasten the door from within and he jerked it open. Penelope who had followed him half way across the yard, saw him stand on the threshold. His hands were at his sides, empty. Beyond him she saw Juan, his gun lifted.

"Juan!" she screamed.

"That's all right, Penny-lope," said old Dan. "Don't you worry none. Juan's never goin' to bore me for doin' what I got to do in the line o' my day's work. Come ahead, kid; better let me carry your gun, hadn't you?"

The two stood intensely still looking at each other, the boy's eyes glittering, the old man's calm and steady. Then all of a sudden the tenseness went out of Juan; his shoulders slumped and the gun muzzle that had been held within two feet of the sheriff's breast was lowered.

"All right, Dan," he said bitterly.

When they rode away, going down through the Goose Neck, Andros alone remained behind. He watched their departure frowningly and seemed tempted to ride after them, but hearing Penelope going to the house turned swiftly to her. She saw the flash of victory in his eyes, but gave not the slightest sign of having so much as noted him.

"Penelope!" he called to her as she ran up the steps.

She had determined not to speak to him. But the sound of his voice brought her to a dead stop; she whirled about and her eyes filled with loathing burned into his.

"Don't you dare ever speak to me again!" she said furiously.

Though he flushed an angry red he spoke evenly.

"I am sorry that Juan is a friend of yours and that he should happen to be taken here. But that is no fault of mine nor am I to blame that he is a murderer, the sort who shoots his enemy in the back! And I am sorriest of all that you take it so; were it not that I love you so that nothing else matters—"

"Love!" she flared out at him scornfully. "You talk of love! You who haven't a shred of humanity in you! Judas kisses Christ and Buck Andros says, 'I love you!' After Bill Mountain saved your life on top of your cowardly attempt to kill him—"

"Damn Bill Mountain!" roared Andros. "Whatever I owe him I'll pay, and don't you forget it! I'll yank him down from his high place and I'll break him flat—and I'll give him a convicted murderer for a brother!"

"No doubt you'll continue to try," said Penelope contemptuously, but his tone carried conviction and frightened her. "But even though you succeeded you'd still be just Buck Andros, you know, and he'd be Bill Mountain!"

"Penelope!"

She turned her back on him and started to go into the house.

"You and your Bill Mountain!" he shouted after her. "You little fool! Suppose you listen to this and think it over when I'm gone: To-day I am going to take White Water Valley away from him, and you—yes, you, by the Lord!—you are the one who has made that possible!"

"Are you crazy?" said Penelope scathingly.

"Like a fox," jeered Andros. "Now run whisper to your Montana friends all I've told you and add for full measure—"

He broke off abruptly; the wave of anger which had flooded him receded, the high colour seeped out of his face and the brightness in his eyes dulled.

"Penelope!" he cried in an utterly changed voice, pleading now. "Forgive me! You drive me mad—I love you so—"

She went into the house and closed the door. A moment he stared after her blankly; then he raked his horse with his spurs and rode away.

CHAPTER 18

Dan Westcott was determined on riding to the Montana home with Juan and though his plan called for heated opposition he insisted on having his way. The two prosecuting attorneys looked at each other in consternation; Harley Prentis opened his mouth to pour forth a tirade, took a good long look at the old sheriff and closed it wordlessly. Whipple however spoke to the point.

"You can't do a thing like that, Dan! It's next door to homicidal folly. Montana Valley will bristle with guns the minute you ride down into it with Juan Montana a prisoner. All hell will break loose—and you've got to remember that I'm holding you personally responsible for the safe delivery of your prisoner at the Montgomeryville jail."

Dan looked at both men out of the corners of his eyes.

"Bill Mountain, he's a frien' o' mine," he said drily. "I ain't goin' to pull any sneaky business on Bill. I'm goin' to look him up the firs' thing an' tell him what's happened an' all about it."

"I warn you you're going to stir up hell-brew of trouble," said Whipple.

"So be as I do," observed Dan very simply, "it

won't be the firs' time. You boys c'n melt outa sight an' let me do this my way, or else you c'n trot along so's you keep your kindly meant word of advice for them as hankers for such. Come ahead, *amigo*," he said in a kindly voice and clapped Juan on the shoulder. "Let's go see Bill."

Prentis spoke up to say:

"Bill Mountain isn't at home. Andros told us that."

"Then me'n Juan will wait," said Dan.

But Bill was at home, having arrived only a half hour before. He saw them from the porch and came down to the garden gate to meet them.

"Hello, boys," was all that he said at first. He took stock of Prentis, the one of their number whom he did not know, nodded to Whipple and Clark, and then regarded both Dan and Juan humorously. The sheriff's face was puckered with worry; Juan, very rigid in the saddle, seemed keyed up for any desperate thing. Bill spoke to Dan, saying unemotionally, "So you ran him to earth for me, eh, Dan?" And while Dan was opening his mouth to explain, Bill put his hand on his brother's knee and gave him an affectionate shake. "It's all right, kid," he said and smiled perfect reassurance.

"Here's the way of it, Bill," began Dan.

But Bill cut him short saying, "Later, Dan. Light down, you boys and come in. You look thirsty." He whistled up a boy from the stables to take the horses. "I don't think I know your friend, Dan," he concluded.

Harley Prentis was introduced as the prosecuting attorney most interested in clearing up the Floyd Pasmore case. He and Bill shook hands gravely.

"This is very irregular, Mr. Montana," said Prentis stiffly. "You understand, of course, that your brother is a prisoner and—"

Bill laughed at him.

"I won't drug your cocktails, Mr. Prentis. And Juan will give you his parole. Tell 'em, kid, that you won't run out on them."

"If you say so, Bill," said Juan reluctantly, and gave his promise. It meant nothing whatever to either Prentis or Whipple, but Dan expelled a long breath of relief.

As they found chairs in the living-room Bill said carelessly to Juan:

"Run down to Ben's office, Juanito, and tell him to step up here and to bring Clay Patten along with him."

Prentis, just easing his portly bulk into a deep chair sprang to his feet, expostulating.

"Westcott! You're turning this into a damned farce! Juan Montana is a prisoner of the law and though I don't belong in your county I swear I'll have you hounded out of office and slammed into the pen if you let him go."

Dan looked at Bill and for once seemed to

hesitate. Bill, who appeared to be enjoying himself hugely, nodded. Dan turned slowly on Juan.

"Didn't you hear what Bill said?" he asked coolly. Juan hastened out. Dan sat down, stretched himself and further infuriated Prentis by that odd little giggle of his. "We'll show 'em, Bill," he chuckled, "how us boys up here c'n tend to things our own way."

A couple of houseboys brought bottles and glasses. Prentis downed his liquor with a snort and shoved his glass back to be refilled. Whipple, who had all the while been regarding his host narrowly, relaxed in his chair.

"I guess, Harley," he said with a sigh, "that we must have got the wrong end of it somehow. I know Bill first rate and he looks to me right now like a man with about four aces up his sleeve."

"You're as right as rain, Whipple," Bill nodded pleasantly. "Of course, I've known all the time that Juan didn't kill Pasmore. He'll never be brought to trial."

"You say he won't!" muttered Prentis. But the first drink had already reacted pleasantly, and he added urbanely, "Fine liquor this, Mr. Montana."

"I'll let Patten spin you the yarn," Bill told him. "He will be with us in a minute. And I want Juan to hear it, too."

"Glory be!" cried Dan and smote the arm of his chair. "Patten's got the kid in the clear, eh, Bill?"

"Absolutely. He has nosed out the man who killed Pasmore."

"Not Andros, Bill?" queried Dan eagerly. When Bill shook his head Dan lay back in his chair and sighed and shook his head. "I knowed it couldn't be—but how a man can go on hopin' even when he knows there's no use!"

"There are other things than murder to put a man behind the bars, old timer," Bill reminded him. "If your luck's better than mine you may be the man yet that gets his rope over Andros' horns."

"I'm prayerful," murmured Dan.

Out of a short silence Whipple said: "Clay Patten, did you say, Bill?" And when Bill nodded Harley Prentis said ponderously, frowning as though at his own admission: "Clay Patten's a good man."

When Juan returned with Ben and Clay Patten the queerest imaginable expression was stamped on his face. Patten had told him; that was obvious enough. The hunted look, so often in his eyes, was gone now for good. But there was no such gladness as Bill had expected to see shining in them. Juan went silently to a chair and sat down with his brow on his hand like a man in deep thought. Bill saw a finger surreptitiously wipe his eye.

"You know now that you are out of all danger?" asked Bill quietly.

"Yes, I know, Bill," said Juan without looking up.

"You know who did it?"

Juan looked up then and tried to smile. But his eyes were bright with something other than happiness.

"I knew all the time, Bill," he said gently.

When the whole story was told Harley Prentis, a hardened tormentor of men's souls, went to Juan and put both hands on his shoulders and said with curious softness:

"You're a damned fine man, Juan Montana—and for your sake I hope we never get the poor devil."

Patten's account was terse and pointed. The man who had killed Floyd Pasmore was a queer, warped fellow—the Indian Amador. It appeared that he had always loved the girl whom Pasmore had betrayed; rather it might be said that Amador had adored her, looking worshipfully at her from afar much as he would have regarded the Holy Virgin. Unsightly and misshapen himself, he buried deep in his heart his adoration and the deeper he thrust it the more did it irradiate his whole being.

His was a sad, quiet, sensitive soul; he was set apart in all things from his people. Often he left them for days at a time, wandering among the mountain solitudes; his goings and comings excited scarcely the least remark. So none had thought to note that he, too, was away at the time when Juan had gone down to Santa Fé.

Patten, with little enough to build upon beyond the fact of the murder itself, conceived and discarded more than one theory before he struck the trail leading him to the truth. He reasoned that with Pasmore's death following Luisa's so closely this might be a case of unrelated coincidence or of indirect cause and effect. Juan had started out to kill the man; others than Juan could have had the same impulse. Who would care like that except someone who knew the girl well? She had lived all her life in Montana Valley. Patten came to Montana and looked around. He returned to Santa Fé and, in a clutter of shacks in the old part of town, found some Indians who knew Amador. They held out a long while but the tighter they shut their mouths the more sure was he. In the end from a woman who had quarrelled with her husband and was in the proper mood to make trouble, he got the first definite fact. Thereafter, thread by thread, he gathered the whole story and wove it into irrefutable certainty. Amador had killed Pasmore, had stayed the night with his friends and had returned the next day to Montana.

"And then," said Bill Mountain sternly, "he sold out to Andros and betrayed Juan!"

"No!" cried Juan, jerking his head up. "No, I tell you! He did not betray me for money;

Amador is not like that! It could have been only one thing on earth to make him do such a thing. Somehow Andros must have learned the truth. He would have gone to Amador and said, 'Look here, I can hang you! You do what I say or I hand you over to the police.' And Andros is like that!"

"Even so, kid," said Bill savagely, "if he'd hand you over to pay the penalty for what he had done—Good God! And you shielding him all the while!"

"Listen, Bill!" cried Juan. "I tell you I know Amador better than you do. In desperation he did what Andros made him do, but he must have felt sure that no Montana could ever be hanged. And at the last moment, had I been taken and tried and convicted, would Amador have sat there with his mouth shut? No! I tell you, No! He could not have done it!"

"How'd you know all the while Amador done it?" demanded Dan.

Juan shivered. The memory tortured him.

"I saw him coming down the stairs as I was going up. He had his gun in his hand. Do you understand? He came down—as I was going up! God have mercy on me! You see now, don't you? Amador had but one beautiful thing in all his life and saw it trampled underfoot by Pasmore! Amador took on his soul the deed I was going to take on mine—*amigos*, I'd rather hang now than see him punished for what I meant to do."

All in the room were for a long time silent. Dan Westcott got up and helped himself to a generous drink, downed it like a shot and started walking up and down, his hands resting on the black butts of his guns. Up and down he went, so deep in thought that the others fell to watching him and waiting for him to speak. He came to a stop at last in front of Bill Mountain.

"I'm gettin' hunches, Bill," he said. "This feller John Andros has been doin' some funny things, looks like, huh?"

"Patten has some more news about Andros," Bill told him soberly. "And about Patty—Remember Penelope's nurse friend?"

"Sure I remember her," said Dan. "She promised to marry me some day when I growed up. What about her?"

"Know her last name, Dan?" Bill asked him curiously.

"Sure I do," said Dan promptly. "Her name was Patty—Patty—Patty Somethin'-or-Other; what was it? It slips me right now."

"Patty Lane," said Bill.

"Well?" said the mystified sheriff. "What of it? A girl's las' name—" He broke short off as the truth dawned on him. "Not Johnny Lane's girl!"

"Yes, Dan. We had her right here in the house and didn't know a thing about it. Andros must have guessed. Remember in what a hurry he shot home? And how right away one of his men came rushing over to ask her to come to him? Only it happened that already she had gone."

"Whew!" The old fellow's eyes opened to their greatest extent. "An' Andros knows! An' does *she* know? An' where is she, Bill? An'—Oh, hell, put me out'n my agony and tell me. You whip her in line an' sign her up an' Andros is done for!"

"Exactly. But if Andros signs her up first, then what?"

"Why ain't she here, man? Where is she?"

"Patten's partner, who is handling this business, located her yesterday. She has been within twenty miles of us for the last two weeks. Andros found where she had gone in California, scared up a patient for her on a ranch between here and Montgomery, and got her up there by having an offer made to her of extra pay. He has been working on her, of course. Perhaps," he ended sombrely, "he has already arranged some deal with her—"

Dan Westcott slapped his thigh and swore. He slapped it again and laughed.

"Andros ain't closed no deal with her yet," he announced positively. "Wantin' to rile me good an' plenty to-day he says mysterious like that he has as good as got the deed to White Water in his pocket. Meaning Patty Lane, o' course. Meanin' also that it ain't quite sewed up yet."

Harley Prentis who had done a good deal of thawing out during the past half hour, sat twirling his glass in his fingers. A broad smile widened his mouth.

"Down in Santa Fé," he said genially, "I've heard tales of how you boys up here in these mountains handle delicate problems. I've a notion that there's a lot of truth in the tales I've heard. If I have got you right, may I make a suggestion?"

"Drill ahead," said Bill.

"It's just this," said Prentis. "If Andros knew who committed the murder and kept silent, he became an accessory after the fact. Further, if he attempted to manipulate circumstances so that your brother was accused of the crime, he became guilty of conspiracy to defeat justice. Now wait a minute!" He lifted a hand that had awed juries. "You begin to refer to a Patty Lane. Everybody knows of the trouble between you and Andros over the Lane estate, so it would appear that this Patty is the long sought heiress? All right. Then the other heir with whom Andros has been dealing is no proper heir at all? An impostor, perhaps?"

"Positively," said Bill.

"Then what?" asked Prentis. "Collusion, subornation of perjury, further conspiracy?" He waved his hand again. "It would appear to an unbiased lawyer from afar that the extremely open-minded Dan Westcott is in a position to stick Mr. Andros in jail for a few days—long enough, say, for an enterprising young gentleman who serves his guests such noble whisky to interview the heiress and conclude the matter?"

"Where's my hat!" yelled old Dan.

There was a general scraping of chairs.

"I'm going along," said Prentis. "I haven't had a day like this since I was a kid. Coming, Whipple?"

"Sure thing," laughed Whipple. But he thought to demand of the sheriff: "What are you going to arrest him for, Dan? And where's your warrant?"

Such suggestions invariably tickled Dan's funny bone.

"I'm arrestin' him on suspicion," he said chattily. "As for the charge, me'n you'll think that up as we ride. Come ahead, Webb. Comin', Bill?" When Bill shook his head, saying that he would not be needed and that he and Juan and Clay Patten were due for a session since Patten was returning home immediately. Dan retorted: "Jus' as well, I guess. No, we won't need you an' I got to leave somebody here to ride herd on my pris'ner. Juan, you stick close an' do what Bill says. I'm makin' him my deppity pro tem."

When the four horsemen rode into White Water Valley the sun had dipped behind the mountains and night was gathering under the big pines. Coming abreast of Penelope's house they saw a light and Dan, bethinking himself, said as he drew rein:

"I got to tell Penny-lope; she'll be worryin'

herself sick over Juan. You boys jus' jog along slow, an' I'll overhaul you in two shakes."

Penelope had heard the horses and came to the door. Seeing who it was and catching a glimpse of the three other figures dwindling away in the dusk, she hurried down the steps.

"Tell me!"

"That's what I'm here for," said Dan with gusto, and launched joyously upon an account of what had taken place.

"How's that for an earful?" he chuckled, gathering up his reins; he had told of Juan as good as clear, of Amador, of Bill's return to take matters in hand. He remembered to add gleefully that at last the heiress to White Water had turned up. "An', come to think of it, it was you, Pennylope, that brung her amongst us! Glory be!—But, shucks, I got to be ridin'. We're all set to hawg-tie Buck Andros afore he c'n gather in the last trick. Addy-ose—"

But he couldn't get away like that! Here he said almost identically what Andros had said before him, that she was responsible for something, very vague, yet very important. And it appeared to be connected with Patty—

"What's all this about Patty?" she demanded.

It was a story which he would have enjoyed telling in detail, but with pressing business calling him, he cut it short and was about to ride away when she checked him most completely by informing him that she expected Patty at any moment.

"Hi? What? How's that?" he exclaimed. He had to know all about it and Penelope, despite Patty's insistence that all was to be *sub rosa*, told him. "We got the worl' by the tail on a steep down-hill drag with the trail greased all the way!" he chuckled. "Look you, Penny-lope, I'm doin' my part, takin' care to cork Andros up for a spell where he can't do nothin' but cuss an' bite his fingernails. You do your part which is, the minute Patty Lane shows up, grab her an' start with her on the run to Bill. An' to-morrow we'll all get drunk. Whoops!"

He tore himself away and sped off to overtake his deputy and the two prosecuting attorneys. He came up with Prentis and Whipple where they were slowly climbing the ridge separating the valley from the Andros property; his squinting eyes made them out as they rose against the sky-line, and also informed him that they were alone.

"Where's Webb?" he asked sharply.

"Rode on ahead," said Whipple. "Said he guessed he'd make sure Andros didn't fade out on us while we were fooling along."

Dan pricked his mount with his spurs and shot by them.

"Come ahead, boys," he invited them. "Webb ain't no man to han'le Buck Andros alone. But I reckon he'll keep his shirt on till we get there."

But Webb Clark was not in the least inclined towards that restraint which is implied in the homely metaphor of keeping one's shirt on. He recalled only too clearly the dressing down which Dan Westcott had given him after the fiasco of his attempted arrest of Juan, and brooded on the part which Andros had played in it.

"The dirty crook played me for a sucker," he growled as he forged ahead of the two lawyers. "Here's where I give him his come-uppance. It's goin' to be me an' not ol' Dan that drops a rope over his horns."

Though those following him rode swiftly now they were not destined to catch sight of him until the journey's end. Having dropped down from the ridge to the more level lands of the Andros ranch Webb once looked back and saw the three dim black figures against a sky in which a single star shone. Estimating that he had a good half mile lead on them he went on at a swinging gallop.

So it was that he came first of all to the group of ugly squat huts constituting the Andros ranch headquarters. As Webb's horse clattered into the bare yard Andros came to his door. His spurs were on his dusty boots; his horse stood at the end of his porch. Webb noted that it was not the same animal he had ridden during the afternoon and judged that Andros was about to do some more riding.

"Who's there?" challenged Andros.

Webb reined in close to the porch.

"Me, Andros. Webb Clark." He added significantly: "Deppity sheriff."

Andros stood very still a moment in the lighted doorway, then stepped swiftly across the threshold and to one side of the door.

"Well?" he asked as curtly as Webb had spoken. "What's on your mind, Webb?"

"A good deal," returned Webb. "You played me for a sucker, Andros, when you made me raid the Montana home tryin' to grab Juan. You knowed that he didn't kill Pasmore. You knowed that the Injun Amador did."

Andros did not stir and did not speak. Webb's only gesture was one which might have escaped notice; merely the closing of a burly hand on his gun butt.

"It's my job to put you under arrest, Andros," he said swiftly. "Now take it easy."

"Arrest? For what? For telling you where Juan was?"

"On suspicion," grumbled Webb, bethinking him of what Dan had said. But he made the mistake of saying too much; he added, meaning to be convincing: "Suspicion of a lot o' things: scarin' up a fake heir to the Johnny Lane estate, subornation o' perjury, conspiracy—"

"What's that?" cried Andros with the first sign of any emotion whatever. "What about the Johnny Lane business?"

Webb laughed at him.

"We know the whole game, Andros," he explained. "You got that Patty Lane girl hid out, an' figger that a quick deal with her will put White Water in your jeans. Mebbe it would, if you was lef' to ramble free. But I'm tellin' you that other folks knows now." He could not refrain from a jeer: "Bill Mountain knows—"

"Got a warrant?" demanded Andros.

"I don't need no warrant."

"You can't arrest me without one; you know that!"

"Can't, huh? You're under arrest right now. Take it eas—"

"Take that!" roared Andros and fired before Webb could draw his gun. Webb grunted as though a fist had struck him in the stomach, and made a weak effort to pull his weapon from its holster. Andros fired a second shot and a third. Webb's bullet-riddled body was slipping from the saddle when upon Andros' ears burst the brittle staccato of horses' hoofs and for the first time he saw three riders bearing down upon him! A yell broke from one of those riders in old Dan Westcott's unmistakable voice. Andros did not stop to argue; he ran along the porch, jumped into his saddle, jerked his tie rope free and lashed his horse into a run. As he dashed towards the shelter of the timbered hills Dan ceased shouting and settled down to shooting. But as far as the sheriff could make out the man whom he had just watched shoot his deputy down had made good his escape.

"Dead," he said heavily a moment later when he rose from his knees and looked stonily at Whipple and Prentis.

"Andros must have gone mad!" gasped Whipple.

Dan shook his head.

"Webb must of let out that we knowed about Patty Lane," he said mournfully. "She was Andros' one high card. He thought that he'd be safe enough killin' Webb, with no witness aroun'. It was jus' his tough luck he didn't know we was right on han'."

CHAPTER 19

The sheriff rode swiftly and alone in pursuit of the fugitive, leaving to Whipple and Prentis the responsibility of caring for Webb's body. Since Andros' precipitate flight had been westward towards the pine-timbered hills it was in that direction that Dan turned, though with scarcely the faintest hope of coming up with his man to-night.

His many years experience with men who sought either to evade him or to wipe him out of the picture stood the grizzled old sheriff in good stead. Emotion had got him by the throat when he bent over his deputy, but he shook it off; towering rage succeeded it and of that, too, he promptly cleared his brain. By sheer force of will in the place of sorrow and anger he reinstated a cold canny shrewdness. He said to himself as he rode and while his eyes pierced into shadows and his ears were cocked against all sounds:

"John Andros is a killer by instinct an' as such was pretty sure, soon or late, to do his killin'. Likewise, he's a fox. He knows now he's done for unless he c'n make a hell-for-leather get-away. He knows it was me yelled at him. He knows I'll have word scattered all through the mountains by mornin' an' all over the county an' clean across the state. Yep, he'll figger on goin' faster'n the mill-sails o' hell. Question is, where?"

He wasted only a few minutes in fruitless search in the foothills, promptly accepting the fact that for the moment his quarry had made good his escape. His course had taken him directly away from White Water Valley, so when he swung south again and turned towards Montana he struck into a trail which gave Penelope's place a wide berth.

She, meanwhile, awaited Patty in growing impatience. The profound hush of the high valleys was like an actual, tangible thing and upon many a solitary evening she had experienced the odd sensation that she was listening to the silence with her soul. To-night it oppressed, and though the hour was one of soft starlight, the stars seemed infinitely more remote than ever before, shining with a frosty glitter. The occasion called for happiness since Juan had made his escape from a burden grown too heavy for him—yet her mind was occupied by Andros and the men riding after him, by misgivings and by an increasing fear that Patty was not coming.

So preoccupied was she that Patty's arrival startled her. She saw the horse first, a calico pony whose glaring splotches of white stood out vividly against a dark hide, as it was pulled up under the pine tree in the yard. Patty slipped out of the saddle and was tying her reins with fumbling fingers when Penelope hurried to meet her. There was so much overflowing the hearts of both girls that they hugged each other excitedly, so much to be told that both were bubbling over with it as they went into the house.

"It's a secret," said Patty.

"I know," answered Penelope. "Come straight into my room. I've a fire burning and we'll be all alone there. Patty!" She squeezed her arm tighter about her friend and asked hesitantly: "You weren't going to marry him, were you? Not Buck Andros?"

"Uh-huh." Patty nodded, her blue eyes never so bright. But it was a feverish brightness with which they shone, bespeaking not merely happiness but also some high excitement. And Patty, with a rather queer little laugh, amended her words with: "I think so!"

Penelope gave her another squeeze and led her into the bedroom. Patty, looking very chic in a deep-blue riding suit and a darker cloak about her shoulders, yanked off the cloak, tossed her small tight hat to the bed and began fluffing her blonde hair. Penelope watched her throw herself down on the bed, then asked soberly:

"You don't really love him, do you, Patty?"

Patty flared up on the instant and came erect with a jerk.

"I like that!" she exclaimed tartly. "Why

shouldn't I love him, I'd like to know? He's the handsomest devil out of gaol and—"

"Patty!" Penelope shivered at the chance words. "Oh, you poor kid!"

"Who, me?" sniffed Patty, and added as she threw herself back on the bed, "Oh, thunder, Pen, let's not get going all wrong. Haven't I come straight to you as my one friend on earth? I've told you I don't know whether I'm happier than a cock-eyed sailor boy in his favourite port, or just plain goofy. He is the handsomest thing—and can he make love? Like a house afire! But the funniest thing, Pen!" She squirmed erect again, finding it impossible to be still two minutes. "When he's with me I could just lie down for him to use for a door mat; and when he's gone I get to wondering. Is love like that?"

"How should I know?" said Penelope hurriedly.

"Unless I change my mind I'm to marry him to-night, Pen."

"You're going to change your mind, dear," said Penelope gravely.

Patty bristled once more.

"Says you!" she said, but nevertheless grew round-eyed at a certain note she detected in Penelope's voice. She demanded sharply:

"What's it all about, Penelope Loring? Why do you look at me like that?"

Penelope told her and Patty's eyes grew bigger and rounder and her red mouth, opened for a gasp, forgot to close. She heard of what had happened this afternoon, of Juan's arrest, the discovery of Amador's guilt, the conviction that Andros had conspired against justice in furthering his own ends, and how the law was already at his heels. To top that off she was informed as far as Penelope's knowledge ran concerning the cause of the feud between Bill Mountain and Andros, of the Lane estate and the long missing heiress—and of the astounding fact that Patty was the heiress in question.

"Me an heiress!" exclaimed a bolt-upright Patty, sure that there was a mistake somewhere since things like this, though of course they happened, always happened to someone else. "Golly, Pen! If it was only true!"

"It is! That is the real reason why Buck Andros—"

"Yeah?" drawled Patty, though her eye showed her excitement grew. She strove to be her own cynical self. "I'm a millionairess or something, am I? And you are not, by any chance the long lost queen of Sylvackia, are you?"

"Listen, Patty! Your father owned all this White Water Valley; he sold it to Bill Mountain's father—Oh, I don't know all the details, but from scraps I've heard I can piece it together. You could make trouble and claim that White Water was still yours; or you could do the fair thing, the thing you're sure to do, and recognise the sale made so long ago. It was for forty thousand dollars; the money with interest has been accumulating in San Carlos for a long time—I think there's about sixty or seventy thousand dollars now—"

"Whoops!" cried Patty. "As my old pal and sidekick, Dan Westcott would say, 'Whoops!' Sixty-seventy grand! If it's true, Pen, then get your duds on and here's me and you on our way to Paris!"

"You see!" said Penelope with a sigh which bespoke some profound relief.

"See what?" Patty demanded.

"You don't love Buck Andros! If you did you'd be thinking of him right now instead of money and Paris."

"I'm not the kind that says good-bye to all her wits when she high-dives," Patty defended herself. "Now, Pen, let's do our level darndest to get all this straight. Tell me—"

"You tell me," Penelope said quickly, "when it was that Buck Andros learned that you were Johnny Lane's daughter!"

Patty shook her head emphatically. Andros didn't know a thing about her father, and there was no use trying to make her believe that he had fallen in love with the heiress and not with Patty's own sufficiently attractive self. But in the very midst of her staunch defence of Andros' motives a flood of light broke on her as she remembered that last day of nursing at Montana Valley.

"The slick devil! Listen to this, Penelope!"

Penelope listened with all her ears and presently declared that Patty must straightway hurry to Montana and have a talk with Bill. But Patty was in no haste; let Bill come to her if he liked but meantime she was going to stop right where she was and Penelope was going to tell her again every single thing she knew about the deal made so long ago between a Lane and a Montana. Where did Penelope suppose Buck Andros was now, and did Dan Westcott really mean to arrest him, and what would happen to him?

"Maybe he didn't know it was the Indian killed Pasmore at all. How could he know, Pen? Maybe there's another side to all this land squabble; there generally is! And maybe I do love the devil after all—and maybe he does love me!"

Penelope bestowed on her a stare of incredulity. "You don't mean that even yet—"

"Would you go back on the man you loved just because he got in a jam?" cried Patty warmly. "Yes, even yet, if I could just be sure that he loves me—that it isn't because all of a sudden I've turned into the girl that holds the golden key. You know Dan Westcott hates him and is an old rascal besides and is like a father to your precious Bill Mountain. You know you're always seeing as Bill sees them. Oh, Penelope!" she wailed, "didn't I write to you that I was all up in the air and needed you? And here you go making a worse mess of things than they were in already!"

So deep were they in their talk that when a little while later there was a clamour of voices outside they gave it not the least attention. That anything was amiss did not dawn on them until Consuela burst upon them, crying: "Fire!" When they ran to the door, fully expecting to see the house erupt into flames all about them, Consuela told them, No, no! It was not here but down at Montana. They should be quick and run to the porch to see. All others at White Water already knew, and the men and boys and some of the women even were on their horses, going to help. It looked like the world afire!

Seen from Penelope's porch the conflagration was of such an order as to give some colour to Consuela's hyperbole. The whole southern sky was an angry red and through the Goose Neck pines, standing jet-black against a lurid background, rose a tall pillar of fire.

Consuela already in the yard urged them to run with her.

"We will go with the other women to the high hill at the Goose Neck where we can see. *Maria Santisima*! It is the barns that are burning with all the hay and the stables, too, and the garage house maybe, and all the fine horses!"

"Hurry, Patty!" cried Penelope, catching Consuela's excitement.

"How could it happen?" marvelled Consuela. "They are always so careful about fire down there. Oh, they are so careful, Senorita! Do you think that some bad man, hating the good Don Bill—"

"Are you coming, Patty?"

"Nothing doing," snapped Patty. "Let the darn place burn. I've got other things on my mind right now."

Penelope looked at her curiously. Suddenly Patty said with an angry sniff:

"You heard what Consuela said. I suppose you'll be blaming this on Buck Andros, too!"

"Why, Patty!—Why, *Patty!*" Penelope's eyes grew big as she stared at her overwrought friend. "Don't you see—"

"Oh, darn!" choked Patty Lane and fled back into the house.

CHAPTER 20

It was George Ladd who was the first to shout an alarm, although almost at the same instant Dan Westcott, returning to Montana, saw flames running up one of the biggest haystacks, and let out an ear-piercing yell. The veterinarian, about to turn in, had chanced to pay a good-night call on one of the polo ponies which had come by a strained fore leg and sniffed something burning; as he stiffened apprehensively he grew conscious of a sudden nervous restlessness breaking out among some of the stable horses in the further stalls, their threshing and snorting leaving him in no doubt that the fire had broken out somewhere in the building. Shouting at the top of his voice he ran out of the polo pony's stall and towards the far end of the stable. As he plucked open a door he saw a broad sheet of flame gush out of the manger of one of the empty stalls.

His voice and Dan's brought men running from all quarters; the door was flung open at the house and Bill Mountain and Juan, followed by the entire household rushed out, while from the little homes of the Indians came many running and shouting.

Whereas at first they supposed that they had to do with one blaze only and that one chance-lighted, an almost instant realisation was afforded them that several fires were already blazing fiercely. The haystack shot its angry pennons skyward, held eyes for only a fascinated second and was ignored for the far greater menace. Bill Mountain's voice as he came running, galvanised the most bewildered:

"The horses! Get the horses out!—Ben! Ben Hodge! Get the hose going! Juan! Tonito! Start getting horses out at the first doors you come to!"

He himself ran on where George Ladd was calling; he plunged into a portion of the stable already filled with smoke where horses were lunging and striking and snorting their terror. Here was one of the spots where a fire had started and already the flames had caught at the beams and floor above and were invading the hay loft. He snatched down a training whip from the wall and began driving the maddened animals out, thundering out his commands to others to drive the horses further afield lest they break back into the stable.

There were those among his people who lost their heads utterly and screamed conflicting orders and made confusion all about them; there were others, Ladd and Dan, Juan and Tonito and a score of quick-witted Indians, who worked from the start with some semblance of reason. When Ben Hodge did not immediately appear it was Juan who called helpers to him and started the fire hose playing on the blaze reddening that portion of the building where Bill was working with the horses. Tonito flashed into action at Bill's side, quick to take the curtest order, equally quick to think for himself; he had secured one of the many patent fire-extinguishers with which the various ranch buildings were generously provided, and for a little while strove with it to combat the conflagration. Realising promptly that he might as well have tried to drown a volcano he cast the implement aside and lent his single-thoughted aid in getting the animals out. A horse reared high above him, its eyes glaring, its upflung hoofs glinting with reflected fire; Tonito dodged and sprang in, caught the animal cunningly by the nose and fought it out into the open.

"Someone has set the ranch on fire!" clamoured the useless, demoralised ones. "Everything will burn! The hay-barn and the stable and the horses—*Ahi*! the fine horses!"

"The garage is burning!" they yelled frantically, as though a great flood of speech might inundate and so put out flames which shot thirty feet in air. An explosion drowned even so frenzied a shouting, but after the explosion they shouted again: "That was the big truck! It is gasoline now; the other cars are burning. Look out, look out! You will be killed, fool!"

And then, as though all this were not enough,

a woman came running and screaming over and over, since so many were already shouting and would not listen:

"The little house of Ben Hodge is burning, too! He is in there! He is dead on the floor. No one can pull him out."

Bill heard nothing of this until later, but Dan Westcott caught what the woman was saying and ran like an agile boy for Ben's quarters. A great volume of smoke threaded delicately with little streaks of fire poured out of one of Ben's windows; Dan dodged in at an open door, saw Ben lying on the floor—or rather saw his boots only, so thick was the room with smoke—ducked his old head down, caught the still figure by the legs and dragged it clear of the cottage. The woman and some others came to see and, when the work was all done, to help, and carried the unconscious Ben Hodge up to the Montana home.

"It is the smoke that has choked him to death," someone said.

"Get him to bed," snapped Dan. "Then you folks look all over the house to make sure fire hasn't started there too. He's not choked on smoke; he has been hammered over the head."

By this time Bill Mountain, working furiously had also organised a score of his level-headed men into a smoothly functioning unit. They got doors open, they led or drove terrified horses out, they got the doors shut again to minimise the draughts. Further their coolness acted towards making some others similarly purposeful in what they did. These drove the stock into the corrals at a safe distance or into the fields.

All the while Juan, directing where the fire hose be used and where men might with some hope of accomplishment employ the patent extinguishers, made a stubborn but uphill fight. Of besting the fire in the end he had not the slightest hope; all he strove for was to keep it in some semblance of control where his brother and the others were at work. Flames began gushing out of the roof at one end of the hay-barn; the heat was so intense that a crowd of fascinated spectators was driven back step by step. Nothing was to be saved there, yet they watched with enormous glittering eyes.

Bill Mountain, his eyes glaring out of a smoke-blackened face, caught Tonito by the arm, saying hurriedly:

"Come with me, Tonito. I am going to the other end. That's where Daylight and Crusader are."

He had glimpsed a red flare through a crack and sped to get the imprisoned horses there into safety before that flare was a vast inferno. He pulled open a door and fell back from the hot blast in his face. All within was the wildest commotion; as he took a deep breath preparatory to dashing in, one of the horses being headed towards the corral broke by the men driving it and almost ran him down, plunging back into the stable. Crusader, the big Percheron stallion had gone stark mad with fear and lashed out with his heels at the newcomer; there was the heavy thud of his enormous heels striking flesh, and Bill saw through the reek of murk the flash of his teeth. The stallion fought and stamped and at last his terrified squeal cut through the babel of sounds like a discordant war trumpet above the din of battle. Whip in hand Bill made his way in; Crusader whirled and struck at him as a long pennon of fire snapped and flickered over his head. There was a halter with its ring about Crusader's high-flung head, and Bill caught it and was swung by it clear from the floor. Yet in a battle that lasted some seconds only, the man had his way; whether it was the whip or his voice or whether at last some sanity came to the big stallion, he was half led, half driven out into the open.

The fight with Crusader was repeated with Daybreak in the next stall. As Bill rushed in upon him a wall was falling; there was the smell of burning horse-hair; the manger was a trough of flame. Daybreak, like Crusader, trumpeted and squealed and struck with fore and hind feet, his savage teeth bared and threatening to lay a man's cheek open. Bill shouted at him, cursing and pleading, avoiding the blows which would have meant death, determined to save this high favourite from his own mad tryst with destruction. Someone came running with a rope; its noose settled unerringly about the stallion's neck and was whipped tight. Others lent their hands and a tug of war resulted in the midst of which, when Daybreak had reared desperately and at last his hoofs came thudding down, Bill Mountain leaped in and sprang upon his back and laid the whip across his rump and so rode thunderbolt out.

As he threw himself to earth, rolling clear and coming up to his feet again he saw several men gathered about a form stretched on the ground. Though they were well withdrawn from the intense heat of the burning building the vast circle of light spread beyond them; he saw Tonito, running swiftly, throw himself on his knees by the quiet form. Men fell aside, making way for him; there was a moment of stillness among them, then Tonito rose and carrying his burden in the clasp of his arms, stumbled away. Bill, realising only that someone had been desperately hurt, was taking a first step towards the quiet group when George Ladd who had seen all that had occurred, put a hand on his arm, saying tersely:

"It's Amador. The poor devil must have been hiding in the hay loft. Got trapped—badly burned—guess it's just as well he jumped for it and made an end. Yes, he's dead, Bill."

Not even Amador's death could long hold men now; those who had gathered about him and seen his body carried away, dashed back to the stable. Juan with his hose whose futility became more obvious at every red moment, was driven back from one spot only to do what he could to retard the fire at another, and now came hastening to lay down a watery barrage where his brother and a handful of men were making the final effort to come at Sultan and some of the polo ponies in the centre stalls. The place was so thick with smoke that the forms of horses and men were mere grey blurs; the walls of the stalls were blazing and fire dropped from the floor boards above. Two men to every horse, that had been Bill's order; in pairs they got every pony out, scarcely breathing while they worked, gulping the air outside. Five men fought with Sultan, and by the time they got him clear the stanchions and ceiling beams were breaking down in glowing cascades. When Bill Mountain fell back from a heat so intense that no longer could any man endure it, shouting to those about him to stand clear, the last horse ran free.

He himself walked apart from the others; he withdrew until he stood at the base of the knoll of which the old home stood, red of roof and window in the strong light, and stood with his hands on his hips, his jaw hard set, watching the walls of his garage crumple, seeing and harkening to the two hissing pyramids of fire gutting his stable and devouring so great a part of his harvest in the big barn, creating in the stead of fruitful garnerings a crackling red hell which spread a black-and-crimson smear across the sky.

"Know who done this for you, don't you, Bill?" said a thin-edged voice.

He turned slowly. The moodiness in his eyes gave sudden place to bright hard anger.

"Hello, Dan. That you? Andros, you mean?" He lifted his shoulders and let them drop heavily. "Likely enough. I doubt that we'll ever know though, Dan."

"Haven't heard about Ben, have you?"

"Ben?" Bill started and grew anxious. "No. I wondered where he was—"

"Come up to the house, Bill. We're all washed up out here."

Tonito came up with them as they were mounting the steps.

"Don Bill," he said heavily. Bill turned and looked at him. "It is about Amador. Will you listen, Don Bill? One minute, that is all. Just you."

"I'll wait inside," said Dan and went into the house.

"I am the one," said Tonito, "who has been hiding Amador all this time. The fire caught him—and now he is dead, Don Bill."

"I am sorry, Tonito—"

"Never mind; it is the way things have to go," said Tonito gruffly. "But I will tell you now: Amador is the one who killed Pasmore—"

"I know, Tonito."

"And Senor Juan?"

"Juan knows; he has known all the time; he saw Amador that night in Santa Fé, and would not even tell me—"

Tonito's eyes flashed; Dan had left the door open and in the pathway of lamp light Bill saw tears rolling down Tonito's face.

"One thing more, Don Bill. Never once did Amador mean to let them hang your brother; I swear it! You believe, *no?* Listen, Don Bill; Amador was not a bad boy, only God made him different from you and me. Here, senor." A suddenly proffered paper was thrust into Bill's hands. "On this long ago Amador wrote that it was he who killed Pasmore; he gave it to me to be sure that it saved your brother." And Tonito touched the brim of his hat and sped away.

Bill Mountain, hurrying into the house, found the sheriff waiting for him in the living-room.

"What about Ben?" he asked anxiously.

"Firs' thing, he's all right," said Dan. "Secon' thing, he's had a close shave. Here's what happened."

When in a few words he had told of the condition in which he had found Ben, the two went together to look in on the foreman; Mrs. Richards had superintended getting him to bed and met them at the door.

"He's all right, Bill," she said in answer to the

look on his face. "He's conscious now, but I don't think he should be disturbed."

"Does he know who hit him?" he asked sharply.

"No. Someone came up behind him while he was sitting at his table. That's all he knows."

Ben, white and sick-looking, grinned rather sheepishly as his two callers came to his bedside. He told them with feeling that all he asked of anyone in the wide, wide world was to tell him who had sneaked up behind him and hit him with a brick house.

Once more in the living-room Bill Mountain turned troubled angry eyes on his old friend.

"What the devil does it mean, Dan? Andros, you say? You didn't find him at home, then? But why should Andros go out of his way to attack Ben? And—"

While he was speaking, the answer to his question was on its way from Santa Fé. Dan had just started to say, "I'll tell you about Andros—" when the telephone rang. The voice from Santa Fé announced in the casual tone of routine business:

"Thought I'd better report back, Mr. Montana. I got you your plane all right. It ought to be showing up 'most any time now."

"Plane!" exploded Bill. "What are you talking about? Who ordered any plane?"

A muffled "Glory be!" burst from the sheriff. He snatched the telephone into his own eager hands and began barking questions. When he slammed the receiver back on the hook there was a new bright glitter in his old eyes.

"God's on our side," he said with a grunt. "Now I c'n tell you the whole dam' story! Buck Andros kilt Webb Clark a little while ago—Keep your hair on an' lis'en!" he snapped, forestalling an interruption. "Andros kilt Webb an' run out on me. He must of headed straight for here, why I don't know onless firs', he figgered I'd never look for him to come this way an', secon', mebbe seein' he was done for he aimed to get all his killin' done while he was at it, an' wipe you out. But on the jump the devil gets him a hunch! He sneaks in on Ben Hodge an' knocks him col', it bein' quieter to crack his skull than shoot him; this he does so's he can grab Ben's 'phone, an' put in that call to Santy Fee for a plane. He says he's Mr. Montana speakin' an' damns the expense, but wants 'em to rush him an air-plane quick. The feller says, 'Where'll I send it?' Andros says, 'White Water Valley!' The feller says, 'Where's that?' An' Andros says where it is an' promises to fix it so the pilot c'n find it all right; he tells 'em he'll have a great big fire goin' at Montana, an' ol' haystack he tells 'em; the pilot will spot that from hell-an'-gone an' will steer north to lan' in White Water—an' Andros promises to have another fire burnin' up there to show him the exac' spot. Which I'd say he's makin' sorta free of other fellers' haystacks an' things!"

"The plane's already on the way—and so is Andros," Bill reminded him. "Ready to ride, Dan?"

"I never was so ready," said the sheriff.

CHAPTER 21

Penelope was standing on the porch where Patty had left her, awestruck by the flaming spectacle which reddened all the south like an angry dawn, when a rider coming in haste from the Goose Neck drew her attention. At first she thought that he meant to ride by without stopping. As though such had been his original intention he checked himself in full flight, swerved and rode to the tree where Patty had left her spotted horse. As he dismounted Penelope hurried to him for news from the fire. He turned sharply at her step; enough light came from her open window for her to see his face distinctly.

"Mr. Andros!" she exclaimed. The instant she recognised him she thought of Patty and decided: "I won't tell him Patty is here."

He did not speak up as promptly as was his custom when with her. He seemed very tense, she thought, his mouth hard set and unsmiling. It was difficult in that light to make much of his eyes. He just stood looking at her a moment; then he looked at the spotted horse and laid his hand on its mane. The most she could make of him was that he was rigid and was breathing hurriedly.

"You have just come from Montana?" she asked.

"Is Patty here?" he demanded, and she detected

the same sort of tenseness in his voice as she had sensed in his bearing.

"Patty?" she repeated. "What makes you ask that? Why should she be here?"

"She is here, isn't she?" He seemed to grow less rigid but remained very alert. "Why don't you answer me?" he asked impatiently.

Penelope heard the tell-tale creaking of a door stealthily opening, and wondered anxiously whether he too had heard.

"You haven't answered me yet! Have you just been at Montana?"

"No. I've come from my place—"

"By way of the Goose Neck!"

"Not exactly. I had callers, Miss Loring, whom I did not care to see to-night, so I walked out on them. I did a bit of circling, came through the Goose Neck and was on my way to see Patty. Luckily I saw her horse and here I am."

"What do you want with Patty?" she asked.

"Indeed, Miss Loring!" He could be as stiff as a ramrod. Then he said, still curtly, "Oh, I beg your pardon. I'm in a hurry tonight. And if Patty hasn't told you you're welcome to know. I've lived a good many years without knowing what love was; all of a sudden I've learned."

Penelope knew then that he had heard the door creak. He had not lifted his voice particularly, yet his enunciation was deliberate and distinct and was meant for other ears than her own.

"In your friend, Patty," he continued, "I have found the one girl on earth for me, Miss Loring. I'd go to hell for her and call it a pleasant holiday!"

"Oh!" said Penelope. What a familiar ring those words had!

"Finding her here is a rare bit of luck," said Andros. "May I run in?"

He asked formally enough but did not stand on ceremony for permission. He stepped by her and ran up the steps. At the top he paused an instant and turned to look back, not at Penelope but towards the Goose Neck. She saw for the first time how tense his face was.

Patty met him in the front room. Her eyes were red and she held a damp handkerchief balled in her tense fingers.

"Oh, hello, Buck," she greeted him airily.

Penelope entered and stood looking at them. Buck Andros, she thought, had never been so wickedly handsome. His tanned face was darkly flushed, his eyes were strangely brilliant—his bearing bespoke an electric recklessness.

He advanced on Patty with his hat in one hand, the other extended.

"Patty! This is the biggest piece of luck a man could have!"

"Oh, is it?" retorted a very sarcastic Patty.

Andros stared at her in silence. Then he turned on Penelope, frowning.

"What the devil's all this?" he demanded. "Have you been trying to come between Patty and me?"

Penelope thought: "Patty is half ready to be a door-mat again. I mustn't let her." So she smiled sweetly at Andros and said "Mercy, no! All I've done, Mr. Andros, is congratulate her on being Johnny Lane's heiress!"

That might have been a body-blow had it not been that the luckless Webb Clark's words had prepared him for their repetition in other quarters. With a wild scheme suggesting itself at a time of vital crisis, his brain was functioning shrewdly. He had always believed in his luck and now saw it at his elbow if only he bore himself both warily and forcefully through a few of the most tremendous moments of his life.

"I don't understand you," he said stiffly.

"You didn't know, perhaps," said Penelope, hoping to lead him into making a statement which Patty would know for a lie, "that she was Johnny Lane's heiress?"

He allowed her to make what she could of as well-controlled a poker face as any man ever showed over a table when he staked his pile on a seven high.

"Why, of course I knew!" he said, and still seemed to wonder what it was all about. "Who on earth didn't know?"

He was so cool about it that Penelope was

momentarily nonplussed. She looked swiftly at Patty. Patty's big blue eyes were opened very wide; they were hungry for the slightest play of expression on Andros' face and began to lose their look of tragedy.

"Patty didn't know, for one," said Penelope.

"What!" he exclaimed as though incredulous.

"Bill Mountain didn't know until to-night," said Penelope. "And I didn't, and Dan Westcott didn't—"

"Oh, come on," laughed Andros. "You're joshing."

Patty had held silent to the limit of her control.

"You're talking to me, Mr. Buck Andros—"

"Bully!" His frown was gone in a flash as he turned from Penelope to her. "Let's talk. And what say we ride while we do it? I've got the surprise of your young life for you, Pretty Patty."

Patty was thawing fast and that surprise he spoke of started a lively curiosity working in his behalf, yet she clung to the tatters of her reserve.

"You know perfectly well, Buck Andros, that I never heard a word about being anybody's heiress. Do heiresses run around playing nurse to a pack of men as mean as bears with sore paws? If I really did have anything to say about White Water Valley—"

"But you've everything to say about it, my

dear!" he told her lightly. "And I supposed that you knew all the while. If you mean to tell me that you stayed all that time at Montana and neither your friend, Miss Loring, nor her friend, Bill Montana, told you—well, it's funny, that's all!"

Penelope felt a little flick of consternation. Before she could speak Patty, though plainly grown uncertain, came straight to the point:

"Did you suppose, Mr. Buck Andros, that by marrying me you could gobble up White Water Valley, too?"

"Great Scott, no!" said Andros. "Why, I gave up all thoughts of White Water months ago! I took it for granted that you'd closed some sort of a deal with Bill Montana! If you haven't, I'm the most astonished man in seven states. Look here! May I ask what the devil all this has to do with my loving you or your loving me?"

Penelope looked at him in wonder. Patty was already regarding him in a sort of hero-worshipping way. Suddenly, Penelope's wits nimble again, she said witheringly:

"Didn't you tell me only this afternoon that I could go tell my friend Bill Mountain that you had him licked—that White Water was as good as yours!"

Andros looked at her steadily; despite his certain knowledge that with every tick of the clock he stood in graver danger, he was maddeningly deliberate. Patty, scarcely breathing, began making a tight twist of her handkerchief.

"I'm sorry, Miss Loring," said Andros at last, very stiff. "I don't believe that you are the sort who would fabricate such a statement out of pure malice; I don't think that you are a wilful trouble-maker. I can only suppose that you were unduly over-wrought at the time, and only half heard. What I told you was that I had Bill Montana licked in the only thing that mattered; and that was the arrest of his brother for the murder of my friend Pasmore. I am quite sure that I made no reference to White Water. As a matter of fact, just now when I told Patty that I had a surprise for her, I had two. One of them is that to-day I have sold my ranch here and therefore have no further interest in Montana or what he does; certainly not in White Water Valley."

"That is a lie!" cried Penelope angrily. "You are trying to make Patty believe a lot of things she would be a fool to believe. And you have known all the time that Juan Montana did not kill Floyd Pasmore but that it was the Indian Amador."

Andros shrugged.

"It is a girl's privilege to call a man a liar," he said with irritating suavity. "As to the other thing, whether a Montana or a Montana Indian committed the actual murder, what matter? They're all in it together." Then he swung about upon Patty. This time, however, he did not smile. "If you think that I'm the sort of man that your friend, Miss Loring, thinks me, there remains only for me to say good night and go."

Patty's trouble was that to save her life she didn't know whether she loved him or not. When he looked at her as he did now, straight into her eyes her heart skipped a beat. Wavering already, she wavered still more. Instantly he played on the strings of her emotions.

"Patty!" he whispered.

"Oh, Buck, I'm such a darned little fool!"

"You are!" exclaimed Penelope vehemently.

"Oh, am I?" sniffed Patty.

Andros stepped close to her and whispered in her ear. Patty's blue eyes grew rounder and bluer, and a rosy flush spread over her cheeks.

"Buck!—Honestly?"

"You'll come? We'll have to take it on the run, Delicious!"

Patty whirled to Penelope.

"Oh, Pen! Wish me luck, there's a dear. We're eloping—in a plane! It's on the way and—" She spun around to face Andros again. "Buck Andros, look at me! I haven't any more clothes, except what I stand in, than a rabbit—"

He caught her by the arm and hustled her out at the door.

Penelope, though she knew it was no use, tried to call Patty back. Her only answer was a breathless little good-bye and, after that, the hammering of the horses' hoofs. For Buck Andros the strain was over, the necessity of squandering precious time was past, and all hope now lay in haste.

CHAPTER 22

Many armed men streamed out of the Montana corrals, riding hard in the hope of coming up with Andros somewhere in White Water Valley. Though the saddle horses were running free there was little delay in mounting them; men on foot drove a herd into a fence corner and roped them at random. It was an angry mob murmuring like a swarm of bees that followed Bill Mountain northward.

With such a rush did they sweep through the Goose Neck that Penelope, riding in haste to the lower valley, was almost ridden down. She swung her horse out of the narrow roadway and called to them as they went streaming by. Bill Mountain whirled and returned to her, urging the others to hurry on and spread out across White Water.

"You, Penelope?" he said hurriedly. "Go on and wait for me at the house. We're after Andros; he has overplayed his hand to-night. He killed Webb Clark and then set fire at Mon—"

"Bill! Why, he was just at my place! He's gone now and he took Patty with him. Wait a minute, Bill! Do you understand? He has Patty and he will force her to give him your valley!"

They had reined their horses close together. He stooped close to her and saw how the starlight sparkled in her eyes and how it gleamed on her wet cheeks.

"He'll not hurt Patty, no matter what he does," he said quickly.

Penelope dabbed at her eyes. "I'm not worrying about her—of course he won't hurt her. But, Bill, he'll steal your valley—and it's all my fault!"

"Don't you worry, Penelope," he said as for an instant his hand rested on her shoulder. Then he wheeled and rode to overtake the others, and along with a tumult of other thoughts came the tingling realisation that those tears in Penelope's brave eyes were for him.

There were a dozen men ahead of him already scattering across the broadening fields and as he passed the school house he heard still other riders coming on behind him. Shouting to make his voice carry above the sound of hoofs, he warned them that Patty was with Andros; if it came to shooting they must have that in mind lest in the dark she fall to a bullet meant for him.

Riding almost neck and neck three horsemen cut across the field to join him. They were Juan and Dan and Tonito, and Juan was asking excitedly:

"Which way now, Bill?"

"Scatter; all directions. And as soon as any man of us hears the plane he's to stop and start any sort of blaze he can manage, haystack or stubble field or shack. Andros has a good lead on us, wherever he is, and our only hope is to confuse the pilot with several signals."

"I hear he's got Patty Lane, Bill?" barked Dan Westcott. "If we let him fly off with her he cuts your throat though we hang him later."

"But he can't do anything," exclaimed Juan. "On the run for murder—"

"Don't go foolin' yourse'f, kid," grunted the sheriff. "Let him get off with her, he'll make her deed the prop'ty to him an afore we c'n ketch him an' hang him, he'll have his las' laugh—"

"Sh!" commanded Bill. "Listen!"

At first they heard nothing but the running horses coming on behind them. Then another sound came throbbing from the skies, a droning hum steadily increasing in volume.

"Scatter and ride!"

Their four horses leaped under them as in a widely extending line they swept northward across the valley, harkening to the throb of an engine somewhere high above, trying to locate it and, most of all, watchful for some sign of Andros.

That sign was afforded them almost instantly. "There he is!" came a reedy yelp from Dan, as eager as the baying of a hound as he sights his quarry. The others saw the bright gleam of fire while Dan's shout was still ringing in their ears, a swift flaring up of flames where towards the northern rim of the valley Andros had made a fallen pine serve him as his beacon.

Shouts rose on all hands as some forty forms streamed across the fields, converging upon a point still at some distance. Some judged that they had a mile to go, others half and still others twice as far; in the night, estimating the distance of a light presents difficulties. But almost at the outset theirs began to seem a lost cause unless at the last moment the pilot should grow deliberate, hesitating to make a landing until the fire grew stronger.

Unfortunately there was no evidence of hesitation. As the signal fire spread among the combustible pine needles and caught at the resinous dead branches, the plane took definite form low down in the northern sky and the roar of the motor burst out clearly above the rumble of running horses. It circled; they saw the tail-light racing across the field of stars. Having dipped earthward it rose in a swift sweep and came circling back. Still at a distance of several hundred yards the Montana men saw it dip again, skim close to the ground, land in a puff of dust made rosy by the fire, and trundle more and more slowly across the stubble. Two dark figures only fitfully revealed, Andros and Patty hand in hand, ran through the fringes of the widening circle of light, hurrying to overtake the plane where it was jolting to a stop.

That it was going to be a close thing Bill

Mountain realised and extorted from his horse the final ounce of power and burst of speed; and what was so clear to him was no less clear to Andros. Dan Westcott, a couple of lengths behind two leaping streaks which he knew for Bill Mountain and Tonito riding neck and neck, entertained the bleak certainty that his quarry was going to slip out almost under his nose unless—and he had small hope in that quarter—the pilot proved to be some degree less quick of action than Andros' eagerness demanded. With sinking heart and rising gorge, riding hard and cudgelling his wits no less than his horse, the sheriff lent his aid towards creating a diversion in the mind of the pilot, become now the man of the moment.

Emptying his six-shooter in the air by way of advertising the fact that there was more at stake to-night than a man's whim to take an aeroplane jaunt, with little assurance that his voice could be heard, the old sheriff began shouting at the top of his voice:

"Hi, there! Pilot! Stop it! That man's wanted for murder—it's the sheriff talkin' to you—hol' everything—"

Others took up the cry, became a clamouring herd of men sweeping onward. Andros and Patty, glimpsed a second only, had disappeared. The plane, a mere spectre of a thing growing dim in the thin edges of light, had started taxying across the field. There was one breathless moment when it seemed to be stopping; an instant later the many eyes fixed so desperately upon it saw it moving more swiftly than ever. With an effortless ease maddening to those who watched in drop-jawed despair, it slipped smoothly into the air, and with a great "who-o-osh!" like an angry snort of defiance shot into a steep climb.

With a rush it gathered speed, rising to the mountains; a blot against the sky it dwindled swiftly, streaking into the east. The glowing taillight became a mocking meteor threading the stars; presently it flickered and dipped and vanished. The hush of the mountain valley returned, unruffled, undisturbed.

CHAPTER 23

Bill Mountain, brooding apart from the others, riding alone across a valley which he had loved since boyhood just as he loved Montana of which it had been a part and which he never wanted to see again after to-night, came to Penelope's house and found her standing by her horse in the yard.

"They got away," he said heavily.

She answered only, "Dan told me," not trusting herself to speak what was in her heart, finding difficulty in uttering the three trite words alone, an uncontrollable huskiness in her voice.

He didn't appear to notice her distress. For a while he sat staring above her head, his bleak eyes upon the high black wall of the mountains over whose barrier Andros had risen so triumphantly. At last, like a man borne down by a great physical weariness, he shifted his body in the saddle, facing homeward. His voice sounded flat when he spoke:

"Climb into the saddle and ride along, Penelope. You'll want to know whether Dan has any luck spreading his net over telephone and telegraph wires; he may have the satisfaction of learning which way they go. Also, maybe you'd like to see Juan; it started out as a big night for the kid."

They rode down to Montana together, Penelope

as preoccupied as he. In the open starlight after they had emerged from the gloom under the Goose Neck pines she made what she could of his grave face.

"The loss of White Water would mean everything to you?" she asked softly.

He drew a deep breath and answered her tonelessly:

"No. It's not as bad as all that. Suppose you should have your right arm cut off?"

"Bill!" she exclaimed, distressed.

He made an arrested gesture which ended in a Spanish shrug.

"I've still got Montana. For a while I'll be crippled a bit. It's good to be young, though, isn't it? There are the good busy years ahead."

"You seem so sure that Patty is going just to be clay in his hands!"

"Can you doubt it?"

When she made no answer he bent towards her, for the first time looking very closely at her.

"It's sweet to have you care so much, Penelope," he said.

Hastily she turned her face away from him as she caught a trembling lower lip between her teeth. Without looking at him she said with a hint of bitterness:

"When I think that had it not been for me, had you never brought me here, this would never have happened!"

More closely than ever he looked at her. Neither spoke another word until they reached the old home. Raimundo saw them coming; he and a couple of men who had returned already from White Water led the horses off to turn them loose in one of the fields. Penelope standing on the porch saw for the first time the havoc which had been wrought here; falling walls still burned fiercely and here and there had crumbled into heaps of red coals. The intense heat beat in her face; the hard bright light drove the dark far afield and made a ghostly flicker of the most distant corral.

Bill Mountain, instead of looking where she was staring with such sad and horror-filled eyes, stood watching her. Feeling his intent gaze she glanced up at his set face; a sob got her by the throat and she broke away from him and ran into the house. He came hurrying after her and caught up with her in the living-room.

"Penelope," he said queerly, "how can you care so much?"

"Care!" she cried passionately. "It breaks my heart! All that beauty brought down in ruin and ash heaps—the work of years undone—and all this that we see just a reminder of the even greater evil to come, the loss to you of White Water Valley—!" She thought almost in a panic that she had been given no right for so great a sympathy—she spoke more guardedly, saying as conventionally as she could manage, “Can one help caring, Bill, when a friend is hurt?”

For a little while he did not speak, but his eyes frowning into hers were so terribly in earnest that hers wavered and fell before them.

“When you said just now,” he said at last with a gravity tinged with something akin to sternness, “that some part of all this might have been different—if I hadn’t brought you here!—I got to thinking, Penelope.”

“Yes?” she asked faintly. The mantel over the fireplace was at hand like a friend; on it was a tiny clay figurine made by one of the Indians, offering itself for her suddenly restless fingers.

“Yes,” said Bill Mountain out of a gravity deeper than ever. “Do you know, Penelope, that the loss of White Water Valley is a very small thing alongside knowing you?”

“You are generous to say so!” She drenched him with a smile made for the occasion and through the smile her eyes sparkled all the brighter for the tears which she wanted to hide from him. “You are just the gallant trooper I said you were, and—”

There came then a flash into his eyes and a new, thrillingly new tone into his voice which startled her and sent scurrying whatever light thing she was going to say. For an instant she kept her eyes lifted steadily and frankly to his; then all of a sudden she lowered them and became busier than ever with the clay figurine, and her face grew a vivid red.

"Penelope!" he whispered, awe-struck.

"What is it, Bill?" she asked breathlessly.

She had never dreamed of seeing Bill Mountain show signs of confusion and grow abashed and hesitant! He spoke with the same awe in his voice that shone in his eyes, stumbling among words.

"Penelope!—It can't be!—A girl like you! You wouldn't—you couldn't—damn it all, Penelope, I'm in love with you!"

"Do you think you are, Bill?" she asked softly.

The clay image slipped from her fingers and broke into many pieces on the hearth. Penelope gasped. "Oh!" and went down on her knees to gather up the pieces. "How stupidly clumsy—" He caught her hands and lifted her to her feet.

"Am I a fool and a mad man to love you?" he demanded huskily.

She could no longer stifle the quivering sigh, long pent up.

"Are you?" she asked softly.

"A man like me," muttered Bill Mountain. "A roughneck like me—" A look of sheer wonder wrote itself large on his face as he read what she no longer made the slightest pretence of hiding in her shining eyes. "You're not laughing at me, are you?—Oh, Penelope, my dear, my dear, are your eyes telling me the truth?"

"Only a tenth part of it, Bill dear," she whispered.

"It's God's greatest wonder!" said Bill Mountain and swept her clean off the floor into his arms. And the wonder increased as her arms, as eager as his, tightened about his neck.

The telephone was ringing. It meant nothing whatever to the two sitting in such hushed intimate cosiness on the couch drawn up before a discreet little fire. But nothing had occurred to-night to soften Dan Westcott's ire or transmute defeat into a radiant victory; he was never far from the telephone and made a leap at it every time the bell tinkled. Now his excited, *"What!"* reached out even as far as the remote distances to which Bill and Penelope had journeyed.

"Bill!" yelled old Dan a moment later. "Bill, where are you?—We got him! The plane's down an' we got him! Where's my hat?"

"Down!" repeated Penelope fearfully as the sheriff bore down upon them. "Do you mean the plane crashed? Was Patty—"

"Crashed, your eyebrow!" snorted Dan. "It was the han' o' the Lord, usin' Wings Smith for fingers, that brought 'em down! Wait a shake an' I'll tell you. Firs', Bill, not wastin' any time, sen' Raimundo runnin' for my horse. In less'n an hour I'll have Mr. John Andros by the slack skin on the back of his neck; he's no fu'ther from us than the Tallant ranch, locked up tighter'n a drum with Wings Smith ridin' herd on him."

Raimundo was sent for a horse and Dan afforded them something more of a detailed story while he waited. Wings Smith, to be sure, was the pilot. He was, if you believed Dan Westcott, absolutely the finest Smith that ever came over the pike. No; Dan hadn't ever heard of him until just now, but the fact remained.

"He wasn't no dam' fool, that's all," said Dan. "No pilot is; them avvyators is the sort o' boys to-day that good cowboys used to be. He had eyes an' used 'em; ears, an' used 'em, too; horse sense an' made it work. The big fire down here looked purty much like the worl' afire to him up where he was. That was O.K. with him at firs', but he noticed other things; he heard us yellin'; he seen a whole band o' men whoopin' it up across the valley; he heard shots; an' when he landed he seen how Andros was almos' jumpin' out o' his skin to get goin' before the party come. Another thing: he'd come, he thought, to pick up Bill Montana. He heard Patty, who was gettin' fearful the las' minute an' wished she hadn't come, sayin' something excited an' callin' him 'Buck.' He speaks up sharp an' says, 'You're Mr. Montana, I suppose?' An' Andros says, 'Sure. Let's go.' An' Mr. Wings Smith was about to say, 'Let's wait,' when he sees the gun in Andros' fis' and the look smeared all over his mug—so he pays to the high card. An' then—"

The telephone rang again; Dan barked: "Westcott speakin'," and then turned to Penelope.

"It's for you," he grinned. "A badly shook-up young lady is on the other en' o' this line right now."

Penelope listened to a hysterical and incoherent Patty:

"Pen! Oh, I never thought to hear your voice alive again in my life. We must have been ten thousand feet in the air when—well, I thought it was the end of the world! Before I got into that beastly plane I was scared—and I knew something was all wrong! I tried to make Buck Andros let me go and he grabbed me and made me come—And the pilot yelled something we couldn't hear and I tell you we were ten miles high and he made a high-sign that the devil was to pay and—Penelope, my heart is in my mouth yet or else that's what I swallowed! We began falling!—the plane went into a side-slip and a tail-spin and a nose dive all at once—and he was just fooling us, Pen, and landed in a big field and jumped out pretending to see what was the matter and the first thing I knew he hit Buck Andros over the head with a monkey wrench or beer bottle or something and took his gun away and here we are at somebody's ranch house where we walked and I'm going to stay until you bring a nice tame team of old horses and a sled to haul me home—"

Dan realized that his horse was a long time coming and went to hasten matters. He couldn't find Raimundo; at the corral where some of the men and horses were he discovered that it was a strangely slow business to get a horse roped, a saddle found and a bridle brought by a man who hurried off for it and turned into a snail. Dan was as quick as the next man in smelling a rat, but could make little of this one. Once in the saddle he rode in haste.

About an hour later Bill and Penelope, sitting in the gleaming of their neglected and dying fire, heard the telephone again. During that hour much had happened. The whole world had advanced into a bright new phase though the rank and file of humanity hadn't noticed. Bill had sat down at the piano and had played, while Penelope stared at him incredulously; he could play with all four fingers on each hand and could even use his thumbs! More than that, he sang to her:

"*Angel de amor*, *tu pasion no lo comprendo*, *Si*, *la comprendo*, *no puedo espresar*—"

"*Novio*!" whispered Penelope.

But the phone rang again and Bill, having kissed her good-bye, went to answer it. Dan Westcott said waspishly: "I'm comin' back to spen' the night, Bill. So's Patty."

"Fine—what about Andros?"

"Tell Mrs. Richards to have me some boilin'

water; I want a toddy. He's dead." Dan clicked up.

He told Bill the story—a part of the story, rather—as soon as he arrived, while a chastened and adventure-satiated Patty was carried off to her room by Penelope. The sheriff did not even remove his hat until the two girls had gone; then he lifted it off gingerly. A bandana handkerchief was tied about his head, and there was dried blood on it.

"He come jus' that close to gettin' me, Bill," he said when he had downed his first toddy and wiped his moustache on the back of his hand. "He got loose, got him a gun somehow an' was makin' a break jus' as I was pullin' up in the yard. We seen each other the same split secon'. He shot a mite firs' an' shot purty good, considerin'. I kilt the son of a gun, Bill."

Bill looked at him steadily a moment, then hastily transferred his gaze elsewhere. He would never forget how Dan had pleaded with him: "Let me cart him off to jail—on the way I'd let him grab a gun an'—"

Dan made himself the second toddy.

"Bill," he said meditatively, "you're a dam' liar but here's happy days."

The rest of the story was told them by Tonito. Penelope had put Patty to bed and returned to say good night—and to linger. Tonito knocked and came in, saying quietly:

"Don Bill, will you talk with me one minute?"

"Alone, Tonito?" asked Bill, wondering at the look in the unfathomable Indian eyes.

"It is you, Don Bill," answered Tonito, "who will judge whether Senor Dan should know."

Dan's old eyes stared at him a long moment.

"Hm-m-m," said the sheriff. "Tonito, you devil! Am I right in guessin' now that mebbe you had a han' in it takin' so long for me to get me a horse saddled to-night?" He neither expected nor awaited an answer; he tucked in the corners of his grim old mouth, stared harder than ever, then abruptly got up and left the room.

"He is smart, that Senor Dan," said Tonito, and shrugged. "He knows already. Yes, Don Bill, Raimundo told me and I rode first to the Tallant ranch. Andros was locked in a room. I set him free!"

"You, Tonito!"

"Yes, Don Bill. I said to him, 'Hombre, I am part Indian, and I am going to kill you.' And I told him, too, that I and my people are the people of Don Bill Montana, the finest gentleman in the world. I said to him, 'I will kill you as Don Bill would kill you in my place.' So I gave him a gun—

"The dirty coward jumped back behind a big tree, quick as a cat. Then he saw Senor Dan coming, and Senor Dan saw him. It was my place to make an end of him—but God made things otherwise. That is all, Don Bill. You will tell the sheriff what you like. I will be smoking a cigarette outside."

As he finished speaking Dan Westcott popped back into the room.

"Didn't hear a word you said, Tonito," he spoke up briskly. "All through now? I'm off to bed; I've did me a day's work an' might start up a headache if I set up too long. I'll say g'night, Bill; 'night to you, Penny-lope. An' night to you, Tonito, ol' man."

With Tonito alone he shook hands and those shrewd old eyes of the sheriff and the jet black eyes of the young Indian met in profound understanding.

As for Penelope, since she had come back to them only to say good night, now was obviously the time to do so. She missed her opportunity, however; she and Bill got to talking about this, that and the other thing; he poked up the fire and they watched the gay little flames, and were two utterly astonished people when after the shortest of all nights the sun broke all records not alone in its unprecedented early rising but as well in the glory of the new daybreak.

Center Point Large Print
600 Brooks Road / PO Box 1
Thorndike, ME 04986-0001 USA

(207) 568-3717

US & Canada:
1 800 929-9108
www.centerpointlargeprint.com